ALSO BY J. B. VELASQUEZ

Sleepers

Every Last One: The Rise of Sylvia Boone

TOURIST TRAPPED

J. B. VELASQUEZ

WILD RUMPUS PRESS

ISBN: 979-8-9875541-0-4

1

____

TOBIAS MUNCH STARED BLANKLY at his computer screen, allowing the letters to blur and drift into one another and then back into words. It was Tobias who put those letters there in the first place and found their manipulation through visual trickery to be of far greater interest than what they represented in the form of language. The sound of throat clearing behind him snapped him back into the florescent-lit, three-dimensional world of corporate malaise.

He swiveled his desk chair a quarter turn to observe his supervisor Carl standing at the opening of his cubicle holding a file folder in one hand and a glazed donut in the other. Carl had not finished chewing the donut when he asked, "You think you're going to be able to finish that troubleshooting section by the end of the day, partner?"

"Yeah. Just waiting on that email from graphics," Tobias replied. He had not emailed the graphics department about anything. Passing the buck had proven to be an effective stalling technique. His good-natured and confrontation-averse supervisor bought it once again.

"Good. We're way overdue on this. Here," Carl said, handing him the blue folder and taking another bite of his glazed donut. "Research on our next project."

Tobias noticed a flake of donut glaze that had fallen onto Carl's seafoam green Oxford just above the left breast pocket. *Almost*, Tobias thought, feeling a twinge of disappointment that it hadn't made it fully into the pressed pocket. Insignificant failures of this kind affected Tobias far more than the average person. "Can't wait," he replied dryly taking the folder and nodding with his lips pressed together in a horizontal line, as if to say *Is that all? Are we done here? I'd really like to get back to zoning out some more.*

Tobias hated his job as a technical writer. Writing user manuals and instruction materials for everyday products like coffee machines, curling irons, and leaf blowers was never his dream. It was never what he thought he'd be doing by the time he was thirty-four. Most of these consumer products were intuitive enough to use right out of the box even without the written admonishment to READ ALL INSTRUCTIONS CAREFULLY, or warnings to only use the product for its intended purpose, or if an electrical product, not to immerse it in water. Other than safeguarding the company from potential litigation, he found his work to be utterly meaningless.

Carl bumped his fist twice upon the top edge of his cubicle wall and turned to walk away. He turned back around extending his index finger skyward. "Oh hey, how's your book coming along?"

Tobias fancied himself an aspiring novelist. Technical writing was only *technically* writing. He had undertaken an epic science fiction fantasy novel for the better part of a decade. Truth be told, he'd been re-writing it for the last six years. The unwieldy tome was down to only 879 pages from a mind-numbing 1422. The meandering intergalactic tale defied any semblance of plot structure and sprawled along self-indulgent curiosities to dead ends before returning to some unrelated branch in time and space.

"It's getting there." He was lying again.

Carl stood there nodding and chewing, his posture limp and unflattering, like a tree sloth forced to stand erect. "Cool, man. I'd love to read it sometime."

"Yeah, of course. It's not quite ready, you know. I still have a few dents to hammer out. It's . . . it's a process."

"I'm sure," Carl said, bobbing his head. "Well, no pressure. I mean, if you ever needed any notes or first impressions, or whatever, I'd be happy to take a look."

"Yeah, thanks. I appreciate it." *Please go away.*

Carl nodded, this time more emphatically. "Oh! Grace brought donuts. They're in the break room if you want one."

"Cool. Thanks." *Goodbye now.* Tobias felt a sense of responsibility to placate what he assumed was some kind of social gesticulation on Carl's part. He almost wished his supervisor was more of an authoritarian and less of a just-because-I'm-your-boss-doesn't-mean-we-can't-be-pals kind of a boss. It felt like a burden.

"Sure thing. Well, I'll let you get back to it. Later dater!" Carl did that fake gun thing with his thumb and forefinger while winking and making a clicking sound from the side of his mouth.

Tobias hated that Carl used this phrase. It was such a goofy thing to say in the first place, but it also reminded Tobias that he wasn't, in fact, dating anyone. If there was anything about Tobias that might have implied he had any proficiency in the dating department, what did that say about Carl?

Tobias was unhappily divorced. His ex-wife Everly Bronson, a bestselling author in self-help and women's issues, used her connections to help him find this job after seven years of supporting him through graduate school and his subsequent yearly recurring cycles of depression. To her credit, she made sure he was gainfully employed and financially stable enough to support himself before she ran off with a publishing executive with whom she'd been having an affair for the last year. Their marriage had been characterized by this inequitable dynamic of unceasing, one-sided support, both financial and emotional. It was Everly who got him into therapy and made sure he was taking his medication regularly.

Despite all her support and caregiving through the years, Tobias remained bitter toward her and his job by proxy. It was yet another example of his ineptitude—another hand-out. He felt he was above the work and yet he was terrible at it. As it turns out, this was his general take on life. Despite evidence that he had failed in almost every aspect of his life, his attitude was aloof and disengaged so that his failures could be easily dismissed as a lack of effort or interest rather than the humiliating swing-and-a-miss. The fact that his book remained in an endless cycle of revision gave him the sense that his lack of success as a writer was only a matter of his untimeliness rather than from any external judgment or objective failure.

The effect of these ongoing revisions pushed the novel's completion further and further into the future. It was always one step forward and two steps back. With every new solution or improvement, he would create yet another problem that needed solving. This created an illusion of progress that effectively kept his depression at bay.

There was one other bright spot in Tobias' mundane and unvaried life. Each weekday on his way to work, he stopped in at the Higher Grounds Cafe outside his building for his regular morning cortado, which he ordered with a half packet of stevia. Usually, he was directed to a buffet table where various sweeteners, creamers, napkins, and thin wooden stirring sticks were arranged. He graciously took the direction to sweeten his own beverage but persisted in including it in his order each morning. As annoying as that was, there was something principled, or perhaps borderline rebellious about it. It was a strange stand to take but it was one he could take without much consequence.

One barista in particular, however, always accommodated this small inconvenience without question or reservation. Mia Navarro, a sun-bleached blonde-haired sprite of twenty-five with a tattoo of a bumblebee on the inside of her left bicep, always seemed to have just heard an amusing anecdote and was trying to be professional in keeping it to herself when she spoke to customers. When she stood at the register awaiting a customer's decision, she bounced slightly, almost imperceptibly, on the balls of her feet. When the customer finally placed their order, Mia gave the impression that they had just made the best decision of their day. To Tobias, this was pure magic.

The highlight of his year was the day Mia recited his order to him as he approached the counter. "Cortado with a half packet of stevia, right?" She beamed wide-eyed, turning her head to one side giving him a sideways look. Her mouth remained playfully agape in anticipation of his confirmation.

"Uh, yeah. You remembered," Tobias said awkwardly straightening his glasses, which did not necessarily require straightening.

"Of course!" Mia smiled. "That's $4.85." She rotated the point of sale register around for Tobias to enter his card payment and floated away to make his coffee. He watched her expertly release the grounds from the bean grinder into the portafilter, tamp the grounds, and latch it into the group head of the espresso machine. She slapped the dispense button and got to work steaming the milk while the espresso dribbled forth into a ceramic demitasse. Steam clouded the sides of the glass cup as she poured the espresso into a Gibraltar. Using a spoon to filter out any froth from the stainless-steel pitcher, she slowly poured the milk in. This was all standard barista artistry, but the best part was watching her take that single light green packet, tear off the top, and meticulously dispense exactly one-half of its granular contents into the beverage and stir it well. That extra care she took, the attention to detail, to Tobias, was an act of love. It was *love*.

He never knew which days he would interact with Mia. Some days she was making the coffees or darting in and out of the back but when she was on the register, his heart raced and a wave of anxiety would wash over him as he entered the coffee shop. Anxiety, as an evolutionary adaptive function, is the brain's way of pushing one toward action. His anxiety was compelling Tobias to *say something!* But he never did. He was both captivated and helpless to act on his desires. Now that she knew his drink order, it was hardly necessary for him to say anything at all. He was content with this plight since it was the most prudent way to remain in good standing with his young muse, who by remembering his coffee order and her willingness to go the extra mile to fulfill it, knew him more intimately than anyone else in his sad, uneventful life.

On his way home from work that day, at a stoplight, Tobias glanced over into the display window of a big-box bookstore. Shockwaves reverberated through his chest. There must have been thirty hardback copies of Everly Bronson's *The Courage to Start Again* stacked artfully into a literary tower of betrayal. It was the first day of her book's release. Although he hadn't read the women's self-help bestseller in its entirety, Tobias summed it up as: *How to give up on the things in life that are hard and take advantage of opportunities to trade up.*

A car horn startled him. The man in his rearview mirror was gesturing forward with his palms face up and mouthing the word, "GO!" Tobias offered a vaguely apologetic wave and proceeded to navigate home to an even more tangible confirmation of his failed life.

Tobias took up residence at the Vista Hermosa apartment complex in a less than desirable part of town where liquor stores, self-storage, and used tire shops were never in short supply. It was the style of apartment building that resembled a 1960's motor inn with geometrically designed metal railing along the second-floor units. The apartment listing boasted poolside views, which was a true claim since the three identical buildings formed a 'U' around a semi-regularly maintained rectangular swimming pool. The same geometric metal railing encircled the pool area, which included several adjustable lounge chairs, yellowed by the sun, and two sets of metal picnic tables with four chairs each, all attached by bicycle cable locks to prevent theft.

Tobias lived on a second floor, 550 square foot one-bedroom unit. He lived minimally, more so from indifference than philosophical principle. Everly was generous in the divorce settlement, giving him most of their furnishings and essential household supplies. She even paid off the remaining balance on his car and student loans so that he could start his new life debt-free. All of this, Tobias regarded as pity and resented it bitterly.

He only selected the essential pieces from their furniture collections, mainly due to the drastic reduction in square footage. He had a bed and a dresser, a couch, a coffee table, and a large desk that took up the entire allotted dining area off the kitchen where he sat for hours either toiling over his book revisions or playing *Ever After*, an online sandbox game. He didn't bother putting up any wall art or decorative embellishments, except for a painted cow skull he bought at a flea market one year, which Everly disallowed from being displayed in their home. He haphazardly hung it, above the couch and off-centered, from a single nail. The ugliness of it, and the rest of the furniture placement, was an apostasy against an oblivious recipient, a performative tantrum no one would ever even notice.

Seeing his ex-wife's book display sent Tobias into a downward spiral of self-loathing. As he entered the modest residence he made a b-line to his desk and started up his computer. His manuscript was open on the desktop screen. His manuscript had been organized by scenes rather than chapters so that he could endlessly rearrange them, creating tedious timeline tweaks. This had become a kind of rudimentary therapy and he felt compelled to toil away, alternating fruitlessly between creation and destruction. It was a neurotic game that provided a placeholder for purpose, in the way that worry provides a route for the anxiety of uncertainty.

The cursor blinked impatiently after the last word he had typed the night before, as if it were mocking him, as if it were dubious of any creativity, any originality at all. He minimized the window and logged into the *Ever After* web portal. He placed a plastic souvenir Viking helmet upon his head and for the next six and a half hours, Tobias was Lord Magnus Magoo, ruler of the Terakaan Empire. He played until his eyes burned, pausing only to urinate or forage for snacks, never once removing that ridiculous helmet.

2

―――――

Tobias had a Thursday 9:00 a.m. appointment with his therapist Dr. Joelle Macintosh. He'd started seeing Dr. Macintosh before his divorce over a year ago. His wife Everly had arranged it. At first, Tobias attended reluctantly, believing it would appease his wife who had been emotionally checked out and preoccupied with her affair partner and the publication of her latest self-help book, *The Courage to Start Again*. He should have seen this as a sign of what was to come but was too engrossed in his own wallowing to put it together. Part of Everly's plan to start again was making sure Tobias, who she regarded as more of an adult child than an equal partner, was in good hands.

At first, Tobias had trouble remembering his appointments and ended up paying a small fortune in no-show fees. He attended with such irregularity that his course of treatment garnered little momentum. It wasn't until Everly handed him divorce papers that he decided to participate in earnest. After several weeks, Tobias was making progress. He was taking his Lexapro consistently and his life had finally stabilized. He was going to work every day and he was paying his bills on time, thanks in part to automated payments. He wasn't happy per se but he wasn't suicidal either.

Tobias entered the three-story red brick office building on the corner of a quaint historic district lined with boutiques, cafes, an art studio, and trendy thrift stores. The lobby was clean and minimal with a large-leafed plant in one corner and a pair of mid-century side chairs in another. A directory board hung on the wall next to the brass elevator doors. The building hosted an architecture firm, a real estate team, a digital marketing company, and a child psychologist. Dr. Macintosh's office was on the third floor, unit 301.

He stepped into the waiting room of Dr. Macintosh's office and sat on a dark weathered leather couch. A wooden coffee table piled high with magazines separated the couch from two cream-colored armchairs. A large picture window framed a mature oak tree outside. An abstract charcoal painting hung vertically on the far wall. A tea station was set up at the other end of the room next to a water cooler. He picked up a year-old copy of *Architectural Digest* and thumbed through the sleek lines of modern construction and Scandinavian furniture.

"Tobias, you may come in," Dr. Macintosh said, standing in her doorway with a warm, inviting smile.

Tobias stood up and dropped the *Architectural Digest* back onto the precariously stacked pile of magazines on the coffee table. The weight of the periodical initiated a landslide of magazines onto the floor.

"Just leave it," she said. "I've been meaning to throw some of those out."

He hesitated. "Sorry."

"It's fine, really. Please, do come in." Her warm smile

was reassuring. Dr. Macintosh was in her early fifties and always dressed more elegantly than any other person in Tobias' life. She wore 1970's inspired turquoise rimmed eyeglasses, which complemented the muted teal paint color of her office walls and various turquoise accent pieces artfully placed here and there. She wore high-waisted, wide-legged, beige trousers with a white sleeveless silk blouse. A rosewood beaded mala hung low around her neck with a golden tassel at the end. She motioned toward the dark gray herringbone fabric couch. "Would you like some tea?"

"Uh, no. No, thank you, Dr. Macintosh," he said as he sat at the far end of the couch and hugged an elephant embroidered throw pillow against his torso.

"I thought we were on a first-name basis," she said pouring herself a cup of tea. She sat gracefully in her tan leather Eames chair. "Please, call me Joelle."

"OK. Sorry." He fiddled with his sweaty fingers, sitting awkwardly upright on a perfectly comfortable couch.

"No need to apologize, Tobias. Breathe with me." She closed her eyes and led him in five deep, cleansing breaths. "Better?"

Tobias nodded. "Yes. I feel better." He settled back into the couch.

"Good." A silence followed, a silence only seasoned therapists are perfectly comfortable sitting in, while Tobias fidgeted with a corner of the throw pillow. He forced his eyes up to meet hers and then quickly over to the bookshelf behind her. He scanned the rows of titles, which were still too distant for him to make out from where he was sitting. "What's going on in there?" she finally asked.

"Oh. I don't know. Work, I guess."

"You guess?" Dr. Macintosh never allowed ambiguity to go unaddressed.

"I was supposed to get this thing finished yesterday but I've barely even started. I just know my boss is going to ask me about it as soon as I walk in the door."

Dr. Macintosh nodded, inviting him to continue.

"I've been phoning it in lately and I'm worried it's finally going to catch up with me."

"This job is important to you," she stated.

"Well, no. I mean . . . I need it, so . . ."

"So . . . so what? Say more about that."

"It's important because I need it but I don't *care* about it. This isn't what I'm supposed to be doing."

"You're supposed to be a famous author."

"Well . . . yeah. At least a published one."

"Like your ex-wife?"

Had it been anyone else, Tobias might have taken this as a jab or an insult. He knew his therapist well enough to know she had no ill will toward him. This was her skillful invitation for him to connect authentically and to get to the heart of the matter. "Her new book came out. I saw it in a bookstore window."

"What did you feel when you saw her book?"

"I don't know." He looked at her and saw that this answer wasn't going to cut it. He bit his lip and looked down as he searched for a better response. "Like . . . like a failure."

"Her success means you're a failure?"

"No. No, I felt like a failure even before she became successful. I mean, she never even wanted to be a writer. That was *my* dream. She was going to teach. And then she had this idea to compile a bunch of her research she'd done for this women's studies class she was teaching. I helped her, actually.

She didn't know what she was doing back then. I was her first editor. I helped her find her voice as a writer. She told me that. When her first book came out, she toasted me at the launch. Said she couldn't have done it without me."

"And that was for *Girl In a Box*?"

"Yeah. I was the one who came up with that title." He scoffed. "Can you believe it?"

"I can. How does that make you feel?"

He thought for a beat. "Used. Like I boosted her over the wall and then I was left standing there on the wrong side."

"What side is that?"

He thought for a beat. "The nobody side."

"The side you've always been on."

"Yeah. When is it ever going to be *my* turn?"

"You want to be on the somebody side."

"Of course. Doesn't everybody?"

"I don't know. But we're not talking about everybody. We're talking about you."

"Right. Well, then yes. I want to be *somebody*. I'm tired of being a *nobody*."

"What's that like? Being a nobody?"

"It sucks. I hate my life." He hesitated. Tobias had been suicidal at different times in his life and early on in his treatment. He didn't want to give her the impression he was headed back to that dark place. "I don't mean it like I want to end it or anything like that. I just . . . I wake up every day and I'm still just . . . here. Taking up space. I go to a job I hate so I can pay for an apartment I hate. It just keeps going, on and on.

"You're tired of it."

"Yes."

"You want something different and you don't know how to

get it." She waited for that to sink in. "How's the book coming?"

Tobias scoffed. "Honestly, it's a mess. I'm all over the place. I follow these breadcrumbs that take me pages and pages in the wrong direction and then I have to figure out how to bring it back and . . ." He made eye contact again. Her eyes were slightly narrowed and she leaned in just enough to give the impression that if he were to fall, she'd be there ready to catch him. "Never mind. Sorry, I'm rambling."

"Stop apologizing, Tobias. You have something to say and I want to hear it."

Something welled up inside him at that moment. A wave started in his chest and rippled up, constricting his throat like a closed fist. His effort to keep the pressure from escaping pushed his eyebrows up toward the center of his forehead and contorted his lips together as if they were being cinched together by a drawstring. He turned his head and wiped his eye with the heel of his hand.

Dr. Macintosh sat patiently, giving him space to experience his emotions. She never interceded or made any attempt to rescue him from his pain, which is what his mother would have done. It was surprisingly validating to have an unbiased witness to his pain. When he finally turned back around, she met his reddened eyes with warmth and curiosity.

"Sorry. I mean . . ." He caught himself. "Sorry, I did it again. Ahhh!"

"It's fine," she said with a forgiving smile. "You're learning."

"I don't know where that came from."

"I think you do."

"Huh?"

"Close your eyes."

He complied.

"Go inside. Where did that come from? Follow it down, way down."

Just seconds into this exercise Tobias opened his eyes. "No, nope! I'm sorry, Dr. Mac . . . Joelle. I can't." He was trembling. The lump had returned to his throat. "It's . . . too much. I'm sorry, I can't right now."

"Let's just sit for a minute. Find your breath . . . Good. Now just stay with that breath as it moves in and out. Don't try to control it. Just stay with it, OK?

Tobias nodded and followed her instructions. His breath made its way around pockets of tension in his chest, throat, and face, slowly ironing them out. After several breaths, he shook his head. "How do you do that? You're like an emotional sherpa."

She laughed. "I didn't do it. You did."

"I feel bad. I'm just not ready. Is that OK?

"You're not disappointing me, Tobias. This is *your* journey. You lead the way. Understood?"

"Yes . . . No! No, I don't know where I'm going! How can I lead the way if I don't know where I'm going? I don't know what to do! I wish you could just tell me what to do. Why can't you just *tell* me?"

"Because that would be cheating," she said. "And you wouldn't do what I said anyway."

"I would. I promise I would. I . . . I trust you."

She took a deep breath. "Listen. You think your problem is that you're on the wrong side of this imaginary wall, that if you could just get to the other side, your life would suddenly improve. Tobias, there is no wall."

"I mean, yeah, I know there's not a literal wall."

"There's not even a figurative one. You made that up. And

you made it up a long time before you even met your ex-wife. Isn't that what you said? Now imagine that you had all the recognition, all the money, everything you believe being a published author would get you. How would you be different? Think about it."

"I wouldn't have to work this stupid job for one. I would feel more confident maybe? Maybe I'd feel confident enough to ask someone out?"

"Do you have anyone in mind?"

Mia's image flashed into his consciousness and Tobias tried in vain to suppress a grin. "Kind of. Maybe."

"Oh? Do tell," she said, matching his budding smile and framing her face with her thumb and forefinger.

"It's stupid. She's way out of my league anyway, so . . ." He shook his head dismissively.

"Go on," she prodded.

"She works at this coffee shop by my work. She knows my order." His smile broke through this time.

"Oh? What's her name?" It's as if she'd caught a big fish and refused to let go.

"Mia. At least that's what her name tag says."

"Mia." She repeated the name slowly, carefully enunciating the vowels, which made him smile again. "And does she know your name?"

He scoffed. "No."

"You said you'd do what I told you to do, right?"

"Oh, God! Wait. You're not going to make me talk to her, are you?"

"How soon we abandon our promises," she teased.

"She'd never go for someone like me. What would I even say?"

"Well, I'm not going to spoon-feed you pick-up lines for Christ's sake!" She smiled.

"No, I know. I just . . . we probably have nothing in common."

Dr. Macintosh picked up a pad of sticky notes and a pen from her side table and wrote down: *We probably have nothing in common.* She handed him the sticky note. "Put this on."

"What?"

"Put it on your shirt."

"Oh . . . kay." He did as she said. "But what—"

"What else do you have? Give me some more excuses."

"Uh . . . she's too young?"

Dr. Macintosh removed her glasses for a second and squinted. "How young?"

"I don't know. Like mid-twenties?"

She put her glasses back on and wrote on another sticky note: *She's too young.* She handed him the note. "Put that one on, too."

He scoffed. "OK."

"What else?"

"I don't know. Um . . . I'm not her type?"

"How would you know what her type is? You've never even talked to her?" She raised her hand, interrupting herself. "You know what? Never mind." She wrote: *I'm not her type.* "Here you go."

"I don't know what this is supposed to—"

"What else? Come on. I'm sure you have more."

"Mmmm, let me see. She probably has a boyfriend."

Dr. Macintosh continued this exercise until Tobias was covered in pastel-colored sticky notes. "Is that it?"

Tobias looked down at himself. "Don't you think that's enough? Yeah, I guess that's it." Tobias examined all of the little notes, some of which he'd added to his pant legs after his shirt ran out of room.

"Good! I'm all out of sticky notes! Now, I'll be Mia."

"Seriously? Roleplay?"

"Yes, seriously." She straightened herself in her chair and pulled her hair behind her ears. "Are you ready?"

"Oh geez. I guess so." He shook out his hands and then rubbed them against his thighs.

"OK, now I want you to be aware of all these thoughts here." She pointed to his shirt and moved her index finger in a circular motion. "You'll have to bring all these with you."

"Wait, I have to wear these into the coffee shop?" Tobias looked terrified.

"Oh dear God, no. You'd make a fool of yourself. No. These are just thoughts, see? You can't get rid of them. You have to bring them with you. Got it?"

"I think so." It did make sense. These thoughts were always there--doubts, second guesses. All these negative thoughts had a significant role in shaping his behavior. They held him back—kept him small. He was more than ready to learn how to break free from their influence.

"OK. I'm ready whenever you are." She got into character by smiling a bit flirtatiously, which made Tobias giggle. "What? Doesn't she smile?"

"Yes. She does. Sorry. Ahhh! *Not* sorry! Uggh."

"Deep breath."

He took a deep breath. "I don't know why I'm so nervous. I shouldn't be."

"No need to should on yourself. Accept it and breathe through it. Yes?"

"Right. Yes. OK. I'm ready."

They spent the last twenty minutes of their session role-playing what Tobias assumed must have come quite naturally to other guys. It took him several minutes to warm up but eventually, he was able to laugh at himself in the safety of her presence. At one point, Tobias suggested they stand because that was truer to life. She used her chair as a prop to represent the counter and stood behind it. She had Tobias exaggerate his fears and they played out worst-case scenarios to build his resilience toward failure. By the end of the session, they were both laughing. He felt an inclination to hug her but thought it might be inappropriate. He wasn't sure.

"I believe you have your marching orders," she said peering at him through the top half of her glasses.

He slowly shook his head from side to side. "I'm still just so scared."

"Of course you are. If you weren't scared, it wouldn't be worth it."

3

——————

Tobias had arranged to come into work an hour late to accommodate his therapy session earlier that morning. He was running a few minutes behind and he was already skating on thin ice with his productivity. He deliberated on whether to stop for coffee on his way in. Although he was feeling a modicum of confidence from his experiential exercises in therapy, he still wasn't ready to talk to Mia. As he passed by the cafe's storefront, he could see that the volume of customers at this late morning hour was significantly reduced. This was enough to persuade him to enter.

Mia was manning the register after all. Anxiety washed over him like a heatwave. He took a deep breath and walked toward the counter. Mia was laughing with a male customer and gesticulating with her hands. Tobias wanted desperately to know the subject of their banter, but he couldn't quite make out what they had been discussing before she took the man's payment. It was probably something cool or clever and he probably didn't have to think about it—it just came out effortlessly because that's how it is for people on the inside. Their interaction ended and the customer stepped to one side. Tobias felt another wave of heat so strong it nearly affected his balance as he stepped to the counter.

Mia pulled a vibrating phone from her back pocket. She turned to another barista and asked him to take over and walked into the back to take the call. She hadn't even seen Tobias standing there. He was watching Mia walk away when her replacement took his order.

"Huh?" Tobias asked as if coming out of a trance.

"What can I get you?" the barista asked a second time, enunciating his words.

"Oh. Um, cortado with a half packet of stevia. To go."

"Sweeteners are over there," the barista said gesturing with his head. "That's $4.85."

He wondered what calamity might have been so urgent as to steal his last occasion for happiness. How important was it? Had someone died? Or was it something as mundane as some inconsequential slice of gossip from a friend? The thought of her leaving him standing there for some trivial pretext hardened his heart toward her. He wished, for the sake of his fragile ego, that someone *had* died. He immediately recognized this as a ghoulish thought, and he loathed himself for entertaining it.

Tobias arrived at his cubicle, slightly sweetened cortado in hand. A yellow sticky note was affixed to his computer monitor: See Carl. *Shit.* If he didn't get fired today, he would be genuinely surprised. He knocked on the open door to Carl's office. Carl was on a phone call, which he ended promptly after waving Tobias in.

"You wanted to see me?" Tobias asked apprehensively.

"Hey, buddy! Listen, I'm gonna need you to start on this new project right away. They moved up the deadline."

"But what about the—"

"Leave it. I'll have Declan finish that up."

"Declan? But he isn't a writer." Declan was a twenty-two-year-old unpaid intern at the company for whom Carl was running out of assignments. The fact that he trusted the intern, who spent most days fetching lunches and delivering mail, with one of Tobias' main job responsibilities only furthered his sense of meaninglessness.

"No, but he needs something to do. Yesterday, I had him stuffing envelopes for Cindy's baby shower. He can handle it."

"Who's Cindy?"

"My wife." Carl turned a framed photo of his exceptionally photogenic wife around for Tobias to see.

"You're married?" Tobias was genuinely astounded. "To her?" Carl had the kind of physique that was both lean and fat at the same time. He was balding yet had the arms of an orangutan, an unfortunate paradox of corporeal existence. His wife, on the other hand, appeared well-proportioned, with radiant skin and a bright smile.

"Yep. That's my Cindy-bun."

Oof, he thought. *Like Cinnabon? So lame.* "And she's having *your* baby?"

"You seem surprised!"

"No, I mean, that's great. Good for you. Congrats."

"Thanks, buddy! You want to come? It's co-ed."

"What? What is?"

"The baby shower! Yeah, she says these days it's totally normal to invite men to these things. Whodathunkit?" Carl laughed exposing his top row of teeth and gums.

Tobias forced a chuckle. "Not me!" He tried in vain to match Carl's amusement. "Wow, no, I don't know. I've never been to one of those. I might be busy, actually."

"I didn't tell you when it was."

Busted. "Right. You know, it's just that I spend most of my free time writing . . . my book."

"Oh, that's right. Well, if you can spare a couple hours a month from Saturday . . . I'm making paella!"

"Oh. Awesome. Yeah, I'll think about it. Well, I'd better get started on this new assignment."

"You got it, dude. Later dater!"

Tobias cringed. He pondered how someone as lovely as Cindy would ever marry a guy who not only looks like Carl but who says things like "later dater," and "whodathunkit." Was either of them even aware of the obvious discrepancy? Tobias took stock of his own subjective level of physical appeal. He was no prize, but he was certain the disparity between his former wife's good looks and his own were not nearly as great. Yet she left him while the likes of Cindy and Carl, as mismatched in aesthetic appraisal as they may have been, seemed to have managed enough success as a couple to warrant procreation. Tobias felt jealous of Carl's good fortune. He wondered what he was doing wrong.

His parents, happily married for forty-two years, lived in the same suburban, four-bedroom, ranch-style home Tobias had grown up in. His father was a retired high school history teacher. His mother, a university administrator. Since Everly left, his mother insisted he come over for dinner on Thursday evenings. It was usually a casserole of some kind, or lasagna, or something equally rich in carbohydrates. Tonight, chicken a la king with a heavily-dressed garden salad from a bag. Tobias had never been impressed with his mother's cooking but lately, it was the only home-cooked meal he was getting.

Arthur Munch was rarely seen away from his recliner, and after 5:00 p.m., without a rocks glass in hand. The only thing that changed about his attire since teaching high school was that he had traded in his brown leather penny loafers for red and black plaid house slippers, still with dress socks. Otherwise, he still tucked his short-sleeved dress shirts, usually overlaid with a sweater vest or cardigan, into tan or gray polyester slacks. He was watching a historical documentary on Nero's sunken city and sipping his Glenlivet, 12-year, single malt Scotch when Tobias arrived.

"Hey, Dad," Tobias said closing the front door behind him as he entered.

"Mmm," Arthur grunted with a weak raise of his right hand, keeping his eyes on the flat screen.

"Good to see you, too," Tobias said under his breath and walked into the kitchen to greet his mother.

"Hi, honey!" Barbara Munch said cheerily, pulling a steaming dish from the oven with floral-patterned oven mitts. "How was your day?"

"Fine." He plucked a crouton from the salad bowl and examined it before popping it into his mouth.

"How was therapy?" Barbara always seemed to have a litany of questions in a queue at all times.

"Fine, Mom," Tobias said irritably.

"You know, I did a little research on Dr. Macintosh and—"

"Mom!"

"Well, did you know she writes a blog for *Psychology Today*?"

"No."

"You should look her up. She's written some really interesting articles."

"Great. Even my therapist is a more successful writer than I am."

"Oh, don't be like that, Toby. You should be grateful to have her as your therapist. She seems very knowledgeable. Do you like her?"

"Yeah, she's fine. Can we not talk about my therapist right now? And yes, before you ask me about it, I'm taking my medicine every day, alright?"

"That's wonderful, Toby. Do you feel like it's making a difference?"

Tobias sighed heavily. "I think so. Can we talk about something else, please? I'm sorry, I just—"

"Of course, honey. So what's new?"

Tobias sighed again. "Let's see. I learned my boss is married and he's about to have a baby."

"Oh, that's nice. You didn't know he was married?"

"No. It surprised me, actually."

"Really? Why?"

"I don't know. I always thought he was kind of a loser and his wife . . . she seems really out of his league. I just can't picture them together."

"Well, I was very much out of your father's league when we met. It's not always about looks, you know."

"Yeah, I know," he said, thumbing the grout lines on the kitchen counter. "How does that happen though? I mean, how does somebody like dad even get your attention?"

"Oh, well he drove this cute little baby-blue Triumph, and—"

"Wait. You liked him for his car?"

"Well, no, not just that. He was a few years older and he was very smart. *So* smart. I'd sneak out of the house with him and we'd go to the Dairy Queen or to the lookout and just talk for hours. He would do most of the talking—if you can believe that! I remember feeling quite intimidated by how much he knew and so I would just listen and ask him questions just to hear him talk sometimes. I could tell he was taken with me and he was very respectful. I'd gone out with cuter, more popular boys but they were just kind of full of themselves. They didn't treat me the way your father did." She gazed nostalgically at their 1979 wedding portrait hanging on the dining room wall. "I guess when it comes right down to it, you want to be with someone that makes you feel good."

"So whatever happened to the Triumph?"

"Your sister came along and we needed a car with a back seat. That's what happened."

"Seems like things were just simpler back then."

"Well, we didn't have all these dating apps you all use these days. Swipe left, swipe right." She chuckled and shook her head. "It's like everybody's dispensable. One person doesn't check all your boxes and, next, you just move on to another, and another."

"Dispensable. That sounds about right."

"Oh, honey, I didn't mean to—"

"No, mom, it's fine. Really. Is dinner ready?"

She placed her hand on his cheek. "Honey, don't worry. You'll find someone in good time. If only you believed in yourself half as much as we do."

"Yeah, I know, mom." He backed away breaking contact. "I'll go get dad."

Tobias passed through the kitchen into the family room where his father reclined, when a familiar color scheme caught his eye. A hardback with glossy teal script on a light peach background sat atop the credenza among framed family photos, the author's name in bold magenta across the bottom: Everly Bronson. Tobias picked up the book and opened its front cover. The inscription read:

To Barb and Artie,

Thank you for all your warmth and support over the years.

You are loved and dearly missed.

Love, Everly Bronson

"Mom!" Tobias called still staring at the inscription and trembling. "Mom, what is this?"

"Oh! That came a few days ago. That was nice of her to think of us."

"Nice?" Tobias was beside himself. "Mom! It's basically a manual on how to leave your husband!"

"Oh, Toby! It's not about that at all. It's about—"

Tobias noticed the book had been dog-eared—page 64. "You've been reading it?!" His voice cracked as the familiar lump returned to his throat.

She stammered. "Well, I just . . . I mean she was kind enough to send us a signed copy . . . I just . . . I . . ." She looked to her husband for assistance. He stood there rattling the remaining melted ice in his rocks glass.

Tobias shook the book in his mother's face and dropped it back onto the credenza so that it made a loud slap and knocked over a framed photo. "I can't stay here. I . . . I need some air."

His father spoke up. "Don't blame your mother. She didn't ask Everly to send her that book. I did."

"What?"

"What?" Barbara echoed.

"I ran into her a couple weeks ago at the farmer's market. She asked how you were doing. Said her book was coming out and she asked me if I would like a copy. I didn't want to be rude, so said I would. And that was pretty much it."

Tobias backed away as if his parents had just removed humanoid masks to reveal their reptilian identities. "I gotta go," he muttered and staggered out the front door.

Even at his lowest point, deep down he knew at least he had his parents' support. Now, he felt, he'd lost that, too. He was afraid to be alone so he went downtown where he could walk around anonymously as a member of society without having to engage as one. He walked past restaurants and nightclubs. Lovers held hands. Teenagers flew by on skateboards. Groups of friends laughed and pushed each other playfully as they stumbled toward their next boozy adventure. Tobias walked with his hands plunged into the pockets of his hooded sweatshirt. The smell of alcohol, car fumes, and urine wafted into his nostrils.

He was deep in thought when he entered the crosswalk. The walk signal was lit but he hadn't bothered to look both ways as his reptilian parents had taught him to do since the age of five. Headlights caught his peripheral vision to the right and the sound of car breaks startled him before he realized what was happening. The impact sent him well into the middle of the intersection. His glasses were flung from his head before it made an audible *thwack* against the asphalt.

A crowd gathered around him and shouts to call 911 and to "get back" could be heard distantly beyond the ringing in his ears. When he opened his eyes, he could see street lights and human heads jockeying for a closer look upon strained necks. Sounds gradually became more distinct. A female figure knelt beside him, the streetlamp obscuring her features. She was crying. "Oh my God! I'm so sorry! Please be OK!" She leaned in closer eclipsing the light from the streetlamp above and Tobias thought he must be dreaming. It was Mia.

4

———————

Within minutes an ambulance arrived on the scene and EMTs carefully transferred his body onto a gurney and into the back of the ambulance. Each jostling maneuver sent pain throughout his body. Clumps of onlookers still lingered on the sidewalks as police taped off the intersection. Tobias caught a faded glimpse between emergency lights flashes of two police officers speaking with a distraught Mia Navarro who was leaning against her car holding her elbows.

They transported Tobias to the university hospital just a few blocks away where they treated his wounds. Tobias was lucky to have survived with a mild concussion, a broken wrist, and superficial lacerations. He was given medication for the pain yet his head continued to throb. He kept thinking about Mia. Despite everything, he felt guilty that he might have caused her trouble. This couldn't have been easy on her either.

Two police officers arrived later that evening to file a report. "You're very lucky, Mr. Munch," the female officer said. "Is there anyone you'd like us to call?"

Tobias was still angry at his parents. He knew his mother would have dropped everything to be by his side. He also knew he wouldn't be able to get her to leave. "No."

"Can you tell us what you remember about the accident?" She clicked a pen and unfolded a pocket-sized notepad.

"I was crossing the street and then I just heard like, a screeching sound. Next thing I knew I was on the ground."

"Did you see the car before the impact?"

"No, just the headlights."

"And you were in the crosswalk when you were hit?"

"Yeah."

"Have you had anything to drink this evening?

"No."

"What were you doing downtown?"

"Nothing. Just walking around."

"Just walking around?" she asked suspiciously.

"Yeah."

"Were you with anyone? Meeting up with anyone?"

"No."

"OK," she said with a slight tilt of her head as if resigned to getting very limited information. "Anything else you can tell us about the incident?"

"The girl . . . the uh . . . driver. Is she OK? I mean, she's not in trouble is she?"

"That all depends on whether you wish to press charges. Do you?"

"No. No, I don't want to press any charges."

"Call us if you change your mind." She handed him her card.

The second officer held out a clear zip-lock bag with tortoiseshell eyeglasses, the frames irreparably twisted at the hinge. One lens was missing, the other badly scratched. "These yours?"

"Yeah. Those are mine." *What am I supposed to do with those?* he thought.

The officer set the bag on his nightstand. "Feel better, Mr. Munch."

They held him overnight because an MRI had been scheduled first thing in the morning to ascertain any further bleeding in his skull. It was only a precaution. After the imaging the next morning, when they brought him back to his room, Mia was waiting there with flowers. She stood as he was being wheeled into place. He thought it very likely that he was dreaming.

"Hi, I'm Mia. I hit you with my car." Her eyebrows drew upward toward the center of her forehead and her mouth twisted to one side. "I wanted to apologize in person." She held out the bouquet of flowers in its cellophane wrapping. Tobias had never gotten flowers from anyone before. It might have been the concussion but he struggled to give context to this unprecedented act of kindness, so he remained awkwardly unresponsive. Mia placed them on the rolling adjustable bedside tray. "The police said you aren't going to press charges. That's . . . that's really cool of you."

"It was an accident," he said.

She sat on the bed and squeezed his uninjured forearm. "Thank you." She gave him a look of gratitude that made him forget his incredible pain. "Oh! I almost forgot . . ." Her face lit up the way Tobias was accustomed to seeing it, wide-eyed and vibrant. Mia pulled a card from a small suede crossbody satchel, which was more fringe than pouch. "It's a gift card . . . for coffee. I know it doesn't exactly make up for running you over. I work at this coffee shop, so . . ." She shrugged and placed the gift card on the bedside table next to the flowers.

"You don't recognize me," Tobias said, attempting to omit any emotional pain from this statement.

Mia tilted her head and narrowed her eyes. "Do I know you?"

"No. I guess not." *Of course not*, he thought. "I'm . . . I'm one of your customers."

Mia's eyes flashed in recognition. "Oh my God! Totally! I just didn't recognize you without your glasses. Holy shit! So that's why you didn't press charges." She smiled widely. "Can't make your morning coffee if I'm in jail!" She giggled.

"Yep. You got me." His ribs had been badly bruised and it hurt him to laugh, so his laugh quickly devolved into groans.

"Oh shit. I'm sorry. No laughing, no laughing." Her face was scrunched up again. "Do you need anything? Water? Morphine?"

"No, it's OK. I'm fine," he said unconvincingly. So far, Tobias felt things were going well. Too well. It was only a matter of time before he made it awkward or said something stupid. It was better, he concluded, to leave on a high note. "You don't have to stay. I know you probably have to get to work."

"Nope! I took the day. I told my boss what happened. That's when I thought I might be going to jail. I should probably text her real quick." She reached into her suede pouch to retrieve her phone. Tobias gazed upon her as her thumbs moved nimbly across her phone's keyboard. Mia's blonde hair was pulled up into a sloppy bun. Her eyes danced in the glow of her smartphone. Even without his glasses, Tobias found every feature of her youthful face luminous and perfect. She smiled as she hit the send button. "There! So, are you getting out today?"

"I think so. As long as the MRI looks OK."

"Do you need a ride?"

"Uhhh . . ."

Mia broke into laughter. "I promise I'm not usually a terrible driver!"

"Oh, no, I wasn't thinking—"

"Sure, sure. No, seriously. It's the least I can do."

"I mean, I don't know how long it's going to be—"

"Tobias . . ." She looked him in the eye and squeezed his hand. "I don't mind. Really."

"I never told you my name."

Mia tapped his hospital wristband.

"Oh, right." *I'm an idiot!* he thought, rolling his eyes at himself. "It's the concussion."

"Uh-huh." She was smiling.

Tobias was having a hard time accepting that Mia was actually enjoying his company and wasn't there purely to appease her guilt. He had to keep reminding himself not to get too excited or read too much into anything. "So how's your car? Any damage?"

"Eh," She shrugged her shoulders. "What's another dent? I actually didn't even check."

"So what happened? Were you just feeling a little homicidal last night?"

She laughed. "Yeah, I was like, 'Who can I murder tonight?' Honestly, I don't have a great excuse. I dropped my phone and I just didn't see the light turn red. By the time I saw it, it was too late." Her countenance was remorseful and contrite at that moment but true to her nature, an effervescent vitality seemed to buoy her up into brightness. "Can I be the first to sign your cast?"

"Sure. Do you have a—"

Mia procured a glittery purple pen from her purse and removed the cap with her teeth. She scratched her name in large block letters, filling in the empty spaces with blue ink.

A knock came at the door and a doctor entered carrying a clipboard. "Mr. Munch? I'm Dr. Burroughs. Your MRI looks good. No additional bleeding or swelling. You do have a concussion, so I want you to take it easy for a few days. Call me if your headaches continue for more than a couple of days, or if you have any other symptoms, dizziness, lapses in memory, things like that. You'll need to schedule a follow-up with the orthopedic to get that cast off in six weeks. Do you have a ride home?"

"I'm his ride," Mia interjected.

"Very well. I'll get your discharge paperwork started. You can go ahead and get dressed."

Tobias didn't actually know where his clothes were and he was too self-conscious to ask. Mia was the one who found them folded on a shelf inside a wardrobe closet. Tobias realized he was wearing only underwear beneath his hospital gown. The pattern on his gown was the kind of design one might find on the upholstery of an airplane seat.

"You're going to need some help getting these on," she said.

"I'll call the nurse," he said, reaching for the call button.

"Don't be silly. I can help you. Here, can you sit up?"

He wasn't totally certain that he could. He complied more so to answer that question for himself. Tobias was struggling to process the fact that Mia Navarro was sitting on his bed and about to see him in his underwear. He wasn't ready for this, but it was happening. She removed his arm sling and then unbuttoned the snaps along his left arm up to his shoulder and untied the string under his right arm letting the thin gown fall to his waist. She carefully threaded his cast through one sleeve while he threaded the other with his left arm. She held the neck hole open, pulled it over his head, and carefully straightened it down over his torso.

He swung sideways and hung his legs over the side of the bed sensing the cool air on his bare thighs. He took his blue jeans in his left hand, the uninjured one, and dangled them down near his feet as if he were trying to catch fish in a net. Mia took over and slid the waistband up to his knees and tugged the legs up over the tops of his feet. When he stood up, he caught the pants before they fell back around his ankles and pulled them up over his underwear. Mia tugged the right side of his waistband up so that they rested evenly on his hips. Tobias managed to snap the top button closed with his free hand and maneuver the zipper up, not all the way but close enough. Mia put on his socks and shoes. He noticed that she had a different method of tying shoes. Not wrong, just different.

The cast was too big to thread through his hoodie sleeve. She placed the sling around his cast and adjusted the straps. She threaded his left arm through the sleeve and wrapped the right side over his sling letting the hoodie sleeve dangle from his right shoulder. She zipped the hoodie up halfway to secure it to his torso. She dressed him in the same manner she prepared his coffee, with great care and respect. It felt nice. He tried to enjoy feeling cared for without jumping to any ridiculous conclusions.

"There," she said. "Don't forget your glasses." She held

them up in their Ziplock bag and twisted up her mouth concealing a smile just under the surface.

"Yeah, I think those are pretty much toast." It didn't take much to trigger laughter in Mia. He wasn't even trying to be funny.

After Tobias signed his discharge paperwork, Mia pushed him in a wheelchair into a parking garage. She helped him into the passenger side of an early aughts, sun-faded, forest green Subaru. She cleared a space in the passenger's seat and floorboard as best she could, throwing empty cups, opened envelopes, and a shopping bag filled with items she had been intending to return, into the back seat. The interior smelled heavily of cannabis with the floral undertones of what might have been Mia's shampoo or lotion. A Ruth Bader Ginsburg air freshener coupled with a rose quartz crystal hung from her rearview mirror. A bumper sticker adhered to the front of the glove compartment read: *All Good Things Are Wild and Free*, in colorful floral lettering.

"Sorry about the mess," she said. Mia started the car and helped Tobias secure his seatbelt. She opened the center console and removed a purple ceramic vaporizer and took a steady draw. She rolled down the window and released the excess smoke from her lungs into the parking garage. "You want a hit?" She offered the small device.

"No, I'm good." He wondered if she had been high when she hit him the night before. Surely the cops had conducted a sobriety test. They would have detected it in her pupils had they checked. A flash of anxiety washed over him as she put the car in reverse and began to make her way to the garage exit. Tobias was not a cannabis user. He'd experimented in college, but it had affected him much more aggressively than his peers. He got so stoned that it was all he could do to ensure the earth remained solidly beneath him. He white-knuckled the experience a few times to maintain credibility with his peers, all the while wishing the relentless spinning would pass.

"So where are we going?" Mia asked. "Where do you live?"

Tobias was suddenly less concerned about her ability to drive under the influence than he was about what she might think of his meager accommodations. He was still struggling to remain aloof and not allow his unrealistic hopes to lead him into disappointment. He convinced himself that what they had shared so far was more than he could have ever expected and that there was no reason to suspect anything would progress beyond this obligatory courtesy.

"Eastside. Almost to the fairgrounds," he said.

"Oh shit. I'll need to get some gas."

"Sorry, I should have warned you it was far."

"No worries!" She pulled into a Shell station. "You need anything? Water? Snacks?"

"No, thanks." He realized he was hungry. He'd left the house before eating dinner last night and forgot to order breakfast at the hospital. It was already past noon.

Mia got back into the car after filling up. "So, Tobias Munch, what do you do? For work?" She took another draw from her vaporizer.

"I'm a technical writer." Hopefully, Mia wouldn't press for more details.

"Cool! What is that?" She seemed genuinely interested.

"Well, you know when you buy something like a blow dryer or a popcorn maker, and it comes with an owner's manual?"

"Yeah."

"I write those."

"Really? Wow! I didn't know that was a thing."

"Yeah, nobody does. I hate my job."

"It can't be that bad."

Tobias shrugged. "I'm writing a novel."

"That's awesome! What's it about?"

Tobias deliberated for a moment whether to entertain her question whole-heartedly. In a few days, she would go back to being a barista and he, her customer. The only difference is that she would know his name. In the end, he figured he had nothing to lose. He spent the entire drive telling his cosmic saga, interrupting only to give driving directions. She was captivated. She'd taken another hit or two along the way and if she was high, he couldn't tell. They pulled up to his apartment complex. "Well that's pretty much it, in a nutshell," he said, wrapping it up.

"I can't wait to read it!" Mia said. *This is what everyone says.* "Let me help you."

"No, I got it. Thanks for the ride. I really appreciate it. I'll see you on Monday morning."

"I think you're the only person who orders a cortado. Most people just order the latte."

"There's less milk in a cortado."

"I *know*. I'm the barista, remember?"

"Of course. Yours is the best, by the way." *Am I flirting? Stop it!*

She shrugged playfully. "I know."

Tobias opened the passenger door and stepped out. As soon he stood up, he felt himself tipping backward and he fell.

"Oh shit!" Mia jumped out and ran around to his side. She slapped his face rapidly. "Tobias! Wake up!"

Tobias blinked. "We have to stop meeting like this."

"Oh my God! You scared the shit out of me." She helped him to a sitting position and then to his feet with his arm around her. Mia walked Tobias up the stairs to his tangerine-painted front door.

"This is me. Thanks again."

"Let me help you to bed. You need to rest."

Tobias reached into his pockets and paused. "Oh no."

"What is it?" Mia asked.

He closed his eyes and dropped his head. "I don't have my keys."

5

———

MIA, true to form, couldn't help but laugh. Tobias was slow to join but sure enough, Mia's infectious joy broke him and he laughed as much as his bruised ribs would allow. "So what now?" Tobias asked.

"Did you leave them at the hospital?" Mia asked.

"I guess so." Normally, he would never have forgotten his keys but he was too distracted by her presence at the hospital to think clearly.

Mia checked for open windows. "Leasing office. They'll have extra keys."

"You mean Bill. He lives in building one." He pointed. "By those vending machines."

"Stay here, I'll check." Mia ran down the stairs and over to Bill's unit and knocked. She turned to face Tobias who was watching from the second floor of building three. She waved happily and bounced on the balls of her feet as she waited for Bill to answer. She knocked again. After a moment, she turned to Tobias and shrugged. She tried to peer into Bill's window before walking back to Tobias. "Do you have his number?"

"It's in my pho—" *Kill me now.*

"You've got to be kidding me!" She laughed again leaning over the metal railing, pretending to hurl herself over it.

"I'm glad this amuses you."

"Alright, alright, let me think. Just come to my house. You can chill there for as long as you need. I'll go back to the hospital and pick up your things."

"No, that's OK. I wouldn't want to impose."

"Tobias." Her tone was suddenly stern. "Don't apologize. I did this, not you. Just let me fix it."

"There's nothing to fix. You've been more than helpful, really. I'll be fine." Tobias felt he was quickly wearing out his welcome. His stomach growled.

"Oh my God, you haven't eaten all day. You must be starving! Come on." She helped him down the stairs and back into her car.

Mia drove back toward the university and pulled up to a historic two-story craftsman, which shared the street with university-subsidized student housing, a record store, a vegan restaurant, a thrift store, and a tattoo salon. A large rainbow pride flag flew from a diagonal flagpole attached to a tapered front porch column. The paint on the blue house with white trim was noticeably peeling. Weeds grew from a large cracks in the sidewalk and concrete stairs leading up to the front porch.

A barefooted, shirtless man in cut-off shorts and a green fedora reclined in a hanging rattan porch chair. He was smoking weed from a bong. "Hey baby," he said coolly, the whites of his eyes pink and glossy.

"Hey, Herman!" Mia said sweetly, the way Tobias imagined she might have spoken to a grandfather. "This is Tobias."

"Sup, playa?" Herman asked.

"Hey uh, sup?" Tobias never felt whiter.

"I hit him with my car!" Mia explained to Herman.

"Oh shit! Yo, you wanna hit this, bruh?" Herman extended the beaker-shaped glass bong toward Tobias.

"Nah, I mean, no, thanks."

"You do you, bruh." He flicked his lighter and pulled another bubbling draw from the bong.

Tobias nodded and followed Mia inside. "Does he live here?"

"Herman? No." She offered no further explanation leaving Tobias confused. Two Asian women a few years younger than Mia, wearing men's boxer shorts and oversized t-shirts, played a video game on the living room couch. His eyes burned from marijuana smoke that hung thick in the air. "Why don't you go ahead and make yourself comfortable. I'll make us some lunch." Mia disappeared into the kitchen while Tobias stood awkwardly in the living room with two women he hadn't yet been introduced to. They hadn't even acknowledged him standing there. Tobias sat on an adjacent love seat trying not to disrupt.

"World of Warcraft?" Tobias asked finally.

The young women were wearing over-ear headphones and either didn't hear him, or they were deliberately ignoring him. Tobias was eyeing an open bag of BBQ potato chips on the coffee table next to a ceramic ashtray containing two healthy marijuana buds, a red and yellow swirled glass-blown pipe, and a lighter. His stomach growled but he thought it better to hold out until Mia returned.

The furniture and decor reminded him of his college

days. A 5' by 5' mandala tapestry of greens, blues, and yellows hung behind the couch. A framed print of Bob Marley, a cliched staple of college living, hung on another wall. A pair of red conga drums stood in a far corner. The built-in shelving held a disorganized collection of books, vinyl records, Buddha statuettes, shoe boxes, and an empty terrarium. He wondered what creature the terrarium housed, which was surely roaming freely outside its designated containment.

"Here you go!" Mia approached him from behind, extending a plate around his shoulder with a vegan BLT and some freshly sliced cantaloupe. He took the plate and she climbed over the backside of the couch, plopping down with her own plate. She sat cross-legged, facing him on the love seat.

"Thanks," he said. She watched him as he took a bite and nodded. "Good," he said, still chewing.

This seemed to please her and she started in on her sandwich. "Have you met Courtney and Frankie?"

"No, not formally," he said.

"Ladies, this is Tobias. Tobias this is Courtney, and that's Frankie."

Courtney said, "Hey," keeping her eyes on the screen. Frankie glanced at him and offered an uninspired up-nod before returning to the game.

"Do *they* live here?" Tobias asked Mia.

"Frankie does. And Khalil. He's at work."

"How long have you lived here?"

"Like two years?" She placed her unfinished BLT on the cluttered coffee table. She stretched and yawned. "I bet you're tired."

"A little." He was curious about her living situation but

every time he tried to get anything out of her, she seemed to change the subject. He wanted to know how she ended up here. How did she meet these people? Who was that guy on the front porch? But before he could ask another question, she beat him to it.

"Do you want to take a nap?"

"OK." The thought of the two of them taking a nap together amused him only for a split second. He knew that's not what she meant and quickly put himself in check. After all that driving around and the lingering effects of his medication, Tobias *was* feeling tired.

She grabbed his plate and set it on top of hers. "Come on." She helped him to his feet and pulled him by the hand toward the stairs. He followed her up to her bedroom. Mia's bedroom was a more pleasant-smelling version of her car. The bed was unmade. Notebooks, art supplies, empty cups, and clothing covered her nightstand, dresser, and floors. "I think you should stay here tonight."

"OK." *What is happening?* he thought. Surely, she didn't mean *in her room.*

Mia unzipped his hoodie and tossed it onto an armchair, already obscured with clothing. She helped him lay down, fluffed the pillows behind his head, and removed his shoes. "Better?"

"Yeah."

Mia laid beside him on the unmade queen-sized bed. Tobias had just spent the last few minutes convincing himself that Mia was only caring for him out of obligation and that when she asked him if he wanted to take a nap, didn't actually mean *with her.* He was having that experience again, where reality as it unfolded in the present moment, was occurring quicker than he was able to comprehend it. *How is this even happening?* he thought. Within moments, however, fatigue had taken over and Tobias fell into a deep sleep.

When he awoke, he was alone. Judging by the orange-yellow light entering from the windows, it must have been dusk. He sat up and placed his feet on the floor. He rose slowly and made his way into the hallway to the top of the stairs. He could hear an intense discussion happening downstairs between Mia and a man. He could tell by his voice that it wasn't Herman. Was this Mia's boyfriend? They were speaking in hushed tones and he couldn't make out the subject matter. Her tone was sharp and acrimonious. Were they talking about him?

A floorboard creaked under Tobias' foot and the discussion halted. He didn't want them to think he was eavesdropping, so he carefully descended the stairs.

"Tobias!" Mia exclaimed. "You slept forever. Good news! The hospital does have your phone and keys. But they wouldn't let me pick them up. They said you have to be the one to claim it. We can go after dinner if you want."

"Cool." Tobias was waiting for an introduction. The tall dark-skinned man with long black shoulder-length hair was standing with his hands on his waist, looking uncharitably at Tobias. His dark eyes scrutinized Tobias, making him feel exposed and intimidated. He was wearing a loose-fitting white linen shirt, sleeves rolled up, with the top three buttons unbuttoned, revealing well-defined pecs carpeted in dark chest hair.

"This is Khalil," Mia said. Khalil didn't respond but continued peering menacingly into Tobias' soul. "He's in a mood. Come on. What are you hungry for?"

"Oh. Anything." He was preoccupied with Khalil and his apparent disapproval. He didn't feel particularly up for going out but under the circumstances, he was eager to escape the tension in the house at present. Mia ran upstairs to grab his shoes and hoodie. Tobias stood at the bottom of the stairs in his socks pretending not to notice Khalil's visual daggers. When Mia returned with his shoes, he slipped them on without tying them and proceeded toward the front door.

"Be safe," Khalil said ominously. Mia ignored him.

"Nice to meet you," Tobias said half-heartedly and then closed the door behind him.

"What was that all about?" Tobias asked as they walked to the car.

"Don't worry about it. Just house drama. So . . ." she said, backing out of the driveway. "Tell me more about this book you're writing. How long did you say you've been working on it?"

"Over eight years now."

"Wow! When do you think you'll finish?"

"That's the ten-thousand-dollar question. It just keeps evolving. I'm trying to shorten it."

"Why don't you break it up into like, a series?"

"That's an option, I guess. I hadn't really thought of that." He had thought of that. Unfortunately, the saga was so convoluted and meandering that there were no natural breaks anywhere in the story. He didn't have the energy to explain.

Mia took another hit from her vaporizer.

"Hey, can I ask you a personal question?" Tobias asked.

She exhaled smoke through a cracked window. "Shoot."

"Are you and Khalil . . . like, together?

"Uh, no!" Mia exclaimed emphatically.

"Do you have a boyfriend . . . or a girlfriend?"

"Nope. What about you? I assume if you were in a relationship, you wouldn't be here with me."

"I guess you're right." He wondered what she might have meant by being here with her. What did she think they were doing? He reasoned that she must just mean that if he *were* in a relationship, his significant other would be the one caring for him and not her. Yes, that made more sense.

"I hope I'm not keeping you from anything." Her eyes widened. "Oh my God! I'm totally kidnapping you! You don't have your phone or your keys. You're injured. I could totally go all *Misery* on you if I wanted!" She laughed.

Tobias laughed nervously. "Where are we going?"

"Riiight . . . here." She parked on the street by an open lot hosting various food trucks. "You want falafel, BBQ, tacos, or . . . sushi?"

"Sushi? From a food truck? Pass."

"Right?"

"What are you getting?"

"Vegan ice cream," Mia said, as a matter of fact.

"Is it any good?" He meant, of course, whether vegan ice cream was as good as regular.

"No, it's terrible. That's why I'm getting it."

"Fair enough. I think I'll try the tacos."

"Solid choice. Meet me by those tables." She pointed to a grouping of red picnic tables.

After placing his order he looked over to where Mia was standing outside the frozen confection truck, which was seductively named Lick. She was bouncing again and excitedly clapping her hands in front of her chin. He puzzled over the ease with which they were getting along. If she was playing him in some nefarious scheme, she was giving an Oscar-winning performance. He almost believed she truly enjoyed his company. The math simply wasn't adding up. Maybe it was better if he didn't stay at her place tonight. Whatever beef Khalil had with him seemed too complicated to deal with. He decided after getting his belongings from the hospital, he'd ask Mia to take him to his car, which was still parked downtown, probably with citations on his windshield. Tobias was a strong believer in cutting one's losses—quitting while one is ahead. It was the safe play.

He watched her from a distance while his order was being prepared. Two men in shorts and flip-flops approached her, one of whom she seemed to recognize. She enthusiastically embraced the tall one, with his hair in a man-bun and a tattoo of a lotus flower covering his left shoulder. He rocked her back and forth in his muscular arms, nearly lifting her off her feet. She was laughing again. She seemed captivated by whatever he was saying, her vivacious smile never abating.

"Tobias!" the taco man called. "Tobias!"

"That's me. Thank you." He took the carne asada tacos to a salsa station where he could continue to view Mia's social interaction. He didn't want to intrude or disrupt their banter. He wasn't feeling social in the least. Finally, she hugged him once more and then hugged the other one who she seemed to have just met. She was still smiling when they walked away and started in on her ice cream as she made her way to a table.

"So what kind did you get?" Tobias asked as he took a seat.

"Blackberry lemon sage!"

Tobias drew the corners of his mouth downward while raising his eyebrows and nodding his tilted head as if to say, *interesting choice.*

"They have crazy flavors there. Wanna bite?" She held out

a spoonful of the lavender-colored confection toward his mouth.

"Uh, yeah. OK." He took a bite off of her spoon and nodded in approval. "That *is* good."

"Told ya. Here. Take my picture." She handed him her smartphone. She placed the spoon backward on her extended tongue. Tobias snapped three photos in succession. She took her phone back and seemed delighted as she scrolled through each one. She selected one and posted it to her Instagram with the mention @lick. Lick's social media feed was nothing but women's tongues.

"So who were those guys?" Tobias ventured.

"Amir, the tall one, he's my yoga instructor. The other one was his brother, visiting from Portland. He works at a dispensary up there."

"You do yoga?"

"Yeah, you should come to a class with me once you get that cast off."

She was there when the doctor said six weeks. Tobias had not anticipated further contact with the young Ms. Navarro outside their routine coffee transactions. He was starting to feel that Mia wasn't playing him so much as just being nice. For Tobias, *nice* carried very little value. When it came to romantic partners, he could take or leave *nice* as long as there was a strong sense of loyalty and dependability. So far, he wasn't getting that vibe from Mia. She was gorgeous and she was nice, but she had such a carefree, devil-may-care spirit that he couldn't see her committing to anything long-term. He could live with that. At least she wasn't playing tricks. Tobias found himself continually recalibrating his expectations.

"Yeah, maybe," he said. "Hey, listen, I think you can just

take me to my car after we get my keys. It's downtown, probably with a parking ticket on the windshield."

"Are you sure?" She raised her eyebrows in concern. "I mean, do you have anyone to help you?"

"No. I think I'm good though."

"Yeah. Totally. Whatever you want." She sounded a bit stung by his suggestion. She dug into her suede satchel and removed a gold-colored vape pen. This was a different device than the dry herb vaporizer she kept in her car. She took a long draw from the pen and turned around on the bench to blow the smoke away from Tobias. With her back turned it appeared as though she was wiping her eye. She sniffled and cleared her throat before turning back around. Her eyes were moist.

"Are you OK?" Tobias asked.

"Yeah, I just got a little smoke in my eye."

Tobias felt guilty but he didn't want to presume she was disappointed to leave him. At the same time, he didn't want to be uncaring or indifferent, so he offered a conciliatory gesture. "I think I would like a hit. I mean, if you're still offering."

"Of course!" Mia seemed to take pleasure in sharing what seemed to be an integral, maybe even spiritual, part of her day to day. "Just push down on that button while you inhale."

The vape pen came with three settings of cannabis oil concentration. She'd had it on the highest setting. Tobias took a healthy drag and immediately started coughing. The coughing exacerbated the pain in his ribs, and he emitted tortured moans between each cough.

"Oh my God!" Mia rushed over to his side of the table and put her arm around him. She rubbed his back until the coughing fit subsided. Outdoor diners turned to see what was going on. Some of them looked concerned. Others knew exactly what was happening and were laughing and shaking their heads in silent ridicule. Once the violent coughing ceased, Tobias felt as if his skull was filled with embers. His arms and legs felt tingly and numb like his skin was slowly evaporating. Tobias Munch was stoned.

6

<hr>

Tobias immediately regretted his actions. He was anxious and felt like every sound or movement was likely to throw him off balance. He could hear Mia speaking to him, but he was too frightened to shift his focus from the color and shape of the lime rind in his taco basket to what she was saying. His breath was shallow, and he was sweating profusely. Suddenly, he had to shit.

"I have to go to the bathroom," he blurted.

"OK, OK. There's porta-potties over there," Mia was pointing to the far end of the lot. "Let me help you."

"No! No! I got it. Just . . ." Tobias was appropriately seated at a conventionally designed outdoor picnic table. It took him a minute to figure out how to extricate his legs from what seemed like a needlessly complex and diabolically config-ured seating structure. He had to think through how he'd gotten himself into such a seated position in the first place in order to reverse engineer his release.

When he arrived at the blue porta-potties, several yards from the eating area, there was a line. All three porta-potties were occupied and there were two people in front of him. The porta-potty company's name adhered above the latrine doors read: Honey Pot. Tobias found this frightfully amusing and he started giggling uncontrollably. He turned to the woman behind him and pointed but failed to articulate what he was laughing at.

His situation was quickly becoming emergent. A heavy-set woman exited the porta-potty to the left and the next person in the queue entered. Tobias was having serious doubts about his ability to maintain command of his bowels for much longer. The door to the porta-potty on the right opened and the next person entered, leaving Tobias next in line. He was trembling so badly his muscles ached. A single tear escaped the corner of his eye. At last, the middle porta-potty door unlatched, revealing the green 'Vacant' designation. Tobias took a single step in the direction of the toilet and his quivering sphincter finally and irrevocably tapped out.

A colossal amount of solid feces slipped unimpeded from his failed anus and into his boxer briefs. A queue of people had already formed behind him. He committed himself to a charade of normalcy and continued stepping robotically toward the newly vacant porta-potty, each step inviting another portion of excrement to be released. Once inside the dark and humid porta-potty, which smelled simultaneously of death and mint, Tobias removed his pants and underwear to assess his situation. He threw his shit-filled underwear into the holding tank filled with alien-blue liquid surrounding an unholy mound of human waste, soggy toilet paper, and used tampons. His jeans, remarkably, sustained minimal soiling.

He reached for the toilet paper only to discover an empty cardboard roll. *Perfect.* Tobias removed his hooded sweatshirt and cleaned himself as best he could with it. Into the holding tank, he dropped the sweatshirt. He emerged from the porta-potty with a new sense of accomplishment, which for the moment, was the only thing helping him survive the shame. He was also feeling a bit more functional in three-dimensional space, still very high, but functional.

Mia waited for him at the picnic table. "Everything OK? Where's your hoodie?"

"I don't want to talk about it."

"OK. Do you still want to go to the hospital?"

"No. Can we just go back to your house? I just want to go to bed. Is that OK?" He couldn't feel his face.

"Yeah, totally. Let's go."

When they arrived at the house, several cars were parked in the driveway and on the lawn, so they had to park across the street.

"What's going on?" Tobias asked.

"Oh, just a few friends hanging out. Don't worry. You can just crash in my room if you're not feeling down to hang. I totally get it. I'll make sure nobody goes upstairs."

"Is that OK? I'm sorry. It's been a while since I smoked weed and I think it just hit me kinda hard."

"You think?" She laughed.

"So lame, right?" *This is so embarrassing.*

"You're funny."

The music coming from the house was loud, even by student housing standards. College-aged kids gathered on the front porch and throughout the bottom floor, spilling into the back yard. Tobias estimated at least thirty people were gathered in various states of dress and chemical influence.

Mia did her best to escort Tobias through the crowd without stopping to hug everyone who greeted her. He could tell that she was well-liked among her friends. And then there was Khalil, standing in a small grouping of party-goers with a tall-canned IPA in hand, glaring at Tobias as he entered the house. *What's this guy's problem?* Tobias caught his eye as he ascended the stairs and quickly looked away hoping to disappear.

Mia helped him into bed, removing his shoes and socks. He allowed himself a modicum of hope that Mia might choose to remain with him that night. She had surprised him enough times throughout the day, shattering his expectations at every turn, that his chances seemed less impossible than he'd originally surmised. She took an empty glass from her nightstand and walked to the adjoining bathroom to fill it. By the time she returned, Tobias had fallen fast asleep.

Two hours later, Tobias stirred when he heard the bedroom door squeak and quietly latch shut. Bare feet shuffled across a wooden floor toward the bed. His heart rate increased with the sound of a zipper and the rustling of clothing being removed and dropping to the floor. The mattress creaked as another body entered from the other side of the bed. Small, delicate hands caressed his torso under his shirt from behind. He could feel with his elbow that distantly familiar sensation of bare breasts as they grazed his back. *It's happening,* he thought. *This is really happening!*

He reached his hand back and touched the warm, smooth skin of an open thigh. Her hand glided down from his chest over his stomach. She tugged on his waistband and unsnapped the button. Her hand thrust into his pants and firmly clasped around his hardening penis, which she began to stroke with a clumsy eagerness. She sat up and grabbed his pants at the thighs and tugged them down. Tobias, now on his back, could see in the moonlight coming in from the windows that the woman who was kneading herself against his fully engorged penis, was *not* Mia.

"What the hell! Who are *you*?" Tobias asked, scooting back toward the headboard on his only good elbow.

"Relax, baby. It's Frankie." Her voice was mousy and her breath smelled strongly of alcohol.

"F-Frankie?!"

"I saw you staring at me earlier today." Her warm, smooth body slithered over his own. She placed his hand on her breast and kissed his mouth, still agape from his confusion. "Don't you want to fuck me?"

"Where's Mia?" He reached sideways and turned on the bedside lamp.

"Seriously?" Frankie scoffed. "Whatever, dude." She climbed off him and hastily put her clothes back on. "By the way," she said, zipping up her pants, "you *literally* smell like shit."

Frankie stomped out in a huff. Tobias sat up and consulted the alarm clock on the bedside table: 12:38 a.m. The music had died down. The din of chatter arose from downstairs. His high had mostly worn off and he was curious about where Mia was or who she might be with. He worried how she might have interpreted what had just happened in her bed or whether Frankie had intended to keep it secret from her. He felt compelled to find her and allay any misunderstanding.

Tobias descended the staircase barefoot to find several groupings of party-goers in clumps drinking beer and smoking weed. He scanned the room for Mia. Frankie was kissing a curly-haired young man who she'd pinned against the dining room wall. She opened her eyes just as Tobias noticed her and smiled, raising her middle finger at him. Tobias poked his head into the kitchen and then the living room. He asked a couple of people where Mia was and neither seemed to know, or they were too inebriated to care.

Tobias walked out into the crisp November air and onto the back deck where a small group was playing cards around a patio table in various states of undress. A skinny underaged boy in nothing but athletic socks and a ball cap covering his genitals was clearly losing. A fire pit illuminated a cluster of pine trees in the distance. He counted six people seated around the fire. They were unusually still, and it appeared from a distance, that their eyes were closed but without his glasses, it was hard to tell. He meandered closer toward the group to get a better look, careful not to appear lurking. Dead leaves and pine needles crunched under his bare feet inviting everyone in the group to open their eyes and turn toward him.

"Tobias?" It was Mia. "What are you doing out of bed?" This was the first time today Mia did not seem thrilled to see him. "Were they being too loud in there?" Apparently, she didn't know about Frankie.

"Oh, no. It's cool," he scanned the group, who gave him the impression he was indeed interfering with something. He offered a feeble wave in their direction. "Sorry, I didn't mean to interrupt. I'll just—"

"You can stay if you want," Mia said flatly. Tobias had the feeling she was only offering out of politeness. The looks on the others' faces seemed to confirm that suspicion.

"Yes, stay," Khalil said turning away from the fire. "Please, join us," Khalil said in monotone that clearly indicated the opposite of his stated words. He looked upon

Tobias with grave intensity. Mia had a look of concern on her face.

"Uh, what are you guys doing?" Tobias asked timidly. The others silently looked to one another.

"Can I talk to you for a minute?" Mia asked, pulling him by the arm several feet from the group.

"What's going on?" Tobias asked.

"Don't take this the wrong way. I'm not sure this is something you'd be into."

"What? What would I not be into?" Tobias strained his neck to check in on the group who were whispering and sneaking glances at them.

"Well," Mia struggled to provide a clear explanation. "It's this thing we do sometimes. It's pretty intense. You had a really strong reaction to like, one hit of weed . . . I just don't think you're quite ready, that's all."

"Well, what is it? Like, drugs? What?"

"Not exactly. I mean, technically, I guess."

"OK. So what were you all doing just now, before I walked up?"

"That's part of it—the meditation."

"Meditation?" Tobias was clearly out of his element and was growing tired of feeling like a bungling maladroit. This was a unique opportunity to bond with Mia and to share a core experience with her—to be a part of her world. He'd already shit himself. What else could possibly go wrong? A whiff of carelessness overtook him. "You know what? Whatever it is, I'm down. Let's do this!"

"If you're being serious, that's not really the vibe you need to be projecting," Mia said admonishingly. This was not the carefree spirit he was used to. "This isn't something you do casually. It's not a fucking beer bong."

"Alright, alright. So show me. Walk me through it."

Mia grabbed his hand and began massaging it while she struggled to explain. "It's like ..."

"Like what?" Why was she being so cagey?

Mia looked up to the sky and exhaled. "Teleportation."

Tobias could only assume she was waxing metaphorical. "Oh ... kay. So where do we teleport to?"

Mia glanced back at the group, biting her lower lip. She bounced on her heels as if she needed to dislodge the next question from her head. "Do you believe in the Afterlife?"

"What? I mean, I don't *not* believe in an Afterlife. You mean like, Heaven?"

"Not exactly. There *is* a place, I guess you could call it Heaven, or the Great Beyond, or whatever. But there's this other place we go first. It's like, an in-between place."

"In-between life and the great beyond?"

"Exactly! It's like a transitional place and it helps people adapt to like, not having a physical body. And when they're ready they can decide to enter the Great Beyond."

"I don't understand. How does that work? Are you saying this drug literally teleports you to this in-between place?"

Mia nodded slowly and deliberately. "Yes, but only for a little while. Eventually, you come back, once it wears off."

Tobias was still dubious of her metaphysical claims. He believed her description of the drug-induced experience to be figurative rather than literal. She looked earnestly into his eyes. It would have been rude to challenge her beliefs, no matter how fanciful. He desperately wanted her approval, and he feared any hesitancy would cause her to rescind the invitation. "OK. I think I can handle that."

"It's not as easy as you think if it's your first time, especially if you're not used to disconnecting from your body on earth. It can really freak you out if you're not prepared."

"OK, well that's what the meditation is for, right?"

Khalil approached the two with what Tobias interpreted as annoyance or impatience. "It's time. Are you in or not?"

"Yes, I'm in," Tobias said.

Mia took his arm and led him toward the fire pit. She sat next to him and continued to hold his left arm while Khalil prepared an extra cup.

"What's he doing," Tobias whispered.

"It's a tea. We call it *La Seta*, which means—"

"Mushroom," Tobias finished her sentence.

"Yeah. You know Spanish?"

"A little."

"So he's preparing the tea and giving thanks. It's a whole thing. When you take the cup, you have to give thanks and set your intention for the journey. Do you have a mantra?"

"A what?"

"Like a phrase or word you can meditate on. You must have a clear focus."

"What should my mantra be?"

"Something simple, like 'open.'"

"Open?"

"Yeah. Use that."

"OK."

"Tobias, are you sure about this? Maybe you should do regular shrooms a few times first and like, build up to this."

"No, I'm good. I want to do this with you."

"OK. Once you start drinking it, you have to keep drinking until it's gone. It tastes fucking terrible, and you'll want to spit it out, but you have to keep drinking, do you understand me?"

"Got it."

Khalil brought a tray with an assortment of ceramic coffee mugs around. Each participant took a cup and held it up to their foreheads, presumably giving thanks. When he came around, Tobias grabbed a yellow mug with the image of Bob Ross on one side and a quote on the other: *We don't make mistakes, just happy little accidents*. He mimicked what all the others were doing. One by one, each participant brought their cup to their lips and began to drink. He looked over at Mia. She was drinking her tea, holding a navy blue NASA mug with both hands. Khalil locked eyes with Tobias and gave a foreboding nod before closing his eyes and consuming his tea.

The smell was repugnant. Tobias held his breath and slowly took his first sip. He could taste a hint of ginger and lemon, which helped the general taste of dirt and what he imagined sweaty socks might taste like. He did as he was instructed and drank the rest as fast as he could. He placed the cup on the ground in front of him. Everyone around the fire pit was laying down, including Mia. She had one hand extended, holding onto his ankle.

Tobias remembered his mantra and repeated it to himself while he stared at the fire. *Open . . . Open . . . Open . . . Open . . .* The fire began to take on a digital characteristic. It reminded him of how fire appears in *Ever After,* glitchy and pixelated. Mia appeared similarly. The contours of her face had disappeared and given way to a more geometric, blocky appearance in binary colors. He turned his head, which seemed to pivot on an overly tightened swivel, back toward the coffee mug. Bob Ross gave him a wink and said, "Here we go."

7

<hr>

IT WAS the sound of birds chirping outside his window and the *wap, wap, wap* of his bedroom ceiling fan that caused him to stir. Tobias woke up in his childhood bed, not the bed he'd left when he went off to college, but the one he had when he was maybe nine or ten. His feet protruded from the bottom of a *Super Mario Brothers* bedspread. When he pulled back the covers, an assortment of Pogs spilled onto the carpet. He had completely forgotten that he used to collect those colorful little cardboard discs. He took in a deep breath expecting to stop once he felt pain in his bruised ribs but there was no pain. He felt vibrant and energized as he stretched both arms above him.

He reached toward the nightstand for his glasses where he'd always kept them. He reached with his right hand, and only then realized it was no longer in a cast. He moved his hand, opening and closing his fist and rotating his wrist clockwise—not broken. He attempted to put the child-sized glasses on his face and then realized he could see perfectly well without them. He could see the contents of his closet on the other side of the room and read the inscription on a soccer trophy displayed on his dresser. He wondered if he'd travelled back in time.

Tobias heard the sound of metal cookware and the sizzle of a frying pan coming from the kitchen just like he'd heard when he was a kid on Saturday mornings. "Mom?" Tobias cried out.

Tobias got out of bed and entered the kitchen—the very same kitchen that he was standing in with his mother just the night before, only without the recent renovations. Mia was standing at the stove in drawstring shorts and an oversized Colorado sweatshirt. She was making pancakes. "Good morning, sleepyhead!" She almost sang when she spoke.

"Hi." Tobias wasn't sure if she was real or just a figment of his imagination. He assumed this was a hallucination. He'd heard of lucid dreaming, when one has some degree of control over their dreaming, although he'd never experienced it before personally. This must be what that is. He thought he'd test the waters and attempt a conversation with this rather alluring hallucination. "Why are we in my old house?"

"This must be where you feel safest," she replied. She glanced at him and giggled.

"What?"

"Your jammies! They're so cute!"

Tobias was wearing adult-sized, yet snug-fitting *Jurassic Park* pajamas, which left him feeling exposed and a bit on display. He pulled a slight wedgie from his butt crack when she wasn't looking.

"Are you hungry?" she asked.

"Not really. Those look great though." He could smell the blueberries and the batter crisping on the griddle. They smelled delicious.

"That was a trick question," she said, pointing at him with the spatula. "We don't get hungry here."

"So why are you cooking?" If he was hallucinating, he figured he must be asking and answering his own questions. He was curious what his answer might be.

"You still have sensory perception. You just don't *need* to eat or go to the bathroom. In fact, you don't even need oxygen."

"So I'm not breathing air?"

"Nope. Everything here is an illusion. Even these pancakes. Here, taste." She cut a bite-sized piece of imaginary pancake and fed it to him.

"Mmm . . . Is that blueberry?" It felt completely real, the smell, the texture. He even felt the sensation of undigested pancake descending his esophagus. How was this imaginary?

"It's whatever you want it to be."

"OK, but I *am* still breathing. Why am I still breathing if I don't have to?"

"Yeah well, you've never *not* breathed before, so you just don't know how to do it. I can show you when you're ready."

"How will I know if I'm ready?"

Mia laughed. "Trust me. You're not ready. Don't worry about it. Just enjoy this. It goes by quicker than you think."

He wondered what it is he needed to be ready for. Why would it be important for him not to breathe? What was the purpose of all this? Enjoy what, exactly? It was nice that his pain was gone. Completely. He took in another deep breath. Yep, still no pain. Was that it? He could eat pancakes in real life. "OK, so what do we do? Can we leave this house?"

"Tobias, slow down. Yes, we can leave but right now this house is the only thing keeping you from losing your mind."

"Where are the others? Where's Khalil?" Far away, he hoped.

"They're at a festival. I decided to follow you here."

"Like a music festival?"

"Yeah, there's music and a whole lot of other crazy shit. I followed you here to make sure you were going to be OK."

"I feel bad. You wanted to go to that festival with your friends and now you're stuck here, on Fox Hunt Trail. We can go if you want. I should probably change."

"No, it's fine. There's a lot to learn about this place so we should be here where you can learn in a safe environment."

"Are you . . . real? I mean, is this really you or are you an illusion, too?"

Mia thought for a moment. "That's a really good question, Tobias. You're on the right track."

He looked at her more closely. She certainly looked real. "Well, are you? Real, I mean?"

"I think so. But how does anybody really know if they're *real*? I mean, isn't it all just like, our perceptions and beliefs that convince us what reality is anyway?"

Tobias reached out and took her forearm in his hand and gave it a squeeze. It was smooth and warm. He felt her pulse in his hand. "You feel real to me."

"Hit me," she said.

Tobias furrowed his brow and pulled his head back. "What?"

"Punch me in the face."

Are you crazy? "No."

"Tobias, trust me. I won't feel it because I know this body doesn't exist. Only my consciousness exists."

"Yeah, no. I'm not going to punch you."

Mia opened a kitchen drawer, closed it, and opened another. "Where do you keep your knives?"

"What?" Tobias didn't like where this was going.

"Never mind, this will work." She pulled a rolling pin from one of the kitchen drawers. Tobias looked nervous. Mia placed her left hand on the counter and raised the rolling pin high above her head.

"Wait. What are you doing?" Tobias cringed.

Mia smashed her hand against the tile countertop with the rolling pin. Her hand flattened out like Play-Doh in the middle.

"Holy shit! Why did you do that?" Tobias was horrified.

Mia peeled her hand from the counter and wobbled it with her other hand. "See, it doesn't hurt." Within seconds her hand puffed up and took on its natural shape. She wiggled her fingers to demonstrate the damage was only temporary.

"Let me try," he said hastily.

"No. You haven't let go yet. You're still connected to your body. It would hurt like hell."

"Come on, give me the thing."

Mia slapped him hard in the face.

"Ow! Why'd y—"

"See? You're not ready. Sorry."

"Alright," he said rubbing his cheek with his hand. "So, how do I . . . let go or whatever?"

"It's not that easy. I can teach you, but we should take it slow. It's not that important that you figure it out right away. We can just chill in this space for a while." Mia looked around. "It's nice here. So this is where you grew up?" Mia sat down at the vintage oak dining table and pushed a chair toward him with her bare foot.

Tobias sat. "Yeah. I lived here my whole childhood until I left for college." He realized he didn't know much at all about Mia's personal life. "Where are you from?"

"I was born in Chile. My dad's a film director, originally from Chile. And my mother was a Swedish actress. They met on the set of this low-budget art film. I lived in Chile until I was like six and then we moved to L.A. My mom still lives there."

"And your dad?"

"He left us right after we moved to California. He ran off with this other actress and now he's this bougie film director up in Toronto. I don't really have much contact with him anymore."

"Oh, I'm sorry." She was opening up now. He didn't want to push too much but it was encouraging to sense her vulnerability.

"No, it's just . . . whatever, you know. So what about your folks?" She pointed to the wedding photo on the wall. "Are they still married?"

"Yeah, for like, forty-something years." He had to admit this was an impressive stat he'd taken for granted.

"Wow. You don't see that a lot anymore."

"No, I guess not." Tobias nodded for longer than was called for and then blurted, "I'm divorced." It had to come out eventually.

"Oh." Mia failed to discern a more appropriate response to this statement. "How long has it been?"

"Officially, it'll be a year next month. She ran off with some publishing exec. She's an author, too—Everly Bronson.

"Wait. You were married to Everly Bronson? The *Girl In a Box*?"

"Yeah, that's her." He wasn't surprised that Mia had probably read it. She was probably a huge fan. *Girl In a Box* was a feminist anthem of a book that *he helped write.* Philosophically, Tobias agreed with every sentence in that book, but he couldn't help worry he was losing points with Mia on the grounds that he was, after all, a man and represented the patriarchy by transitive property. He could have taken the high road and praised his ex-wife's work. Instead, he took the low road. "She got really successful and sort of left me in the dust."

"That's rough. Maybe it's for the best though. For you, I mean."

"I don't know. It's been pretty brutal this past year. I'm in therapy."

"Well, that's good! You're healing. Things are bound to get better and better. I mean, you're writing this amazing book, right?"

"I wish I had your optimism." He really did. It was nothing short of magical.

"You just need to believe in yourself. You're only limited by your own beliefs."

"You sound like my therapist."

Mia laughed. "Life doesn't have to be as hard as we make it out to be. That's what this place taught me. Everything is temporary. Everything is . . . *illusion.*"

Tobias furrowed his brow in reflection. "But I can't smash my hand in real life."

"You can't smash your hand *now.* Reality is just a projection of the mind. If you believe there will be pain, there will be pain."

"What if I can't help it? I mean, I still have instincts."

"Not instinct. *Programming,*" she said, drawing out the last word. "You have to *de*-program yourself."

"But *how*?" Tobias was getting the feeling this conversation was just a big circle.

She handed him the rolling pin. "Here. Hold it out in front of you." He took it from her with some hesitancy. "Now let go." Tobias released his grip of the rolling pin and it dropped to the carpeted floor. "Just like that," she said. "It's exactly the same thing. Letting go is letting go."

Tobias was dubious. He couldn't articulate a rebuttal but his resistance was evident.

"Let's try something else," she said, pinching her chin between her thumb and forefinger. "Stand up. Here. Stand up on this chair." Tobias did as she asked. "OK, now from there, jump to the floor." Tobias jumped down. "Easy, right?"

"Yeah." *What is this supposed to prove?*

"You didn't even have to think about it. OK, now don't freak out. Trust me, OK?" She grabbed his hand and turned him toward a hatch in the wall that Tobias could have sworn wasn't there before. "I want you to do the same exact thing you just did from the chair. Ready?" Mia pulled down on a lever with both hands and opened the airplane hatch. A gush of wind hit him like a tidal wave. He looked around the room, which had transformed into the hull of a Cessna 182. He looked down from the open hatch to see a miniature version of his hometown through wispy clouds.

"Are you kidding me?" Tobias yelled over the sound of rushing wind and the high-pitched whirr of the small plane's engine.

"Jump!" Mia yelled. "Just like you did before!"

"I can't!" he yelled.

"Yes, you *can*!" she yelled back.

"Shouldn't I have a parachute or something?"

"You mean this?" Mia pulled a parachute pack from a

compartment. Tobias nodded emphatically. Mia threw the parachute out the window. "It's *imaginary!*" she yelled. "This is all in your head!"

"I'm afraid!" Tobias yelled.

A loud popping sound came from the front of the plane followed by a sputtering. Tobias looked out the windshield and the propeller had stopped. Smoke was billowing from the single engine at the nose of the plane. He could feel the plane's descent. It was diving down toward the broad side of a mountain ridge. "Holy shit!"

Mia cocked her head and shrugged as if to say, *what now*?

Tobias backed up to the other side of the hull opposite the hatch and shook his head.

Mia yelled, "Looks like you're going to die anyway. Do you want to die from something you chose or something that chose you?"

"I don't want to die at all!" he screamed. This was a true statement. In fact, it was true even in the darker moments in his life, which is ultimately why he never succeeded in taking his own life. While Tobias Munch knew he feared death, he also equally feared life. Not wanting to die, in fact, was not the same thing as *wanting to live*.

"Looks like you made your choice," Mia yelled and then back-dove into the pale blue sky, disappearing through layers of cloud.

"No!" Tobias reached with his hand but it was too late. The mountain grew closer. Tobias looked toward the open hatch and then back to the quickly approaching mountain. He shut his eyes and fell into a fetal position on the floor of the hull. He covered his head and screamed, "Aaaahhhhhhh!"

By the time he'd stopped screaming, he was back on the

floor in his mom's kitchen. He opened his tear-filled eyes and sat up still catching his breath. Mia was sitting with one leg crossed over the other on the countertop playing with the tips of her hair. Tobias wiped his tears, slowly picked himself off the ground, and crossed his arms. "OK, I get it now," Tobias said, looking down in surrender. "I'm not ready."

Mia smiled compassionately and shook her head. "That's OK. Listen, I don't know how much time we have left here." A wall clock tick-tocked in contrast to the silence that followed.

"What should we do?" Tobias finally asked nervously.

"Can I see your room?"

"Sure."

Mia delighted at the retro toys and decor that were all the rage around the time she was born. She picked up a Game Boy from the top of his dresser, examining its rudimentary physical buttons and small screen size. She tested out a Bop It, laughing at its simplicity and then at herself for not managing to keep up. "What's this?" Mia asked, picking up a Stretch Armstrong off the floor.

"I'll show you. Here, take his legs." Tobias took the arms of the malleable doll and pulled. "Pull harder!" They were nearly five feet apart when Mia shrieked and her infectious laughter caused her to drop it.

"Hey! Is that a Super Nintendo?!" Mia asked elatedly.

"Yeah, you wanna play? I have . . . let's see . . ." Tobias knelt in front of his 32" Hitachi CRT television and sorted through a shoebox full of game cartridges. " . . . Tecmo Bowl, Super Mario, Zelda, Ninja Turtles, Street Fighter II . . ."

"Street Fighter! I'm gonna kick your ass!" Mia's enthusiasm bubbled over. They played for what felt like two hours laying side-by-side on their bellies, propping themselves up on their elbows. Tobias found Mia's smack-talk endearing. It was the first time he'd ever been called a "little bitch" by a girl, and he was thoroughly enraptured. When she lost, she feigned an exaggerated pout that quickly unraveled into laughter. She shoved him and he shoved her back. Tobias couldn't remember the last time he'd had an interaction so easy, so lighthearted and playful.

Right in the middle of a climactic digital fistfight, Mia began to lose control of her avatar. She was pushing the controller buttons yet her commands were not represented on the screen. "Uh oh," she said.

"What is it?" He looked over at Mia and she seemed to be glitching and fading.

"Time's up," she said. "Did you have fun?"

"One hundred percent. Can we come back?"

"Of course. It feels a bit tingly when you start to go," Mia said, her voice crackling and breaking up like a cell phone out of network. "Just remember your mantra and try to let go. See you soon!" She flickered and glitched another moment, and then she was gone.

8

———————

TOBIAS SAT up and braced himself for his return. He turned off the TV and sat with his back against his bed, hugged his knees, and recited his mantra. After a minute or two, he opened his eyes and leaned his head back on the bed, looking up at the ceiling fan. He felt good—happy. He gathered the Pogs that had fallen onto the floor, examining them with glee. He smiled as he reflected on his time with Mia, and for the first time, felt a sense of hope. He thought when he returned, maybe he would ask her out properly. Nothing too serious—something casual and fun. Pedal boats maybe, or a carnival, the ones with those hokey midway games where he might try to win her a giant plushie.

His daydreaming was interrupted by the doorbell. Tobias froze. The doorbell rang once more, followed by knocking. Tobias slowly got up and tiptoed to the living room window where he pulled back the curtain just enough to peek out onto the front porch. A fashionably dressed man in a denim jacket and newsboy hat stood with his hands in his jeans pockets. He looked a bit older, late forties maybe, and hip.

Mia hadn't given any instruction about visitors. He knocked again. "I know you're in there," the man said. "I just want to talk."

Tobias took a deep breath. The man looked friendly enough. He walked to the door and opened it, leaving the screen door locked. "Can I help you?" Tobias asked timidly.

"Hey, man, you got a minute?"

Tobias didn't technically know the answer to that question. He was expecting to disappear any second. "Who are you?"

"My name is Remy. Can I come in?"

Tobias remembered what Mia said about staying in the house. He knew he wasn't ready for whatever might be outside. He unlocked the screen door and pushed it open, allowing Remy to step inside.

"Thanks, man," Remy said looking around, hands still in his pockets. "This a nice house. Lemme guess, your childhood home."

"Yeah, how'd you know?"

"I don't know too many grown-ass men who wear dinosaur jammies." Remy gave a kind of weak chuckle that indicated more pity than ridicule.

Tobias was suddenly self-conscious. "I woke up here in these. I didn't pick them out or anything."

"Right," Remy said dismissively. "What's your name?"

"Tobias."

"You a tourist, right?" Remy asked.

"Come again?"

"A tourist. You're here for . . . recreation. In other words, you ain't dead."

"Oh, yeah. No, I'm not dead. Just visiting. Are you . . . dead?"

"Now that's just insensitive," Remy said curtly.

"Oh, I'm sorry. I didn't mean—"

"I'm just fuckin' with you, man!" Remy said with a puckish smile. "Yeah, man. I'm dead."

"I'm uh . . . I'm sorry?" Tobias didn't mean for it to come out as a question. This was the first time he'd ever met a dead person.

"It is what it is. We all gotta go sometime. Am I right?" Remy was looking around the room like he was in a museum of 90's interior design.

"True enough. So how long have you been here?"

"You mean when did I die?" Remy asked. "'Bout two months ago."

Tobias carefully considered his next question. "Would it be rude to ask, like, how it happened?"

"I was shot by the police."

"What did you do?" Tobias asked, ignorant of his privileged assumption that Remy had somehow caused the incident.

"*Psshh*. What did *I* do? Man, I didn't do nuthin' except be black on a fuckin' Tuesday. My car was in the shop that week, so I was riding my bike home from work. I seen this cop car coming up behind me so, you know, I don't wanna get hassled or nuthin', so I make a right on the next street. I'm thinking, just get out the way, let 'em do their job, right? That's when they hit the siren and they pulled up ahead of me and cut me off. I almost crashed into the side of the damn cop car! They jump out the car, pistols out, yellin' at me to get down, and I'm still tryna get off the bike. My pant leg got caught in the chainring. So I reach down, you know, to get it loose and I hear *pop, pop, pop, pop!* Next thing I knew, I was walking through that archway."

"Holy shit! That's crazy."

"I found out later, after I got here, they got a tip on some dope dealer in the neighborhood. I guess they figured any nigga would do."

Tobias shook his head. "That's terrible." He was well aware of an epidemic of police violence against blacks but he'd never met anyone anywhere close to it, much less a victim.

"The worst part is, they knew they fucked up, so they put a knife in my hand to make it look like I was tryna come at 'em. That way they could claim self-defense."

"How did you find out about all that after you got here?"

"From the viewing room," Remy said.

"What's that?"

"It's like a computer lab where you can go and watch what's happening down there. You can even go back in time. Some people never leave the viewing room. They just sit up there watching their family and their friends day in and day out. They can't let go."

"Why are you still here?"

"I'm waiting for the trial. Once those cops are convicted, I can finally let go. That's why I'm here, actually. I was kinda hoping you could help me out."

"Me? How?"

"Evidence. I was reviewing the incident in the viewing room and I noticed a light in an apartment building across the street. This kid was up there with his phone out and he was recording the whole thing. If I can get that kid to come forward, maybe they'll see what really happened and put those crooked cops in jail. I can't talk to him from up here but you can, once you go back."

"You want me to find this kid and convince him to turn his video over to the police?"

"Yeah. I got his information right here." Remy pulled a folded piece of paper from the breast pocket of his denim jacket. "Will you do it?"

Tobias could think of several reasons *not* to but none of them were any good. The honest truth was that Tobias simply didn't care enough about this dead man's mission to clear his name. He was much more concerned about getting back to his own life—to Mia. Under the circumstances, however, it didn't seem worth it to tell the truth. Kicking a man while he was already down wasn't his style. Besides, who knows? Maybe he'd change his mind. What was a dead man going to do from up here if he didn't follow through anyway. He nodded and took the paper from Remy's hand. "OK. Sure, I'll do it."

"Thank you! I'd say I owe you my life but . . ." Remy chuckled.

"Ha-ha. Good one." Tobias folded his arms and nodded. "Hey, how did you know I was just visiting anyways?"

"'Cause you parked your house in the barrens. When people die for real, they go through the archway. Most people stay within the city limits—where the action is. You came in through a backdoor—through a portal. That's why your house is in the middle of this desert."

"Desert?" Tobias looked out the window. Vast stretches of sand dunes rolled toward the horizon in every direction. This gave him a queasy feeling.

"Is this your first time?" Remy asked.

"Yeah," Tobias looked confused. "Hey, how long have we been talking? I'm supposed to be back by now."

"Time is a little strange up here. I'd say 'bout half an hour, give or take?"

"I was here with a friend, and then she went back, right before you got here."

"Everybody's different. Don't worry, it don't last forever."

"I'm sure you're right," Tobias said trying to mask the queasiness he felt in his stomach. "Do you meet a lot of us? Tourists?"

"Nah, not a lot. Most of 'em just tryna relax. Don't much want to get involved with our problems. I don't blame 'em. Be careful though. A lot of folks ain't too cool with the whole death appropriation. It's offensive to a lot of folks."

"I hadn't thought about that. I guess I can see how it could be seen as a bit disrespectful."

"It don't bother me. I'm not sure I totally get it though. I mean, why? Why'd you come here anyway?"

Tobias smiled. "There's this girl—"

"Oh, alright, now I get it." Remy gave a kind of half chuckle. "Say no more."

"I have a question," Tobias said.

"Shoot."

"If you die, and let's say you don't have any unfinished business keeping you here, how long does it take to . . ."

"To disconnect?"

"Yeah."

"That depends. Everybody's different. Some people walk right on through. My theory is they were already pretty spiritually evolved so this is just like a checkpoint. For others, they'll stay here for generations. Ain't no time limits. Leaving is always a choice. But," Remy held up his index finger, "once you go through that door, you lose your memory. You become a blank slate. That's what so many people have a hard time letting go of. Letting go of the body's a piece of cake, but your identity, your ego, that's another ball game."

"What about reincarnation?" Tobias asked.

"What about it?"

"Does anyone ever come back? Like in another form?"

"I don't know what happens after you pass through the door. I guess it's possible. It don't make no difference. You wouldn't know anyway."

"But *something* happens. I mean, why go to a transitional place if there's nothing to transition to?"

Remy shrugged. "I guess."

Tobias squinted. "I always thought when you died, you'd finally have all the answers."

"Sorry to disappoint."

"So what else is there to do here, I mean besides avenge your murder?"

"Whatever you want. They got mini-golf, fro-yo, kayaking, you name it."

"You're messing with me again." Tobias wasn't sure what to expect from the Afterlife, but he imagined it was more dignified than common recreational diversions.

"No, man, it's true. There's a concierge and everything. It gets old though, after a while. How many days in a row do you want to ride go-karts and eat birthday cake? Those things are fun down there because you can't do it every day. You have to go to work and shit."

"That makes sense," Tobias said, nodding. "What did you do for a living? On Earth?"

"I was a musician. I played rhythm guitar for Ophelia Day, the jazz singer. We had a standing weekend show at Reed's Lounge. I played in a bunch of other bands coming up and did some recording stuff here and there. I also volunteered at this non-profit teaching guitar lessons to underpriv-ileged kids. I do miss that. What about you? What do you do?"

Tobias felt self-conscious about his day job and didn't feel like explaining it. "I'm an author."

"Anything I mighta read?" Remy asked.

"No. I haven't actually published anything yet." That wasn't true. He'd published countless consumer product owner manuals. "I'm working on a sci-fi fantasy novel right now."

"Cool. Cool. Like with aliens and shit?"

"Yeah, there are aliens, and space battles, and intergalactic romance. It's going to be epic."

"That sounds dope."

Tobias felt uneasy and tired of making chit chat. He sighed deeply. "This is weird. I just feel like that tea should have worn off by now. How long can this last?"

"Don't ask me. I never tried it. Didn't even know it was a thing until I got here."

"Hey, you think I can go to that viewing room?" Tobias asked. "I want to check in on Mia."

"Yeah, you need an access card. I can get you in. But uh .. ." Remy looked Tobias up and down. "You ain't goin' dressed like that, are you?"

Tobias tugged down on the crotch of his pajamas. "No, of course not. I'll just go change." Tobias turned to walk toward his bedroom.

"You know you don't actually have to *change* your clothes. You can just ... change."

"Come again."

"Like this." Remy blinked his eyes and he was suddenly wearing a three-piece suit. He blinked again and he was wearing a basketball uniform, then a spacesuit, then a Copa Cabana gown with fruited headdress, a bear costume, and finally back to his stylish hipster look. "You try it."

Tobias blinked his eyes but nothing happened. "It didn't work."

"You have to think of the thing you want to change to in your mind and then blink," Remy said, nodding his head a little on the word blink.

Tobias imagined himself in his usual get up—T-shirt, jeans, sneakers, and a hoodie—and then blinked hard. He tried a second time with no change. "Maybe I just need to practice some more," Tobias said.

"Nah man, look. Relax your shoulders. OK, picture in your mind what you want to wear. Got it?"

"Yeah."

"Alright. Now just—"

Tobias blinked and . . . nothing. "Sorry."

"Don't sweat it. Here." Remy blink nodded and Tobias was now wearing a respectable outfit that he would have never chosen for himself given his limited sartorial sense—khaki chinos, a navy blue blazer over a pressed white button-up with leather slip-ons. "What you think?"

"It's a little dressy," Tobias said surveying his new threads.

"Really? OK hold up." Remy blink nodded again and his blazer and button-up combo was replaced by a navy pull-over with the sleeves pushed up to his elbows. The loafers were replaced with brown leather sneakers. "Is that more to your liking?" Remy asked with a smack of sarcasm.

"Better, yeah." He usually wore jeans and t-shirts but he didn't want to push it and he felt comfortable enough in Remy's selection.

"You wanna call 'em or should I?"

Tobias looked up from examining his attire. "Call who?"

"Uber," Remy said matter of factly.

"Uber? You have Uber here?" *Does Uber know they have Uber here?* Tobias thought to himself.

Remy nodded. "I got it." Remy pulled out his smartphone and ordered the car. Seconds later, a black, driverless Prius pulled up in front of the house. Previously, there had been nothing but sand beyond the sodded front lawn. Now there was a street. "Well, come on. Let's roll."

9

JUDGING by the expanse of sand dunes that existed when he initially got into the car, Tobias was prepared for a long drive. However, it didn't take long before the dunes gave way to streets, buildings, and people. The interior of the city was a lot like any other American city he'd been to but without the noise, trash, and awful smells. Everything seemed new and unblemished, as if it were newly constructed. It was well-populated, multigenerational and ethnically diverse, but not crowded. They must have traveled no more than four city blocks before stopping at a large gray building with blue reflective glass windows along the bottom floor. The sign above the front awning of the building simply read: LIBRARY.

Tobias followed Remy into the building, which smelled exactly like every library he'd ever been to—woody with a hint of almond. Rows upon rows of bookshelves lined every wall of the interior. In the middle of the room, between all the perimeter shelving, was an open pit with four rows of desktop computers. There must have been thirty stations altogether and roughly a third were occupied. Most of them did not acknowledge them as they walked in—too preoccupied with their screens. Some looked up for a moment and went back to their business. Tobias wondered if he looked out of place. Remy sat at an empty computer and pulled another chair over for Tobias. He logged in waving his unique access card in front of a scanner. *Welcome, Remy* appeared on the monitor.

"What's her name?" Remy asked.

"Mia."

"Mia what? What's her last name?"

"Oh. I—I don't know her last name. I think it's Spanish."

"Well, *that* really narrows it down," Remy quipped sarcastically.

"Put in my name. Tobias Munch."

"*Munch?*" Remy raised an eyebrow and glanced at Tobias.

"Yeah, just like it sounds." There was a more flattering pronunciation of his last name, which was shared by the Norwegian painter, Edvard Munch, who famously painted *The Scream*. This pronunciation was more like *MOONK* but no one in his family ever adopted this decidedly classier version. Tobias had become bored with the childish jokes levied upon his surname his entire life. He often ignored or feigned obliviousness to any mention of it.

Remy typed in his information and up popped a photo of Tobias with his name, age, and a few other identifying details. At the bottom of the screen, there were options to see a live feed or to enter dates to view previously recorded content. Remy clicked the live feed button and a video box opened up in full-screen.

Tobias was laying on the ground under Mia's backyard pine trees. A feeble output of smoke arose from the remaining embers of that late-night campfire. "That's Mia!" She was pacing back and forth. No others were present. She stopped and looked in the direction of the street and then ran toward it, off-screen. "Can you follow her?"

"Yeah, check this out." Remy moved the cursor to the right edge of the screen until the camera caught up with Mia again. He positioned the cursor over Mia and her name appeared above her head. "Navarro," Remy said. "Mia Navarro." He clicked her name and an option box appeared that read: *Switch to Mia Navarro? Yes. No.* Remy clicked *Yes*, and the camera centered on Mia and followed her around the side of the house to the street where an ambulance had just parked.

She waved to the medics and motioned for them to follow her, and she ran back to where Tobias was laying. The medics knelt around him, taking his vitals. One medic opened his eyes with a gloved thumb and forefinger and shined a penlight into his pupils. He conducted a forceful sternal rub and when Tobias remained unresponsive, they quickly transferred his body onto the gurney and into the back of the ambulance. Mia climbed in behind him.

"Oh shit! Oh shit! Am I dead?" Tobias asked.

"I don't know, man! This is crazy." Remy kept his eyes glued to the screen.

"Is that why I haven't gone back? Did I die?" His heart pounded in his chest.

"Shhh! We are in a library!" Remy said in a forced whisper. "Calm down. If you was dead, they wouldn't be rushing you anywhere. Right?"

"Yeah, I guess you're right. Shit! Why did I agree to do this? I'm such an idiot!" A bejowled older woman with red cat-eye-framed eyeglasses, sitting diagonally across the table from Tobias, shot an admonishing stare.

"Shhh! They will kick us out, man!" Remy said. "Lower your voice."

"Is there a way to find out for sure? Like, a registry or something like that?" Tobias asked.

"There *is* a registry! Hold up." Remy minimized the video and opened up another window. He did a search for *current residents*. This generated an infinitely long list of names, which could be sorted by arrival time, departure time, last name, and so forth. He typed in Tobias Munch and hit enter . . . *Search Results Not Found.* "Looks like you still alive my friend."

"Oh, thank God! So why am I still here?"

Remy opened the live feed up again and watched as they arrived at the ER and transported Tobias inside. Mia followed close behind but was asked to remain in the waiting room while they wheeled Tobias back to the intensive care unit. Remy hovered the cursor over Tobias and selected the option to switch from Mia back to Tobias.

The nurses worked quickly to start an IV and placed an oxygen mask over his face. They attached a skull cap with electrodes to monitor his brain activity. The monitors displayed information that neither Remy nor Tobias were qualified to interpret. Tobias' body lay motionless in the same hospital he'd just been discharged from the day before. Tobias listened in as doctors explained his condition.

He didn't understand everything that was being said but from what he gathered, the official cause for the coma had nothing to do with the substances he'd ingested earlier that morning. The swelling in his brain from the concussion had not abated as the doctor expected it would, given the proper rest. Over the course of the day, the increased swelling had caused his brain to push down onto his brain stem, damaging his reticular activating system (RAS), the bundle of neurons responsible for wakefulness, which acts as the connection between the conscious and the subconscious.

Interestingly, the marijuana he'd smoked earlier most likely delayed the onset of the coma to some degree. The cannabinoids actually increased blood flow and inhibited inflammatory compounds in his brain, staving off the impending effects on his brain stem. Of course, this was only temporary. Tobias felt some relief that he hadn't caused the coma. Had he not taken La Seta, he would not have ended up here in the in-between. He'd simply be on pause until he came out of it. At least, he was glad to be conscious, somewhere.

"Come on, man," Remy said, standing up to stretch his legs after some time. "Let's go get a churro or something. This shit's depressing."

"Remy, I can't leave. I have to get back there."

"Whachu think you gonna do from up here? You got to trust those doctors to do their jobs. In the meantime, try to live a little."

"You think that's funny?" Tobias said with an irksome tone.

"Ya know, I wasn't trying to be, but now that I hear it out loud, that shit is kind of amusing." Remy grinned despite the absence of a reciprocating audience.

"You go ahead. I just want to stay a little longer." Tobias propped his head up with his elbows on the table.

"Suit yourself. But don't stay too long or you'll end up like Patches over there." He pointed to an elderly man whose spine seemed to have adapted into a permanent viewing position.

"I won't. Hey," Tobias turned to face him. "Sorry I can't

help you out now. Looks like I'm stuck up here, for who knows how long."

"It's cool, man. There'll be another any day now." He was referring, of course, to another tourist.

"Hey, how do I get in touch with you?"

"Check your pocket."

Tobias reached into his front pocket and removed his phone. It was his phone, the one he'd left at the hospital the day before. He unlocked the lock screen and it opened to Remy's contact information. When he looked up again, Remy was gone.

Tobias turned back to the monitor. His parents had just arrived. His mother held his hand and burst into tears while his father stood despondently by her side.

Mia was sitting in the corner of the room when they entered. She stood to introduce herself. "Mr. and Mrs. Munch? Hi, my name is Mia." She sniffled. "I was with your son when this happened." She had been crying. Tobias thought she was beautiful even with a reddened face and those puffy eyes. "It's all my fault. I'm so sorry."

"How do you know my son?" Barbara asked, wiping tears from her face.

"I was the driver who hit him the other day. I came here the next morning to apologize and we ended up spending the day together after he was discharged. He was supposed to be resting, so I wanted to make sure someone was watching him. I guess I didn't do a very good job."

"Well, why didn't he call us?" Barbara asked and turned to Arthur, whose quiet stare immediately answered her question.

"I don't know. He just didn't mention it. I think he thought he'd be fine. I did." Mia said. "I'm so sorry."

"They said he had THC in his system. Our son does not do drugs. Did you give him marijuana?" Barbara asked, sounding like a high school vice-principal.

Mia looked at the floor and crossed her arms. "Yes."

"I think you should leave," Barbara said sternly, another tear trickling down her cheek. Mia nodded and quickly made her way to the door without making eye contact. Before she stepped through the door, Barbara added, "You might need to think about contacting an attorney."

If only his mother knew how much Mia meant to him. He would voluntarily get hit by ten more cars for the chance to be with her. He didn't know his mother to be a litigious person but these were unprecedented circumstances.

"Excuse me, sir." A middle-aged woman who, by her prairie-style dress and condescending mannerisms, could not have been anyone other than the librarian, stood behind Tobias staring down her pointy nose at him. "You do not have permission to be here."

Tobias stammered, "Uh . . . I . . . I was ju—"

"You were just using someone else's account for services you have not earned." She took control of the mouse and clicked on the account tab, which pulled up Remy's photo and account information. "I take it you are not Remy Williams."

"No, ma'am. He was here with me just a minute ago."

"Sir, whoever you are, I'll ask you to kindly leave the premises."

Tobias skulked out of the library and down the curiously litter-free street with nowhere to go. He passed a cafe with outdoor seating. Diners stopped their conversations to watch him pass. They weren't rude or hostile but he had the feeling they could tell he didn't belong. This was a familiar feeling for Tobias. He felt the same way at Mia's house last night among her friends. He felt similarly in most social settings, in fact, always wondering what it was that gave him away.

A professional-looking man, a little older than Tobias but fitter and dressed in a business suit walked toward him at a brisk pace. His dark hair was shiny and crisp with an abundance of product. He, too, was looking curiously at Tobias as he passed him. "Hey! Hey, are you a tourist?"

Tobias stopped and turned without answering the man who was slowly walking back toward him.

"Can you help me? Please. My name is Jake. I need to get a message to my daughter. There's a key to a safety deposit box. I need to tell her where it is so she can get it before my ex-wife finds it. She doesn't know I'm dead yet, but she'll find out soon enough and when she does—"

"Woah! Woah! I'm not . . . I'm sorry, I don't actually know when or if I'm going back."

"What do you mean? Tourists always go back." He sounded desperate.

"I'm in a coma." Tobias realized he had a card up his sleeve—a coma card.

"Oh. Sorry. Sorry to bother you," Jake said, and before walking away, added, "I hope you pull through."

"No worries. Good luck." Tobias thought to stop him again as the man walked away. He wanted to ask how he recognized him as a tourist but the moment passed and the man had disappeared.

The sound of a bell caught his attention. A red trolley car was approaching behind him from the direction of the library. It stopped right in front of him and a few passengers disembarked. He had never ridden a trolley before, and since he had nowhere to be at the moment, decided to see where it went. He hopped on just as the trolley was pulling away and remained standing holding onto a grab strap. He noticed the sideways stares from other passengers. One older gentleman shook his head in disapproval. A teenage girl giggled unmercifully. Others pretended they didn't see him at all. Both the attention and forced lack of attention made him uneasy. *What are these people staring at?*

The trolley stopped at various points along its route and passengers would disembark while others climbed aboard. He wondered what business these passengers might be tending to, here in the in-between. Surely nobody had jobs to go to. None seemed to be in any hurry. In the distance, a large gleaming white archway loomed. *This must be where new arrivals come,* he thought. He could see several people, more than could fit onto the trolley, gathered at the next stop. They appeared more animated, conversing with one another and consulting brochures.

Tobias decided to get off to explore further. He walked toward the archway, as several people walked past, too preoccupied to notice him. Some appeared disoriented, some sad. Others were mesmerized and awestruck. A woman in a white uniform had her arm around a crying woman seated on a bench between two topiaries. He slowed his pace as he tried to make out what they were saying but was unable to decipher anything clearly.

Everyone seemed to be moving in the opposite direction, away from the towering archway. They were all coming from a massive flat-roofed building that seemed sunken into a lush, green landscape. Topiaries, sculptures, and benches surrounded a majestic stone fountain in the middle of a large courtyard just outside the building's steps. Several doors lined the main entrance of the building, except no one seemed to be entering. Tobias surmised that this was not, in fact, the building's entrance, but its exit.

He sat on a bench near the fountain and watched as people exited the building. He could feel the mist from the crashing water behind him on the back of his neck. White uniformed people waited at the top of the stairs to greet and assist as people of all ages and ethnicities emerged from the building with pamphlets and folders in their hands. The white-uniformed assistants would happily answer questions and often referred to pages in the informational packets the people were holding.

He could still see the archway on the other side of the building, except that from the courtyard, the building obscured all but the very top of the arch. He could hear faintly beyond the dominant sound of crashing water in the fountain, a hollow tone, low and steady, like a giant Tibetan singing bowl—ominous yet eerily inviting. He stood to decipher more clearly from where the sound was originating and as he moved further from the fountain, determined it must have been coming from the front side of the building. Tobias felt compelled to seek it out.

Tobias surveyed the landscape surrounding the building and could see a small clearing near the base of the building on the left side, at the top of a hill. He walked toward the left edge of the courtyard away from the flow of pedestrians who seemed too preoccupied to notice him. He took a look around to see if anyone was paying attention before stepping over the low-roped barrier and slipping into the densely wooded thicket, dried leaves crunching under his feet. He climbed toward the top of the hill using boulders and trees to assist his ascent, occasionally slipping on the moist surface. The resonate sound had become dominant at this level and he could no longer hear the water fountain in the courtyard. His curiosity pulled him forward.

When he arrived at a clearing, he reached a chain-link fence, which blocked his advancement toward the front of the building. From this vantage point, he could see the left side of the archway. There didn't seem to be any other roads or structures beyond the archway, only blue sky, clouds, and rolling hills in the distance. The inside of the archway, however, was blurred around the edges and grew darker toward the middle. He stretched his neck to get a closer look into the opening of the archway and could only describe what he imagined to be outer space.

Tobias tried to pull himself up onto the fence to get a better look. There appeared to be a cylindrical tunnel made of what reminded him of the aurora borealis. He could not see into the tunnel itself but at its opening at the base of the archway, one by one, human figures appeared.

"Excuse me, sir?" A pleasant-looking woman in a white uniform was standing behind Tobias. She had a kind face, simultaneously youthful and wise, and the innocent haircut of a school girl. Her eyes exuded compassion. "Are you lost?"

10

Tobias looked around and stammered. "Where am I? What is this place? What's that?" he asked, pointing toward the archway.

The woman's name tag read, *Maggie*. She smiled kindly. "Would you like a closer look?"

Tobias nodded. Maggie held out her hand and when Tobias hesitated, gave a reassuring nod. Tobias took her hand and was immediately transported to an open area between the massive archway and the front of the building. His knees buckled as he regained his bearings. The towering stone archway stood two to three stories tall. It looked like it was made of ivory or marble maybe. The low resonate tone was soothing and seemed to carry a vibration Tobias could feel in his teeth. Tall cypress trees lined either side of the courtyard, which was less ornate than the one at the building's exit on the other side.

Tobias watched as a person materialized at the mouth of the cosmic tunnel. It was a gentleman, which Tobias estimated to be around eighty years old. The man stepped cautiously into the courtyard and took in his surroundings with some trepidation. He continued observing the empty courtyard as he advanced toward the front gates. Although he appeared old, his gait was like that of a much younger man.

Once the man passed through the gates, Maggie took his hand and Tobias found himself standing just inside the foyer by an oval desk. Another assistant in a white uniform, a short-haired young man, was seated there to greet the old man as he approached the desk. His name tag read, *Peter.* Tobias scoffed quietly at this. *Like St. Peter?* Maggie glanced at him and said, "It's just a coincidence." Could she read his thoughts?

"Name?" Peter asked the old man with a warm smile.

"Burt," the old man said, "Burt Nichols."

Peter consulted his computer monitor. "Nichols . . . Nichols . . . Yes, here you are. Burt Nichols, born April 12, 1941, in Montgomery, Alabama to Sid and Martha Nichols."

"That's me," Burt said.

"Welcome, Mr. Nichols. You'll report to Conference Room D just down this hall." Peter pointed to his right. "Here's your access card." Peter handed the old man a lanyard with a standard swipe card attached. "The next orientation will begin in ten minutes."

"Ah, just to be clear," Burt said. He placed both hands on the counter and leaned in. "Am I dead?"

"Yes, Mr. Nichols," Peter said, smiling. "I assure you all your questions will be answered in the orientation. Would you like a fresh-baked cookie?"

"What?" Burt asked.

Peter held out a warm chocolate chip cookie in a brown paper sleeve. Burt took the cookie with some hesitancy and turned to walk down the hall. Maggie smiled and gestured with her head for Tobias to follow the old man.

They arrived at the designated room and stopped at a folding table, which held a handful of blank name tags, two black sharpies, and a bowl of individually wrapped mints. Mr. Nichols filled out a name tag with his first name in all caps, *BURT*. He peeled it from its backing and stuck it onto his shirt before entering the room. They followed Burt inside where white plastic folding tables had been arranged in three rows on either side of a narrow aisle. Blue folders and spiral-bound presentation booklets were placed at each seat. Two other participants of similar age to Burt, sat at opposite tables looking over their orientation materials. A projector was set up on the front table, projecting the presentation's title slide, which read *Welcome to the Afterlife!* Burt took an aisle seat in the second row and began leafing through the contents of his folder.

Tobias stood in the back of the room feeling awkward and imposing. He looked at Maggie, who nodded and smiled. She leaned toward him and whispered. "Orientations are customized by cause of death. This one is for those who have died of health issues later in life. Pretty standard." Tobias nodded. He wondered if Remy had attended an orientation with other murder victims. Probably so.

The presenter arrived and took his place at the front of the room. "Welcome everyone! My name is Dylan and I'll be leading you through your initial orientation today. I know you have lots of questions, but please hold your questions to the end of the presentation. OK, let's get started."

Dylan advanced through his twenty-five-minute slide presentation with the ease of an experienced tour guide, complete with off-color puns that earned laughs from only one participant in the front row. For the most part, the presentation consisted of a tutorial for an app that had been automatically downloaded to everyone's phones when they arrived. It contained all the information that had been provided in the participants blue folders, plus various tools for navigating the in-between, including Uber, which Tobias was surprised to have discovered earlier. He hoped someone would have asked about this but they didn't. For newly deceased people, they seemed to accept this new dimension without much protest.

Ten minutes were devoted specifically to procuring real estate. Another five to the variety of restaurants and recreational diversions. Tobias wanted to learn more about letting go of his body. As he understood it, this was the whole purpose of the in-between—to let go of the body in preparation to the Great Beyond. All Dylan said about this was, "You'll find that after some time you may find your bodies quite limiting, like a caterpillar tight in its cocoon. Don't worry about that. When you're ready to break free, you will. There's no pressure. Enjoy your time here and when you're ready, you'll know." When he finished his final slide, he asked, "Are there any questions?"

The participants looked around the room. An elderly woman raised her hand. Dylan acknowledged her. "Yes, ma'am. Esther."

"So how do I change my age again?" Esther asked looking down at her smartphone screen.

Dylan smiled warmly. He must have grown accustomed to coaching the elderly through challenges with technology. "Do you see the icon there with the face on it?"

"Yes, the purple one?"

"Yes, ma'am. Click the icon and you'll need to give the app permission to use your phone's camera."

"OK," she clicked a button. "Oh! It's me!" Esther said, delighted to see herself on the screen.

"Yes, ma'am. Now do you see the slide bar there on the bottom where it says 'Timeline?' You can drag that to the left and you'll see your image change as you go back through time."

Tobias watched Esther transform as she played with the slide bar. She settled on the thirty-two-year-old version of herself. "This is the year I met Charles. This is the age I was when he fell in love with me."

"You look lovely," Dylan said. "All set?"

"Yes, sir. Thank you," Esther said admiring herself on her phone's screen.

"Anyone else? Other questions . . . Yes, sir. Uh, Burt."

Burt was looking at a menu from a barbeque restaurant that had been included with several others in his blue folder. "It says here 'All You Can Eat.' Is it truly unlimited brisket, or do they stop you after your fourth trip to the meat station?"

"In the Afterlife, there are no limits to either the supply of grilled meats or your capacity for consumption."

"Same with the ice cream?"

"That is correct, sir."

Dylan continued scanning the room for hands, prompting for further questions. "Well, if there are no more questions, we can be dismissed. If you do think of any, you may consult the concierge app on your phone. Have a wonderful Afterlife, folks!"

"Do you have any questions?" Maggie asked as the participants gathered their materials and slowly filed out of the room.

Tobias considered for a moment which of many questions cycling through his mind were most urgent. "Can . . . can you tell I'm not dead?"

Maggie smiled compassionately. "Yes."

"How? How can you tell?"

Maggie placed a finger over her lips as she considered how to respond. She looked Tobias up and down. "It's your body."

Tobias looked down at himself. "What about it?"

"It's like . . . Did your high school have a mascot that danced around on the football field during games?" Maggie asked.

"Yeah. It was a bulldog."

"Well, you know how everyone knows it's just a kid in a bulldog costume?"

"Yeah."

"It's like that."

Tobias was confused. "I look like I'm wearing a bulldog costume?"

"No, a person costume."

Tobias looked at his hands. "I look like I always do."

"That's what *you* see," she said.

"But you look normal, too. Everyone here looks normal."

"To *you* they do. It's hard to explain. These newcomers, they might not see the difference. But for those of us who have been here longer, it's pretty obvious."

"That's why some people look at me funny and others, like the ones leaving this building, don't seem to notice."

"I'd say that's accurate." She nodded in concurrence.

"Listen. I need to go back. Do you have any idea how I can get back into my body on Earth? I'm in a coma down there."

"I'm sorry. I don't have any experience with helping

people go the other way. Here." Maggie handed him a welcome packet. "Try to enjoy yourself while you're here. I'm sure it won't be too long. Besides, just because you go back to your body on Earth doesn't mean you'll automatically snap out of the coma. You're better off up here than being comatose. Don't you agree?"

"I guess you're right. But what if I don't wake up. What if I die down there?"

"Then you'll end up here anyway. Take advantage of this. Very few get this opportunity. I'm sure you're in good hands down there. I bet once you're home, you'll start to miss it up here. Good luck, Tobias." Maggie extended her hand for Tobias to shake. As soon as he squeezed her hand, he found himself standing in the courtyard in front of the large fountain once again.

The trolley was approaching in the distance and a queue of newcomers had formed at the stop. Several people were gathered around a directory of the city with colored transportation routes and a red dot near the archway labeled: *You Are Here*. Tobias thought about that for a moment. *I am here*. How could he be both here and also down there, on Earth? How could he exist in two places at once? The notion was disorienting, and he took a seat on a nearby bench.

"Are you gonna swim wif the sharks?" A young boy was sitting on the bench swinging his legs back and forth. He must have been seven or eight. Tobias hadn't seen him there at first.

"What?"

"Are. You. Gonna. Swim. Wif. The. Sharks?" The boy tilted his head sideways to the left and then to the right to punctuate each word.

"Uh, no. That doesn't sound like a very good idea," Tobias said.

"Yes, it does," the boy said plainly. "They don't bite. Plus, you can hold your breath to infinity. Aquaman's gonna teach me."

"Right. Of course," Tobias said, playing along. "What's your name?"

"I'm Finn."

"That's fitting," Tobias said. The boy stared at him blankly. "You know, because shark fin. Nothing? OK, well, is today your first day in this place?"

"Yep! Look what I can do!" Finn hopped off the bench and started spinning with his arms outstretched and accelerated faster and faster until he was a blurry, child-sized tornado. When he finally stopped, he teetered to the right, leading with his head, and fell over. "Woah," he said holding his head.

"Are you OK?" Tobias said half standing with an outstretched hand.

Finn laughed. "Did you see that?!" He slowly picked himself up, still a bit unsteady.

"Yeah, pretty cool!" Tobias wanted to ask how he died but couldn't think of an appropriate way to bring it up. He decided it was probably better if he didn't know. He was already pretty bummed out to begin with and learning Finn's tragic ending wouldn't help. Plus, if for whatever reason Finn didn't know he was dead, Tobias sure didn't want to be the one to break it to him. "So, Aquaman's gonna take you swimming with sharks?"

"Yep! Wanna come?"

"No, I'm good." Tobias looked around wondering who might be tasked with supervising young Finn. Surely, he wasn't alone here without parental guidance. "Hey, can I ask you something?"

"Sure," Finn said, probing the opening of his nostril with an index finger.

"Where are you going to live?"

Finn shrugged reflexively and after a moment blurted, "Probly in my realm."

"Your realm?"

"Yeah, I made it. You know, in *Ever After*."

"Oh! You play? I play *Ever After*! Are there other people in your realm?"

The boy nodded. "Kory. He's a llama. And a tortoise named Shell. You can come if you want. You can live in my castle. It has a water slide and everything. You have to watch out for the fox though. He always tries to dig up the diamond garden. There's a spell that can hypnotize him for a little while. I'll show you."

"Where is it? Your realm?" Tobias wondered if Finn understood he meant in real life and not on a computer or game console. He was willing to concede that an eight-year-old might not actually know the difference.

"It's over there," Finn pointed toward a crystal blue sea, which Tobias could have sworn was not there a minute ago. He looked closer toward the horizon and noticed a small island in the distance. A rainbow appeared in the sky descending down onto the island. "But you can only get there by shark," he said emphatically.

"That's the *only* way, you say?" Tobias said playfully. He pointed toward the rainbow. "Are you sure you can't slide down that rainbow?"

Finn's face brightened. "You *can* slide down that rainbow! Or you can ride a shark. There are *two* ways to get there."

The distinct sound of a Harley Davidson motorcycle engine approached from the main road. The rider was a long-haired, shirtless man with nautical tattoos covering his muscular arms and torso. He stopped the motorcycle right in front of them and revved the engine. A golden trident adorned the gas tank. He whipped his long, dark, wavy hair from his face and looked to Finn with intense sea blue eyes. "You Finn?" he shouted over the rumbling and popping of the Harley's idle engine.

Finn nodded, dumbstruck.

The man held out a helmet, painted blue with shimmering translucent scales. "Let's ride!" he called.

Finn looked at Tobias with eyes like coasters. He took the outstretched helmet and placed it on his head. Finn's most favorite aquatic superhero pulled him up by his arm onto the back of the motorcycle. Finn wrapped his arms around the rider's torso and squealed in revelry as they sped away.

11

———

Tobias looked out toward the sparkling ocean. The last time he'd been to the beach was with Everly. It was a quick weekend visit to Martha's Vineyard for a friend's wedding about three years ago, before the affair. He recalled feeling happy that day. At least, he wasn't depressed. He could have sworn Everly was happy, too. He remembered how she had laughed at something he said as they walked along the beach in the cool night air. He couldn't remember the joke but that might have been the last time he felt connected to Everly. This was the wedding where she was introduced to the man she would eventually marry. The man who would give her the courage to start again. He had to admit, it *was* a good title.

Tobias took out his phone and pulled up Remy's contact info. He hesitated before hitting the call button and determined texting to be less intrusive.

How about that churro? This is Tobias.

He waited a full minute for a reply and when it didn't come, decided to take a walk down through the boardwalk. It had all the trappings of a typical beachside boardwalk, like Venice Beach in L.A. or Mission Beach in San Diego, but without the congestion. The salty smell of the ocean mixed with hamburgers and sunscreen filled the air. *Sunscreen?* he thought. *Why? Is that even the sun?* He looked up into the sky. Seagulls squawked overhead. Young, tanned beach bodies played volleyball in the sand. Surfers paddled out toward the horizon. A Speedoed juggler in face paint and yellow boots passed him by on a unicycle. His phone buzzed. It was Remy.

Yo, where you at?

Boardwalk.

Meet you at Sal's in five.

Tobias looked up and saw a round, hairy man sitting at a sunglasses stand. He was wearing a *Where My Beaches At?* tank top and pink flip-flops. His unruly beard was accessorized with colorful beads. "Excuse me. Do you know where I could find Sal's?"

The man pointed further down the boardwalk to a thatch-roofed sandwich and smoothie shop with umbrella-shaded outdoor tables. "You gotta try the Pakalolo." He gave a chef's kiss to his fingertips. "It's perfection!"

"I'll keep that in mind," Tobias said.

"Hey man, you like these?" He held out a pair of retro Wayfarer sunglasses, in light blue.

"I'm sorry, I don't have any—"

"You're kidding, right?" He laughed. "They're on me, brother."

Tobias remembered from the orientation that money wasn't a thing up here. "Do you have them in a different color?"

"I have all the colors, my friend." He swept an up-faced palm over his inventory with pride.

Tobias selected a pair in mat black and tried them on. "These?"

"Now you're talkin', brother!"

"Thank you."

"Right on!" He waved as Tobias walked toward the brightly painted sandwich shop.

Remy was sitting at an outdoor table with a red smoothie in his hand. He had changed into beach attire—board shorts, flip flops, and an open short sleeve Hawaiian patterned button-up. "Nice shades, T!" he said as Tobias walked up to the table.

"Thanks for meeting me," Tobias said.

"How you settling in?" Remy asked.

"I got to sit in on an orientation, so I think I got the basics. I met this little kid. He was maybe seven or eight? It was like he felt right at home here. He wasn't scared at all. He said he was going to live in this realm he created in a video game and that Aquaman was going to teach him to swim with sharks."

Remy nodded. "Little kids live in their imaginations anyway. For him, this *is* heaven. He can finally do anything he ever wanted to do. And it'll come natural, too. I mean, he won't have to try to let go like we do. He'll never get sick or be in any real danger now that he's dead. He won't even need to eat or sleep so he can stay up as late as he wants to."

"So he'll be just fine all by himself? Won't he miss his parents?"

"I hate to say this, T, but you bummin' me out."

"Sorry. I seem to have that effect on people."

Two blonde-haired men on longboards skated past. A group of young, tan-skinned women in bikinis and flat bellies bounced up to the order window. "These people aren't really this young, are they?" Tobias asked.

Remy laughed. "Nah, man, them bitches old as fuck. It's a little disappointing once you realize that. But still," he shrugged, "nice to look at."

"It's like everything here is just . . . imaginary," Tobias said.

"I don't wanna fuck with your brain too much, but it's actually the same down there."

"What do you mean?"

"You got plenty of time to figure that out. Even if I could explain it, you need to come to that conclusion on your own."

Tobias was confused and frustrated. He'd spent his entire life wondering what others seemed to inherently understand that he never could. He always felt as though other people seemed to have some special knowledge and he was invariably late to the party. He was always on the wrong side of the wall. Always a tourist.

"Do you know anything about ghosts?" Tobias asked. "I mean, is that a thing? I figured if you can't find a tourist to be your messenger, maybe you could deliver that message yourself, you know, as a ghost."

Remy took a sip of his smoothie. "You want one of these?" Before Tobias could respond, he turned to the proprietor who was wiping down a nearby table. "Hey man, can we get one more of these?" The man nodded and returned inside. Remy addressed Tobias in a hushed tone without looking at him directly. "Listen here. That shit's dangerous."

"Have you ever—"

"Nah, nah. Fuck that. A ghost is someone who gets stuck. Like you is here. It's someone from *this* side that gets stuck down *there*. You feel me?"

"Not really."

"Here, the goal is to get used to your freedom, to lose your body, which you don't even actually have. All you have to do is learn to let go of the *illusion*. Down there you have to materialize. You have to will yourself into the material world when you ain't got no body to start with. It's a lot harder. Plus, once you are able to materialize enough to do some shit, you can't get back through the veil. Yo ass gets stuck. But there is a way to communicate through a guide."

"Like a medium?"

"Exactly. They can open up a channel. But it has to come from the other side. That's the problem. Someone has to be looking for you specifically."

The proprietor brought over the smoothie and placed it on the table. Tobias took a sip and pondered. "How do they contact you?" Tobias asked.

"How does anyone contact you? On your phone, brah."

"Really? OK, well, if they were to call you, then you'd have their number, right?"

"I guess. Shit, I don't know! Nobody's ever tried to contact me up here."

"Do you know anyone who has made contact?"

"Yeah. I do." Remy pulled out his phone and scrolled through his contacts. "Masha Rabinovich. She plays the viola in a chamber ensemble. She visits with her family on the regular."

"Can we talk to her?"

"Yeah, they fixin' to play down at the park. Maybe we can catch her before they go on."

When they arrived at the beautifully manicured park several people were scattered across the grass surrounding a white gazebo. They were reclining on blankets, nibbling on cheese, and sipping wine while the ensemble tuned their instruments.

"That's Masha over there," Remy said. Masha was wearing a black dress with lace around the collar and sleeves. She looked mid-to-late-forties with tremendous arms and an ample backside. Her hair, dark and wavy, hung loosely upon her broad shoulders. Her expression appeared focused.

"Maybe we should wait until after the performance," Tobias said. "She looks busy."

"Nah, man. Come on." Remy walked up to the gazebo and placed his hands on the railing next to where Masha was seated. "Hey, Masha! What's shakin'?"

"Remy!" Masha exclaimed as she stood, placing her viola in her chair. She carefully made her way through instrument cases and music stands, down the gazebo steps, and embraced Remy with a motherly fondness. "You come see Masha play?" Masha asked in a thick Russian accent.

"You know it, girl! Hey, this my boy Tobias."

"Hello," Masha said with a welcoming smile.

"Hi," Tobias said. He felt immediately comfortable in Masha's presence. She reminded him of his maternal aunt who always made him feel treasured. "It's nice to meet you."

"He had a question and I thought you might know the answer," Remy said.

Masha smiled. "Yes? What is question?"

"Well, I understand you use a medium to talk to your family."

"Yes," she said.

"I wondered if there was a way to contact that medium."

"Medium must create channel. Like telephone operator."

"Right," Tobias said, unsatisfied. "But you can dial 0 to get the operator. Is there a way to dial zero to speak directly to the medium?"

Masha laughed. "Is not perfect metaphor. You see, medium must create unique channel to speak to anyone on this side. Otherwise, too much noise. You understand?"

No, he thought. Before he could press for an alternative solution, the director ascended the gazebo steps and Masha turned and nodded toward him.

"I must go. You will stay? Listen to Masha play?"

Tobias nodded and looked to Remy. "Yeah. Sure, I'd love to." After all, he had nowhere else to be.

Masha returned to her seat. The conductor tapped his baton on his music stand and the ensemble raised their instruments. What followed brought Tobias to tears. It was the most angelic melody he'd ever heard. He closed his eyes and allowed the music to transport him. The notes initially entered through his ears and seemed to fill his entire body with a soothing vibration. Eventually, he felt as though the music was emanating *from* his body. When he opened his eyes, the musicians had been replaced by luminous beams of light. He looked around and what was there before, the gazebo, the trees and shrubs, the park benches and lamp posts, remained as faded images, like overexposed film negatives. All the people on the lawn, including Remy, had transformed into gleaming beams of pure, white light. He looked down toward his body and was nearly blinded by his own radiance.

When the music ended, Tobias found himself back in his body and everything appeared as it were before the music began. He joined in the applause and turned to Remy. "Was it just me, or did we all just—"

"You saw the light?" Remy replied.

"Yeah."

"You starting to see the truth."

"Why did it change back?" Tobias asked.

"It didn't. You did. The music allowed you to disconnect for a moment but then when it stopped, you reverted back to your normal perceptions. You'll get there. Don't worry. You see what you need to see when you need to see it. Feel me?"

"Not really," Tobias said. "How long does it take most people to see the truth? To see things the way they really are?"

"Don't worry about most people. That's the problem. You can't compare your unique path to someone else's. It don't work like that."

Dr. Macintosh had said something very similar on more than one occasion. Tobias couldn't argue with the soundness of the claim but he tended to forget it when it mattered most. His instinct forced him to look to others for direction on how to behave in a given context. He'd been instructed his whole life to simply *be yourself* but he didn't have any idea how to do that. *How do I be myself?* he would think. *Show me.*

Remy continued. "You ever been to Seattle?"

Tobias shook his head.

"There's this public art installation in Capitol Hill. They embedded these cast bronze footprints, well, not feet but like the bottoms of shoes, you know what I'm saying? They're embedded into the sidewalk, arranged in a pattern of dance steps with numbers on each footprint and arrows pointing to the next step. They have 'em for like, the Tango, the Waltz, the Cha Cha, all them old school dances, right? I was sitting in this coffee shop one day, looking out the window and people would stop and like, put their feet on these footprints and try to follow the steps but you know, there ain't no music or nothin'. They was just goofin' around, ya feel me? Now, I don't know what the artist had in mind when he put those in but it hit me like this. Ain't nobody gonna learn how to dance by tryna step on footprints in the sidewalk. It's not like they the wrong steps. They technically correct. But you just don't learn to dance from following the instructions. You know what I'm sayin', brah?"

"Sort of," Tobias offered.

"There ain't no footprints in the sidewalk for how to live your life. You just got to let that shit unfold."

"It's just that some people seem to already know the steps."

"I know it probably seems that way, but I promise you, they don't."

"I guess I'll take your word for it."

"I ain't asking you to. You either will or you won't. Like I said, it's up to you to figure that shit out in your own time. Wherever you are though, that's exactly where you supposed to be. So don't sweat it."

But I don't want *to be here,* Tobias thought. He wanted to be on Earth, with Mia. Here he was learning these deep spiritual truths about life and death and all he could think about was what he wouldn't give to have a chance to take Mia on a real date, in *real* life, not here in this imaginary place. He finally felt like he had a chance to be happy and the universe literally took that chance away. It felt like the Peanuts cartoon when Lucy swears she won't move the football and Charlie Brown stupidly believes her. Right when he's about to kick the ball, sure enough, Lucy pulls the football and Charlie Brown falls on his back. It was a classic. Tobias Munch was a cosmic joke.

Tobias looked up toward the sky. It should have been

getting dark by now. The musicians were putting their instruments away as the audience mingled amongst each other with friendly smiles on their faces. Masha approached them with her viola case in hand. "I hope you enjoy music," she said smiling.

"It was beautiful," Tobias said. "It was . . . luminous."

"Oh, Masha so happy you enjoy! We play every night here. You will return, yes?"

"I will."

"Lovely as always," Remy said, giving Masha a big hug.

Masha turned to walk away and then turned back toward Tobias. "You know, there are other ways to contact loved ones on Earth."

"Really?" Tobias asked. "How?"

"Transmutation," she said slowly. "You can temporarily visit Earth in another form like butterfly or hummingbird."

"My aunt Mona always said every time she saw a bluejay that it was her daddy coming to check in on her," Remy said. "I always thought it was just her way of coping with the loss. I never thought it could be true."

"What about a bumblebee?" Tobias asked.

"Sure," Masha said.

"A bee?" Remy asked dubiously.

"Mia has a bumblebee tattoo on her left arm," Tobias explained. He wasn't sure what the significance of that tattoo was but she must have chosen it for a reason.

Masha took out her phone and scrolled through her contacts. "Here she is. Selma Olivera." Masha shared the contact to his phone. "Selma can help you."

"Thank you!"

"Good luck!"

12

T OBIAS WAS eager to get back to Earth again, even in the form of a flying insect. He longed to see Mia in person and wondered what he might say to her after all that had happened. Tobias called Selma Olivera who spoke in a thick Columbian accent. He explained his predicament—how he traveled to the in-between via La Seta and got stuck when he fell into a coma. She was intrigued and enamored with Tobias and his quest for love. She sent him her location and he summoned a ride. Remy opted to sit this one out since he needed to get back to the barrens to await the next tourist.

Selma's house was a large Spanish style hacienda with a red-tiled roof and gated courtyard in front, spilling with flowering foliage. He stepped out of the car and walked through a wrought iron gate onto the stone-paved courtyard adorned with potted plants and water features. The sun was still high in the sky. Butterflies danced among fragrant blossoms. Birds chirped mirthfully and chased one another from one side of the courtyard to the other in a game of tag. He knocked on a large turquoise wooden door, which was already open. He heard a voice from inside. "Please come in!"

His eyes were drawn to colorful tile accented archways and architectural niches everywhere he looked. Saltillo floors of deep orange gleamed in the sunlight from a large picture window into another plant-covered patio out back. Dark wooden artisanal furniture displayed colorful handcrafted objects. Through the corner of his eye, he caught a black figure down the hallway ascending up a curved staircase. "Hello?"

Tobias cautiously made his way down the hall and up the staircase. He entered a large salon lined with floor-to-ceiling bookshelves, a roaring fireplace, and antique furnishings. Glass doors opened up to a balcony at the far end of the room. "Hello?" Tobias asked again, a little quieter this time. He saw the black figure moving behind an antique chaise. He leaned to his left to get a closer look when a shimmering black jaguar pounced toward him. Tobias screamed and fell backward to the floor. The jaguar approached slowly and placed a hefty paw on his chest.

"You must be Tobias," the jaguar said looking directly into his eyes.

"Don't eat me!" Tobias pleaded, straining his face toward the floor, and struggling in vain to remove the paw from his chest with both hands. He could feel individual claws pressing into his tender flesh.

"Have you forgotten? There is no hunger in this place." She removed her paw. "I am Selma."

Tobias scuttled backward and pulled himself to his feet. He stood behind a wingback chair and watched Selma circle back to the chaise, onto which she sprung gracefully and reclined.

"You scared me," Tobias said.

"I apologize. Fear is an adaptive response on Earth. It is essential for survival in such a hostile environment. It has very little value here. When you cannot die, there is nothing to fear. I expect you will learn this soon."

Tobias watched with astonishment as the jaguar changed its shape. Selma's human form was only slightly less intimidating. A black silk robe draped over a curvaceous olive-skinned body. Long legs ended in a pair of strapped sandals, toenails painted blood red. Her long, wavy, jet-black hair hung loosely between ample breasts. Her husky voice produced a strong Columbian accent. He judged the former jaguar, now human vixen, to be around fifty years of age. "There," she said. "Now you don't have to be frightened."

"S-s-so, ah, how does this transmutation thing work?" Tobias asked warily.

"Have you considered the form you would like to take?"

"A bee," Tobias said with certitude.

"That's a new one. OK so here's how it works. It's not technically transmutation. You don't actually *transform* into a bee. It's more like VR. Do you know what that is?"

"Virtual reality?" Tobias asked.

"Jes, exactly. First, we make an agreement with the creature on Earth to use its body for a short period of time. It is important that we have their consent." She opened a cabinet and took out a wooden box. She lifted its lid and turned it toward Tobias. "You simply put on the goggles, which will allow you to experience everything the bee experiences. You can guide its movement with this." She handed him a matching white video game controller.

"You're kidding," Tobias said with the VR goggles in one hand and the game controller in the other.

"What do you mean?" Selma asked.

"VR is still pretty new on Earth. Have you always used this technology?"

Selma smiled knowingly. "Human perception is already a virtual reality. This just makes it more familiar to you."

"Gotcha." Of course, Tobias didn't fully understand what she meant about human perception. It was good enough for him to temporarily suspend his disbelief so he could get back to Mia.

"First we need to locate the girl." She procured a phone from her bra. "What did you say her name was?"

"Mia Navarro."

She typed her name into a search bar and hit enter. "Ah-ha! There she is. Higher Grounds Cafe." Mia appeared as a red dot on a map.

"Yes! That's where she works."

"OK, now let me see if any bees are in the area." She entered the word *bee* into a search field, selected a range of *1 mile,* and hit enter. "Aye! There are so many!" She circled a cluster of tiny dots nearest the cafe and submitted a group request. Within seconds she got a flurry of responses. "You are in luck! Are you ready?"

"So . . . just put these on?" Tobias asked examining the device.

Selma assisted him with the goggles and switched them on. She placed the controller in his hands and led him into the wingback chair. "Now I am just going to initiate the pairing. One second . . ."

"Oh! I'm in! I'm . . . whoa! Everything is so big!"

"Take a moment to orient to your surroundings before you take flight."

"Too late! I'm flying! I'm doing it!" Tobias soared up toward the treetops in a nearby park.

"Easy! Take it easy. Try landing."

"This is amazing! Whoa! I'm super high up." He could see the roofs of buildings for a city block. Cars looked like toys on the grid of streets below. The sound of his wings reverberated in his ears.

"Push up on the right button to go down," Selma instructed.

"I know, I know. OK, I'm coming down now." He could see the entire park from his vantage point. He guided the bee back down toward an old man reading the paper on a park bench. He landed atop the old man's driver's cap.

"Be careful around humans," Selma said. "Remember, you're a bug. People like to squish bugs."

"Got it." Tobias guided the bee toward a cluster of bushes with small purple flowers. Although from his viewpoint, they were quite large. Another bee alighted from another portion of the bush and approached him. He'd never seen a bee that close before and at such a massive scale. It looked utterly sinister with monstrous eyes and fur—everywhere. Tobias was terrified at the alien creature now inspecting him without regard for personal space. Right when Tobias decided he'd had enough, the neighboring bee flew away.

"Is everything OK?" Selma asked.

"Yeah. I just got a close-up of what I must look like. Remind me to avoid mirrors."

"OK, well, now that you seem to have the hang of it, can you see the cafe?"

Tobias flew up and oriented himself toward the main street. "I think so. I think that's it over there." He could see the dumpsters behind the building. The name of the cafe was stenciled on the back door. He flew toward it and landed on a wooden pallet leaning against the back wall. It occurred to him that he hadn't thought through any coherent plan. At that moment a teenage barista emerged with a full trash bag in each hand, pushing the door open with his butt. As soon as he stepped away from the heavy door it slammed shut before Tobias could navigate the bee through it. He waited for the boy to toss the bags in the dumpster and positioned himself at the top of the door frame out of sight. When the teen opened the door again, Tobias quickly flew inside and positioned himself on a high metal shelving rack.

He took a moment to orient himself and concluded he must be in some kind of storage room. Stacked boxes, whole-sale bags of coffee beans, and rows of flavored syrup lined the shelves. Cleaning supplies, a mop station, and a utility sink occupied the far wall. It was tidy and organized for such a small space. A swinging door with a round window led to the coffee bar and the rest of the cafe. He'd already missed his opportunity to make it through the swinging door safely. He flew onto the ledge of the round window. The clock on the wall read 12:56.

There she was. Mia was stocking a retail shelf with ceramic coffee cups and travel mugs from a cardboard box. She made sure that all the handles were facing the same direction and the store's logo faced out. When she'd finished that, she wiped down a table and straightened the chairs around it. Mia removed her apron and floated toward the coffee bar taking an iced beverage from another barista. She lingered in a brief chat and then waved goodbye. *Here she comes*, he thought.

Mia pushed through the swinging door and turned to a

wall-mounted tablet where she clocked out before backing into the heavy back door with her coffee in one hand and her phone in another. Tobias quickly flew through the door just before it slammed shut. He flew up a few feet above her to see where she was headed. She remained focused on her phone as she walked toward her car, which was parked in an adjacent parking lot. *Here goes nothing*, Tobias thought and landed at the top edge of her phone.

Mia simply shook him off. He landed again in the same spot. She shook him off again. "Go away!" She continued to double-tap and scroll through her Instagram feed undeterred. This time Tobias landed on the straw as she lifted the cup toward her lips. He watched as her perfect, enormous lips opened and envelop his furry body. She immediately spit him out and continued spitting and wiping her tongue with her sleeve. "Gross! Stupid bee!"

Mia got into her car and Tobias managed to fly inside before she closed the door. He perched on the backside of her headrest and took some deep breaths while Mia started the car and pulled out of the parking lot. This was proving to be much more difficult than he imagined. Mia reached into her center console and removed her vaporizer. *One more time*, he thought and landed on the mouthpiece of the smoking device as she raised it to her lips. This time, however, she noticed him and flung him into the instrument panel on her dashboard. Tobias shook his furry body and flew directly toward her face stopping inches from her nose and yelled, "Mia! It's me, Tobias!" Of course, all she heard was *bzzz, bzzz, bzzzz!* She began swatting at him with her hand and then with her apron. Tobias maneuvered as best he could away from her attacks and thought himself to be fairly adept until suddenly, he saw black.

Tobias removed the goggles from his head and asked, "What happened?"

"You killed that poor bee, that's what happened!" Selma scolded. "Good luck finding another bee host."

"Maybe that wasn't the best form after all," Tobias conceded.

"I had my doubts."

Tobias thought. "What about a dog? Dogs are pretty good at communicating with people, right? Like Lassie."

"No! Killing a bee is one thing but a dog? No way, José. Not on my watch."

"I didn't kill that bee. *She* did. I doubt she has the heart to kill a dog."

"I suppose you're right," Selma said. "But it's going to be a lot harder to find a dog that is not on a leash or behind a fence." She pulled out her phone and did a search. "Wait. I don't believe it."

"What?"

"I think I found your canine host. He must be a stray. Aye! Dios mío! He is adorable! Look at that face!" She turned her phone screen toward him. The dog was a mixed breed terrier of some kind with scruffy gray whiskers and in need of grooming.

"Yeah, he's perfect. Will he do it?"

She tapped her phone and waited for the response. Her eyes flashed. "He is willing! Put your goggles on and I'll get you paired."

Tobias placed the VR goggles over his eyes and sat back in the chair. A moment later he could see a monochromatic dog's eye view. He was moving along a sidewalk in what appeared to be an older neighborhood. He didn't specifically recall any of the houses, but he had the sense he'd been there before. He had a sense he was moving in the right direction. It was the smell, and it became stronger with every step. It was Mia. He increased the dog's pace. Tobias had no idea how far away she was, but he knew he was getting closer.

Two corgis on leashes barked at him from across the street. Their odor was oddly compelling, and he had the urge to investigate but he steeled his resolve and stayed the course. He noticed plenty of other smells in the neighborhood. Some were familiar but had a richer quality to them. There were no *bad* smells. He was surprised by the alluring odor of fresh dog feces someone had neglected to scoop. To humans, dog poop registers as a single note, more or less—repulsive. Through a dog's nose however, poop has many layers. It's complex and nuanced. Tobias realized he had stopped and was completely absorbed, enraptured by this steaming pile of dog shit. *What am I doing? Come on! Get it together.*

He continued down the street and made a left at the intersection. After another block, there it was. He ran as fast as he could toward the 1920's craftsman with peeling blue paint. He ran up the cracked concrete steps to the front door and barked. He jumped vertically, spun around, and barked again. He scratched at the door and barked. The door opened.

"Oh my God! Aren't you a cutie!" Mia squealed. "Are you lost?" Tobias barked. Mia reached down and pet his head. "No collar? Are you hungry? Wait here." Mia closed the door. Tobias stood eagerly on the welcome mat wagging his tail. Mia returned and squatted to place a plate of sliced vegan hot dog on the mat. Tobias ignored the food and jumped into her lap. She scratched him behind both ears. "Oh! You are so sweet! Where do you live, Mister?"

She smelled like coffee, marijuana, and a combination of

various essential oils and botanical beauty products. Tobias was loving this attention, but he needed to stay on task. He needed to get her to think about him, Tobias, not the dog.

"Are you thirsty?" Mia asked in a syrupy baby voice. "I get you some water. Wait here."

As soon as she opened the door to go back inside, Tobias darted into the house. He smelled another familiar scent— his own. He ran up the stairs and into Mia's bedroom. His shoes were still on the floor next to her bed. He grabbed one sneaker in his mouth and ran back downstairs.

"No, silly! That's not yours!" Mia scolded playfully and laughed. "Give me that!" She took the shoe from his mouth. Tobias barked. "We don't eat shoes, silly." Tobias jumped up and snatched the shoe from her hand and ran with it toward the back door. He scratched at the back door and turned toward Mia.

"Oh, you want to play? Fine but not with that shoe." Mia looked around the room. "Here, how about this?" She picked up a hot pink disc from Khalil's disc golf bag. She took the shoe once again from his mouth and opened the door. Mia threw the disc across the lawn. "Go get it!" Mia called. "Get the frisbee!" She placed the shoe on the patio table and ran toward where the disc landed in the grass.

Tobias stood on his hind legs and grabbed the shoelace dangling from the side of the table and pulled it down. He ran with it to the cluster of pine trees where they had gathered to ingest the psychedelic tea. He dropped the shoe near the fire pit where he sat and barked.

Mia slowly approached the dog. She furrowed her eyebrows. "What are you trying to tell me?"

Tobias sat in the same spot he sat in when they drank the tea. He barked and thumped his tail on the ground. He picked up the shoe with his mouth and placed it back down again.

"I don't understand," she said.

He whimpered and placed his head on top of the shoe.

"Tobias?"

13

———

TOBIAS PERKED up his ears when she said his name. He sat up and lifted a paw for her to shake.

"Is that really you?" Mia asked, taking his tiny paw into her hand.

Tobias barked enthusiastically.

Mia got down on both knees. "Can you understand me?"

Tobias barked.

"This is so weird," Mia said out loud to herself, holding the sides of her head with both hands. "If you're really Tobias, bark twice."

Tobias barked twice.

"OK, roll over."

He rolled over.

"I can't believe this is happening. Are you . . . dead?" Mia asked with a look of remorse.

Tobias shook his head back and forth.

"Are you still . . . up there?"

Tobias looked up at the sky and barked.

"You must have gotten stuck when you fell into a coma.

133

Oh my God! I've been so worried about you." She pet his head. "I'd go back but I'm out of tea." She tapped her lips with an index finger. She looked at her watch. "Maybe Khalil has some left. He'll be home soon. Come on!"

Mia sprung to her feet and ran back into the house. Tobias followed closely behind. She ran up the stairs and into Khalil's room and started opening dresser drawers and rifling through his belongings. She looked under his bed and in the drawer of his nightstand and then went to his closet. Mia pulled a chair over and stood on it to see what was stored on the shelf above the hanging rod. She opened shoe boxes and plastic storage bins.

A distinct odor registered like an olfactory beacon in Tobias' snout. He ran directly into the closet and pressed his nose into the back left corner. He barked and pawed at the wall. Mia got down off the chair and shined her phone's flashlight into the dark corner. A piece of the drywall had been cut into a small square roughly six inches wide. She used her fingernails to gently pull the cutout piece from the wall. Mia shined her light into the hole in the wall but didn't see anything. She started to reach her hand into the hole and then hesitated and pulled it back again, fearful of any critters that may have been hiding in there. She shook both her hands and made a high-pitched moaning sound. Mia closed her eyes and plunged her hand into the hole and felt around. Her eyes popped open, and she pulled out a crumpled paper sack. Mia opened the sack and pulled out a ziplock baggie. "Bingo!"

"What are you doing, Mia?" Khalil stood behind her with his arms crossed.

Mia emerged from inside his closet with the ziplock in

her hand. "I'm sorry! I have to get back. Tobias is still up there."

"Whose dog is that?"

"*This* is Tobias!" She gestured toward him with open palms.

"Excuse me? Mia, are you OK?"

"Somehow, he found a way to contact me from the in-between. I know this seems bananas but it's really him." She turned to Tobias. "Go ahead, show him."

Tobias barked and raised his paw.

"All dogs do that," Khalil said, unimpressed.

"He found his shoe in my room and took it straight to the fire pit. Then he found where you were hiding La Seta. It's him, I swear! Once we got to the in-between, Tobias fell into a coma and got stuck up there. I need to go back, pleeease."

Khalil looked at Tobias with a frown. "You could have just asked me," Khalil said, looking around his bedroom. "You didn't have to tear my room apart."

"I'm sorry," she said with a heart-melting apologetic smile. With that face, Mia could get away with murder. "Please?"

Khalil got down on one knee and peered into Tobias's eyes like he was searching for a hint of humanity. His eyes were dark and intense. Tobias made his best puppy dog eyes and lowered his head in submission.

Khalil sighed. "Fine. Just don't use it all. We're running low."

"Thank you!" Mia wrapped her arms around Khalil's neck and kissed him on the cheek.

"I don't get it," Khalil said. "What do you see in that guy anyway?"

She looked at Tobias and cocked her head to one side, smiling. "He's kinda cute, isn't he?"

"No, I mean . . . never mind."

Tobias followed Mia downstairs to the kitchen. He sat patiently at her feet while she prepared the tea. When it was done, Mia brought the steaming mug into the den and sat on the couch with her legs crossed. Tobias hopped up on the couch and laid his head in her lap. Mia closed her eyes and breathed deeply while stroking his head. After a few minutes of meditation, she raised the cup to her forehead in gratitude and then drank the entire cup. She kept her eyes closed as she lay next to Tobias and cuddled him.

Tobias removed the VR goggles and stood. "I did it! She's coming!"

"Oh, that's wonderful. I'm so happy I could help," Selma said taking the goggles from him.

"What now?" Tobias asked, looking around the room as if Mia was supposed to somehow appear there. "Where is she?"

"I don't know," Selma said, shaking her head.

"She drank the tea. When does she get here? How do I find her?"

"I don't know," Selma said, shrugging.

The barrens! Remy said something about a portal. "I have to go! Thanks for your help! I really appreciate it," he cried as he ran back through the house into the front courtyard. He opened his Uber app and realized he needed to enter an address before he could summon a car. He was sure the barrens were off the grid. At that moment his phone rang. It was Remy.

"Yo, T! I was hangin' out in the barrens waiting for the next tourist and guess who just arrived?"

"Mia? Is she with you?"

"Yeah, man! She's right here. Say hello."

"Tobias?" Mia said. "Where are you?"

"I'm not sure exactly," Tobias said. His heart was beating heavily in his chest. He held the phone with both hands as if he might drop it.

"Meet us at the pier by the big Ferris wheel," she said.

"OK. I'm on my way." He hung up and typed "Ferris wheel" into the Uber app and summoned a car.

When he arrived at the pier, his palms were clammy and his face flushed. When he first met Mia, it caught him off guard. He didn't have time to feel nervous. Plus, he had no expectations. He had zero aspirations for any kind of romantic connection with Mia when he met her because at that time, she was only a fantasy—a dream. It was different now. She came back for him. This was intentional.

The sun was finally beginning to set in the distance as carnival lights illuminated the pier and the big Ferris wheel. A crowd had gathered around a stocky Peruvian gentleman furiously blowing away on a traditional Andean panpipe. He was accompanied by a guitarist and a percussionist. The melody was upbeat and joyful. People clapped and nodded to the driving downbeat with smiles plastered on their faces. Among the celebratory crowd, Mia was dancing with her eyes closed, free and without inhibition.

"Mia!" Tobias called, cupping his hands at the sides of his mouth.

She opened her eyes to see him waving and she smiled widely. She took him by the hand and pulled him into her rollick. Tobias wasn't much of a dancer. In fact, he was terrible at it. He locked eyes with Mia and felt her exuberance and delight so deeply that he forgot everyone's eyes were on them. He began to move his body in response to hers. Whatever self-consciousness that might have accompanied such behavior in the past was no longer present—not here, not with Mia. He felt a sense of freedom he couldn't remember ever experiencing before. His movements accelerated and grew demonstrably greater in expression. His legs and arms flailed about rhythmically without any thought or agenda. When the song ended, Mia practically stumbled into his arms.

"That was amazing!" she cried.

"I kind of lost myself there for a minute!" Tobias exclaimed.

Remy was standing in the back of the crowd with a muted grin on his face. He gave Tobias a wink. "How did you find each other?" Tobias asked Mia.

"It's like he knew I was coming. He was at the portal when I arrived."

Remy joined them and slapped Tobias on the back. "That was something," he said.

"Oh," Tobias said coyly, still catching his breath. "Thanks. So I guess you've met. That's crazy, right?"

"I knew it was Mia right away," Remy said. He turned to Mia, "I thought he was exaggerating but you are even more lovely than he described." Of course, Remy had seen Mia before from the viewing room. He was just being charming.

"Aw!" Mia exclaimed and smiled at Tobias.

"Well, listen, kids," Remy said, "I'm gonna leave you two to catch up. It was lovely to meet you, Miss Mia. I do hope we meet again. Tobias, you be good now." He winked and patted him on the shoulder.

"See you, Remy," Tobias said. "And thanks!"

Remy gave a casual two-finger salute and walked away.

The sky was dark now. The bright lights along the Promenade encouraged celebration and merrymaking. Mia wore a Bohemian-style dress and beaded sandals. Her hair was loosely pulled back at the sides with a single long braid down the back. Her brown eyes danced with excitement. "How did you do it?"

"Do what?" Tobias asked.

"How did you turn into a dog?"

"Oh. It's called transmutation. I went to this lady, who was also a jaguar. Anyway, she has this app that can put you into the consciousness of any willing creature on Earth using VR technology. I was also the bee in your car."

"Oh my God! That was you? I'm so sorry! Did I hurt you?"

"No, no. I mean, you straight up murdered that bee but no, I didn't feel a thing."

"Oh thank God! That was pretty ingenious though. I never would have even thought of that. So how are you getting along up here? Have you been able to let go of your body yet?"

"Earlier I listened to this symphony in the park, and I could see myself as a beam of light. But it only lasted until the music stopped."

"That's a start!"

"Yeah, it was pretty cool. Listen, I'm sorry about my mom. I saw what happened in the hospital from the viewing room."

"You saw that? I'm pretty sure she hates me, right?" Mia forced a pained smile.

"She'll come around. She thinks the drugs had something to do with the coma."

"They didn't?" Mia asked.

"No. I heard the doctors talking. I would have gone into the coma regardless. They shouldn't have let me go in the first place."

"Well, that's a relief. I guess it doesn't matter. I mean, it's been what, five days and you're still in a coma."

"Wait. What? You were just here this morning."

"Uh, no. That was Saturday. You went to the hospital on Saturday. It's *Thursday*."

Tobias was stunned. It felt like a long day. It should have gotten darker a lot sooner but it certainly hadn't been five days. "This is the first night since I got here. It's been daytime the whole time."

"That's because they only do night like once a week. You don't need sleep here. Haven't you noticed you aren't tired or hungry or haven't had to go to the bathroom since you got here?"

"So nighttime is . . . just for fun?"

"Yeah!" She laughed.

"Still, it doesn't seem like I've been here all that long."

"This place is trippy, right?"

"Thanks for coming back. I . . . I missed you." His words trailed off at the end and he averted his eyes.

"Aw! Of course! If I had known you were still here, I would have come sooner. I had no idea you'd be trapped here. That's so crazy." There was a pause. "Listen," Mia said, grabbing Tobias by the hand. "I hope you wake up soon but in the meantime, it's important that you try to let go. That's what this place is for—to get used to not having a body. You might as well learn what you can while you're here, right?"

"Sure. I'll try." He wasn't lying but clearly this was something Mia was a lot more concerned about than he was. He would have agreed to just about anything if it meant he could spend more time with Mia. "Do you think you could come back to visit?"

"Yes, of course! We're low on supplies but I can probably get some more by next week."

"So that would be . . ." Tobias calculated in his head, ". . . like two days my time? I can handle that."

Mia laughed. He couldn't get enough of that delightful sound. She smiled and tilted her head to one side. Her eyes reflected the lights from the Promenade. "What do you want to do?"

"I . . . I don't know."

She looked up at the big Ferris wheel. "Wanna ride that?"

"Oh, I'm not good with heights."

"Yeah, I remember." She giggled.

"OK, no, you're right. I can't stay afraid forever. Let's do it!"

"Seriously?" Her eyes sparkled. Mia grabbed his arm and nearly pulled it out of its socket as she led him toward the Ferris wheel. She climbed into an orange-painted gondola and pulled him in after her. The stars, or whatever they were, shimmered brightly in a cloudless sky. The moon was unusually large. Its color slowly transitioned from a deep violet into magenta and then to orange. Mia could not contain her excitement as they ascended. She settled her gaze upon Tobias who was holding onto both sides of the cage. "Isn't this amazing?" Mia asked.

"Yeah," he said unconvincingly.

"Watch this!" Mia exclaimed. As their gondola ascended to the top of the wheel it detached from its joints and floated gracefully into the night sky.

"Wooooah my God!" Tobias exclaimed as they soared over the city lights. The moon cast a sparkle over the water. The sky above was littered with stars, or what passed as stars.

A comet darted across the dazzling sky. He breathed shallow breaths and clutched the sides of the metal cage.

"Relax, Tobias," Mia said in a soothing voice. "We can do anything we want here. It's pure freedom!" Her eyes sparkled and her smile radiated brighter than the stars above them. "There's nothing to be afraid of. Give me your hands."

Tobias hesitated before releasing his grip. He placed his hands in hers—soft, delicate, and warm. He kept his eyes on her face, more so to quell his fear and maintain a sense of balance. Her smile was reassuring and completely relaxed in the face of such perilous antics. He thought to himself, *everything is fine. She knows what she's doing. Just be cool. None of this is real. None of this is real. None of this is real.*

14

———

THEY TALKED FOR HOURS, walking along the beach, stopping only to watch the sunrise. By the time the sun, or whatever it was, came up again, Mia had faded away. Tobias felt, for the first time, that his life was starting to make sense. This life suited him much better than his life on Earth. He started to think this coma was the best thing that ever happened to him. Mia actually wanted to spend time with him. In the beginning, this would have been impossible to comprehend. After last night, his nagging doubts had all but vanished.

He strolled back toward the boardwalk with the heels of his shoes dangling from his index and middle finger. There were fewer people milling about after the festive evening. When he reached the boardwalk, he sat on a blue bench facing the beach, stretching his arms across the back. Surfers in black wet suits like skinny seals were already paddling out. A family of sea gulls descended upon an overturned bag of popcorn in the sand.

"Fun night?" Remy stood next to the bench with two coffees and a playful smirk.

"Oh, hey!" Tobias took one of the coffees. "Thanks!"

Remy sat. "Well?"

Tobias took a sip of the hot beverage, nearly burning his tongue. "It was amazing. We talked all night. It was just so . . . easy."

"So you guys just *talked*?" Remy asked with a sideways leer. "You guys didn't . . . you know—"

"No. No, I mean, the thought did occur to me. You know, like, maybe I should make a move or whatever. But we just kept talking and I wanted to hear everything. Have you ever just been like totally in sync with another person? Like every word, every look, every pause, it all just feels—I don't know, meaningful?"

Remy slowly nodded, his expression somewhat distant. "Yeah, I know what you mean," Remy said at half volume. He kept his gaze on the surfers in the distance.

"I've never felt that way before—even with my ex." Tobias realized he'd never told Remy about his divorce. "I was married before. I thought I was in love with her at the time but now I'm not so sure. Everly—that's her name—she was kind of out of my league. She was beautiful, ambitious, outspoken. She took chances. Not like me. I followed her around like a lost puppy. She asked me one day, after we'd been dating for two years, if I was ever going to propose. At the time, it felt like it would be stupid *not* to marry her. I didn't think I'd ever find anyone like her again. So, we got married. But I can't say I ever felt this way about her—the way I feel about Mia, that is. I was always trying to catch up to her. I always felt like I was falling short, always several steps behind. With Mia, it feels like we're right here." Tobias clasped his hands together, fingers interlaced. "You know?"

"I guess you don't find that every day," Remy said.

It occurred to Tobias that he'd never asked Remy much about his life on Earth. "Were you married?"

"Yes, I was. But we was separated when I died. I kind of fucked up my marriage a long time ago. I hadn't even spoken to her in probably five, six years."

"What happened?" Tobias asked.

"I cheated. A few times actually. It's no excuse but I was playing a lot of shows at the time, and we'd stay out pretty late. There was always some girl hangin' round lookin' for some attention. It was way too easy if you ask me. Easier than it should've been. After a while, I stopped trying to hide it and she finally had enough. But like I said, it's no excuse. Carla was a good woman. She didn't deserve that, and I knew better."

Tobias bristled at Remy's confession of infidelity. That was the cause of his own divorce. Could anyone ever really be trusted? Remy, a working musician and Everly, a bestselling author. Why would people like that need to cheat? He started to consider the notion that maybe infidelity was another perk to being successful—something he wasn't, and maybe that's why it seemed so unconscionable to him. Then again, Remy did seem remorseful.

"No kids?" Tobias asked.

"Nah, man. She had some fertility issues and I never really pushed for alternatives. At the time, kids weren't exactly part of my lifestyle as a musician, so it didn't bother me much, but I know she was pretty sad about it—for a long time. I think she woulda made a good mom."

"Do you ever check in on her from the viewing room?"

"I did at first, out of curiosity. She came to my funeral so that was nice. I wasn't expecting that. She's with some other dude now—fuckin' car salesman. Seems happy enough, I guess. Probably doesn't think about me too much anymore. That's alright though. I'd rather it be this way. One less thing I gotta worry about. You know what I'm sayin'?"

Tobias nodded. He wondered if Everly even knew what happened to him, that he'd been hospitalized and in a coma. How could she? She was in the middle of a national book tour. She probably never thought about him either—probably glad to have him off her plate, off her radar. This triggered a sadness buried deep inside, which he immediately reburied. He sniffled and clenched his fists. *Fuck her.*

"Hey man, you ever been surfin' before?" Remy asked.

"No. You?" Tobias replied.

Remy shook his head. "No. I say we change that right now."

"But I don't know how." He didn't know how because surfing is the kind of activity that requires one to let go and surrender to the ebbs and flows of life with equanimity and grace—qualities Tobias had never embraced.

Remy chuckled. "That don't matter! If you can see it in your mind, you can do it. It's not like you can drown." Remy set his coffee down and blink nodded into a wet suit. He was holding a baby blue surfboard. "Come on. You do it."

"OK. Can you help me out with the—" Tobias nodded his head and blinked indicating he still hadn't figured it out.

Remy blink nodded to change Tobias into a wet suit, only his surfboard was white with thick yellow and orange stripes down the middle. "How do I look?" Tobias asked looking down at his skintight get up.

"Like a surfer!" Remy said, nodding in approval. "Race ya!" Remy slapped Tobias on the back and took off toward the shore. Tobias ran after him. Remy pranced into the cool surf and dove chest first on top of his board, paddling toward the waves with his arms. As the next wave swelled toward him, he held the board with both hands and positioned his feet underneath him. He slowly stood with his arms stretched out for balance. Tobias did exactly as Remy until he found himself underwater, trying to figure out which way was up.

Tobias coughed up salt water, clutching the top of the surfboard to keep himself afloat. He looked on as Remy reached out to skim a ten-foot wave with his fingertips. The water wall curled behind him and fell back onto itself. Clearly, Remy must have done this before. There was no way this was his first time. Tobias made a few more attempts closer toward the shore but never stayed up more than a few seconds before the surfboard slipped from under him.

When Remy had had his fill, he joined Tobias who sat on his surfboard in the wet sand throwing seashells back into the ebbing tide like a pouting child. "What happened?" Remy asked, wriggling a finger in one ear to get the water out.

"I don't know. I couldn't stay up. I thought you said you never surfed before."

"I hadn't."

"You're telling me this was your first time surfing?" Tobias asked incredulously.

"I swear to God!"

"Why couldn't I do it? I did just like you up until I tried to stand up."

"You got me. You supposed to be able to do anything here on the first try."

Two young women in bikinis sat on beach blankets in the shade of a pink and green umbrella, a blonde and a redhead. "Hey studs!" the redhead catcalled. The other giggled and flipped her blonde hair. "Want a beer?"

Remy looked at Tobias and shrugged. "Why not?" They

carried their surf boards over and sat next to them. The redhead handed them each a can of beer from an ice chest. Remy cracked his open and raised his can. "Cheers!"

The young women giggled and initiated superficial and flirty small talk. One of them, the blonde, kept touching Tobias on his arm and pulled a piece of kelp from his hair. After his night with Mia, Tobias wasn't especially interested in engaging in Afterlife romance with anyone else. They were both knockouts by any standard, and still in their twenties. He wondered if their age and beauty were artificially rendered from the aging app that automatically downloaded to everyone's phone when they arrived in the in-between. The blonde woman sitting closest to Tobias squeezed his knee and he jumped.

"Can I ask you ladies a question?" Tobias blurted.

"You can ask me anything you want," the blonde said in a breathy voice, leaning in and pressing her breasts together between her arms.

"How . . . how old are you?" Tobias asked.

The redhead scoffed and turned toward the blonde who backed away from Tobias and muttered, "Rude."

"I'm sorry," Tobias said. "I didn't mean to offend."

"Come on, Jennifer," the redhead said, and they both got up and stormed off in a huff, brushing sand from their tanned posteriors.

"Smooth," Remy said sarcastically, shaking his head.

"I guess that answers my question," Tobias said. He felt bad for calling them out but figured they were the ones trying to be something they're not. They were the ones being deceitful. He should be the one storming off, not them.

Remy finished his beer and crushed the can in his fist. "Don't sweat it, man. Hey, you want to get some waffles?"

Tobias wasn't hungry but waffles sounded good. "I do, actually."

I know this great little place. Remy summoned a car and blink nodded them back to their usual attire. They arrived at a 1950's style diner and he could smell the waffles and coffee from the sidewalk. Inside, the Chantell's bellowed doo wop harmonies from a jukebox. They took a seat upon red vinyl stools at the front counter and a pretty, doe-eyed waitress with an entire can of hairspray in her hair handed them laminated menus. "Coffee?"

"Please," Remy said perusing the menu as she poured coffee from a glass carafe. "We'll take the chef's special."

"Two specials, coming up!" She ripped a sheet from her notepad and placed it in the short order window behind her and yelled to the cook, "Two specials!"

Tobias looked around the restaurant. "This place is the real deal," he said. "Very authentic."

"Wait 'til you try these waffles. They're phenomenal," Remy said.

Tobias felt unusually comfortable around Remy. It was unusual because Remy was cool. Tobias was definitely not. Tobias maintained a longstanding and unwarranted resentment toward cool guys. It was another example of being on the wrong side of the wall—the uncool side. But Remy didn't seem to acknowledge any such wall. He didn't carry the burden of even knowing the difference. It was this burden that came to define Tobias' entire life.

Remy had finished roughly half his waffle when he noticed something outside. "Hey, now." He placed his coffee mug on the counter and swiveled in his barstool. "It's a tourist!" These opportunities didn't come around every day. His primary mission in the in-between was to find a tourist to help him uncover the truth about his murderer down on Earth and when the opportunity arose, he had to attend to it.

"Where?" Tobias asked looking in the direction that Remy was now glaring. He saw people walking on the sidewalk—nothing out of the ordinary.

"There!" Remy said. "Can't you see that one guy out there? In the baseball cap."

"Who? That guy right there?" He pointed at the very normal-looking man waiting patiently at a crosswalk with his hands in his pockets.

"Yes! Can't you tell he's . . . different?"

"No. Not really. How can you tell?"

Remy slid off the barstool. "Sorry man, I gotta catch this dude before he fades. I'll catch up with you later!"

"Sure! Good luck!" Tobias called out as Remy rushed out onto the sidewalk. Tobias watched him jog across the street to catch up to the alleged tourist who seemed a bit startled to be approached by a complete stranger. Tobias wondered what his opening line might have been. *Good luck, Remy*, he thought to himself, shaking his head.

"Order up!" the cook called. The waitress placed his plate in front of him along with silverware rolled in a white napkin. He turned back around and cut himself a syrupy bite. They *were* phenomenal. *Is that cinnamon in the batter?* The waitress came by to refill his coffee. "This is really good," he said with his mouth full and pointing to the plate with his fork. He savored the mouthful and swallowed, satisfied. He looked around the diner again, admiring the attention to detail. Even the cash register—it could have been a working prop right out of a James Dean movie set.

He noticed an elderly man in a beige windbreaker sitting in a booth at the back of the diner. It was the iconic mustache and curly brownish-grey disheveled hair that triggered the flash of recognition—*Chester Lang?* Tobias had read at least twelve Chester Lang novels and collected essays by the time the prolific author died in 2007. Lang was the first author he ever truly felt connected to as a malcontented youth. He wondered what he might have to say to such a literary giant. Would it be inappropriate to ask him to read his manuscript? Would he even give him the time of day? He figured he would never have the chance to ask him on Earth. It was now or never.

Tobias nervously made his way to the table. "Excuse me, sir? Mr. Lang?"

15

———

THE SAGE NOVELIST removed a soft pack of Pall Malls from his inside pocket and extracted a single cigarette with his lips before looking up at Tobias. "That's me," he said with the unlit cigarette in his mouth. He patted his pockets in search of his lighter, which he'd forgotten he'd placed on the table next to the condiment caddy. Tobias picked it up and flicked the red plastic lighter, cupping the flame with his other hand. Chester lit his cigarette and sat back in the booth. He gestured toward the opposite side of the table, inviting Tobias to take a seat.

"It's a great honor to meet you, sir," Tobias said, sitting down. "I think I've read your entire catalog."

"I sure hope it wasn't a waste of time," Chester said dryly. His voice was raspy and deep and sounded as if it was being filtered through a sack of wet gravel.

"Oh no, sir! You're my absolute favorite author. In fact, you inspired me to become a writer."

"Well, then it certainly *was* a waste of time." A hint of a smile danced at the corner of his mouth. It was the kind of dry humor Tobias had come to expect from the great satirist. "What's your name?"

"Tobias. Tobias Munch."

Chester took a long drag from his cigarette and turned his head to exhale. "What are you doing here?"

"Excuse me?"

"You're obviously not dead. What are you doing here—in the in-between?"

"I'm in a coma." Tobias looked down at himself wondering what it was that gave it away.

"You don't say," Chester said, scratching at the stubble on his age-spotted cheek. "So, Tobias, what kind of writer are you?"

"Science fiction, mostly."

"No, I don't mean what do you write about. I mean, *you*, as a writer. What kind of writer are *you*?"

"Oh. I . . ." Tobias furrowed his brow. "Sorry. I don't know what you mean." Tobias was stumped by the question and suddenly felt, once again, like an imposter.

"Well, besides my oh-so-inspiring body of work, what motivates you to write? Why do you do it? Why does it matter?"

"I guess it's a chance to make my mark. I've always wanted to be an author but you can't call yourself an author unless you've published a book. So, until I publish my book, I'm just taking up space."

"That's it? That's what you want your whole life to be about?"

"Well, yeah," Tobias said. Surely, if anyone could under-stand that, it would have to be Chester Lang.

"I think that's the saddest thing I've ever heard," Chester said with a pained look on his face.

Tobias was confused again. "Why?"

"You think my life was about writing? Hell no! My life was about *living*. Living was the meal. My books were just what came out the other end." He leaned to one side and farted—low and dry as if honked from a beat up trombone.

Normally, Tobias would have thought that was hilarious but he was too perplexed to react. "I thought you loved writing," Tobias said.

"I did! Just like I loved a good bowel movement. A good bowel movement can be quite enjoyable but it's not a life purpose. I hope you have a better reason than that."

The same waitress from before came over and refilled Chester's coffee. She was slim with painted fingernails and didn't bother to hide her gum chewing. She turned to Tobias. "Can I get you anything, sugar?"

Tobias was thankful for the interruption. "Uh, just coffee. Thanks."

"You got it," she said with a wink and walked back to the kitchen, her hips swaying rhythmically under a baby blue polyester skirt.

Chester leaned toward Tobias and grinned. "Pretty little bird, ain't she?" His unkempt, overgrown eyebrows jumped up and down cartoonishly to emphasize his point.

Tobias nodded but inadvertently shrugged simultaneously as if to concede. *Sure. Why not?*

"Would you believe we're the same age? In fact, she used to pour my coffee when I was living in Indiana, before I published my first novel. I fell head over heels for this girl but I never could pluck up the courage to ask her out. Even after I moved across town, I'd take three buses just to see her each morning. Then one day, she was gone. I heard she got married and moved to Kansas or Kentucky, or someplace.

Never heard from her again. Until I died, that is. And here she was. She still doesn't know who I am."

"That's incredible!" Tobias said. "Why don't you say something?"

"No, no, no. It's better this way. I was twenty-eight years old in 1950 and for a better part of that year, I was obsessed and tortured. I'd dream about escorting her to the movies and out for burgers and milkshakes and we'd laugh like idiots all night long. I'd dream one day we'd get married and buy a little house in a respectable neighborhood. She'd bake pies in the kitchen while I pushed a lawnmower outside on the front lawn. Then we'd have a baby and then another, and another." He took another drag of his cigarette. "I'd lose myself in these fantasies, in the yearning. Looking back, it was the yearning that made me feel alive. It doesn't get any better than that."

"But you could have everything you ever wanted now, in this place. Why not make it happen in real life?"

"I already had my real life and I don't regret any of it. But when you have something tangible you lose the anticipation, see? If I asked her out, all that nervousness, all those knots in my belly, that all goes away. I'll start to take her for granted. She'll nag me about my smoking and drinking. I'd have to spend holidays with her uptight parents, wearing some moronic-looking sports team jersey they bought me and pretending to give a shit about football stats. Sure enough, I'll find myself longing for someone else, someone less . . . *real*. No thanks." He poured an excessive amount of sugar from a glass, flap-top sugar dispenser into his coffee and stirred it.

Tobias reflected on his own yearning for Mia before all of this. He just couldn't see it from Chester's point of view. For Tobias, all that pining was pure agony and, by his own assessment, a little pathetic. No, he much preferred the reality of being in a face-to-face relationship. He was finally getting what he'd been dreaming about all this time, and he couldn't comprehend how that was less preferable to the unrequited yearning itself.

The waitress returned with Tobias' coffee. "Here you are, sweetie."

"Thanks. Hey, um, can I ask your name?" Tobias asked. He could feel Chester shifting in his seat.

"It's Beth. Let me know if you need any—"

"Hi, Beth. This is my friend Chester. Chester Lang? Maybe you've heard of him?"

Chester was glaring at him and pursing his lips together.

"Nice to meet you, Chester," Beth said with a courteous nod. Did she really not know who Chester Lang was or was she just being polite?

"That's enough!" Chester hissed under his breath and then flashed a pained smile in Beth's direction without making eye contact.

"Did you ever live in Indiana?" Tobias asked, ignoring Chester's admonishment.

"Why yes, I did. It's been a spell," she said. "Why do you ask?"

"Well . . . Chester? Do you want to take it from here?"

"No. Now stop it!" Chester said and kicked Tobias in the shin.

"Oooh kaaay," Beth said, wrinkling her forehead and forcing a smile. "Holler if you need anything else." She turned and walked away.

"I told you I didn't want to meet her!" Chester chided. "Didn't you listen to anything I said?"

"I'm sorry. I just thought, you know, maybe if you got the ball rolling—"

"I shouldn't have said anything. Forget it." Chester took a drag from his cigarette. "What did you want anyway?"

Tobias blew it. He never imagined his little intervention would make him this upset. "Look, I'm really sorry. I didn't mean to put you in a weird position. I'll just get going." He started to slide out of the booth.

"Wait a minute. Sit down," Chester said. "I know you didn't come all this way just to ruin my Afterlife. What did you want?"

Tobias slid back into the booth. He played with his fingers and cautiously ventured, "I was hoping you could give me some writerly advice. I can't seem to finish this book I'm writing. I've been working on it for eight years and every time I try to wrap it up, I just keep creating more problems."

"You want me to read your book?"

"If it's not too much trouble," Tobias said and then added, "Sir."

"I'll read your book. But I need you to know something. I'm not going to sugarcoat it. If it stinks, I'll tell you it stinks. You got that?"

"Yes, sir!" Tobias couldn't believe it. "Thank you!"

"You got it with you?" Chester asked.

"Yeah," Tobias pulled out his phone and opened the Files app to locate the Word document saved there.

"No, no, no. I'm not reading it off some rinky-dink phone screen. If you want me to read it you need to print it out." Chester Lang was a notorious luddite who wrote everything he'd ever written either by hand or on his trusted Smith-Corona 2200 electric typewriter, well after computers had become ubiquitous. "There's a print shop across the street," he said pointing behind him with his thumb.

"Of course. I'll just go print it out real quick. I'll be right back!" Tobias was eager to accommodate the great Chester Lang and feared the opportunity might dissolve if he'd waited a moment longer. He ran across the street to a print shop and located the self-serve commercial printers. He followed the instructions to upload the file from his phone. Usually, there is a step to swipe a credit card before starting the print job but in this case the machine simply prompted him to push the green button. A few minutes later all 879 warm pages sat in the printer's output tray. He looked around the store for an employee out of habit. He knew intellectually there was no cost for the service, but his instinct remained. Once he confirmed there was no one there, he snatched up the pages and ran back across the street.

Beth was filling Chester's coffee mug when Tobias walked back into the diner. The old man craned his neck as she walked away. Tobias smiled and shook his head before interrupting his salacious ogling. He placed the printed manuscript on the table and slid into the booth. "I really appreciate this, Mr. Lang."

Chester put out his cigarette and cleared his throat. He placed a pair of brown square-framed glasses on his face and slid the manuscript toward him. He took a look at the title page. "*Odessy Intergalactic* by Tobias Munch. Have you ever considered using a pseudonym?" Tobias shook his head. "Never mind. Alright, well, meet me here tomorrow, same time."

"You're going to read it in one day?" Tobias was bewildered.

"You haven't been here very long, have you? Time kinda does its own thing around here. Don't worry, you'll get used to it."

"I don't know what to say. Thank you, Mr. Lang. I'll see you tomorrow!"

Tobias left the diner feeling hopeful about his writing career but it didn't take long before self-doubt crept in again and he worried that his writing might prove to be pure garbage. He figured it was better to hear it from a dead expert than to release it to a mercilessly critical living public. As far as he knew, the dead could not leave negative reviews on Amazon.

Tobias felt inspired to get started right away. He figured he'd need a place to write once he'd heard Chester Lang's feedback. He could never write in a library or a coffee shop. He got too distracted by the people around him—always wondering if they were silently judging him. He needed his own private space. He wondered where Remy lived. He never mentioned it. If you never have to sleep or use the restroom and the weather is always perfect, one might never actually need a place to live. He remembered the boy, Finn, who created his own residence in the in-between from the *Ever After* realm he created on Earth. *How did he do that?*

He opened the concierge app on his phone, which had appeared mysteriously on his home screen after he audited the newcomer orientation. He scrolled through a menu of options: Entertainment, Transportation, Food and Dining, until he saw a link for Home Listings. He had the option to select a home based on available criteria like square footage, number of bedrooms, all the standard search criteria that might have been available on a typical real estate site with the exception of price. Every style of residence, from sprawling estates to urban lofts to cookie-cutter tract homes, was available. There was also an option to either upload digital home plans or to create your own house. As far as he could tell, there were no limits to the size of the home or available materials to choose from.

As fun as it might have been to create his own residence without restrictions or limitations, as he had done many times in *Ever After's* sandbox mode, Tobias wasn't particularly invested in the long-term occupation of a permanent residence. Any of the available listings would have sufficed to provide the privacy he needed. He scrolled until a property overlooking the ocean caught his eye. It was a small, coastal cottage on the edge of a grassy cliff. A checkbox indicated that the oceanside property came fully furnished. At the bottom of the listing, a large green button read: *Move in!* He clicked it and animated fireworks displayed on his screen with the words: *Congratulations! Welcome to your new home.*

He called a car and entered his new address. The driverless car winded its way up a mountain road and then onto a private unpaved drive. The simple cottage sat at the end of the drive and blended into the natural coastal landscape among towering oleander and Japanese maple. Tobias walked up to the arch-top front door, which was painted a vibrant blue, juxtaposed against the white plaster exterior walls of the cottage. He turned the antique doorknob and to his surprise, the door was unlocked. Apparently, there was no need for home security in the in-between.

The house was fully furnished, as advertised. It wasn't how Tobias might have furnished it, but interior design was not a priority. The furniture was simple yet functional, neither contemporary nor outdated. He poked his head into the kitchen and the home's only bathroom, neither of which were of any use to him at all since he never got hungry or had to go to the bathroom.

A pair of French doors off the main dining room looked

out onto the sparkling ocean. He stepped through the doors, which led to a flagstone patio with a small wrought iron bistro table and two matching chairs. At the end of the patio, a steep and winding staircase of uneven railroad ties led down to the rocky beach. The sounds of crashing waves and seagulls permeated the salty air.

His phone chirped in his back pocket and he retrieved it. He pulled his head back in disbelief. A notification appeared on the Lock Screen alerting him to his meeting with Chester Lang. It was already tomorrow.

<h1 style="text-align:center">16</h1>

WHEN HE ARRIVED BACK at the diner, Chester was sitting in his usual booth. He was smoking a cigarette and staring thoughtfully out the window. "I can't tell you how much I appreciate this, Mr. Lang," Tobias said, sitting down across from him. "So, what did you think?"

Chester remained silent for longer than Tobias was comfortable. "What are you trying to say?" Chester asked finally.

"Come again?"

"I read the whole damn thing and I still have no idea what it's about."

"Well, the main character is exiled from his home planet, see? And he's in search of this new kingdom he's been promised. But, of course, everything goes wrong and he gets sidetracked with all these minor quests and—"

"Let me stop you there," Chester said. "I read it. I know what happens. What I don't know is *why* it's happening. What are you trying to say?"

Tobias sat pensively for a moment. An unfinished

thought began to escape his mouth and he quickly suppressed it once he realized he was only guessing and that he actually had no clue what his own book was about. After eight years of writing, he had no clue.

"Is there anything in here that reflects your own life?" Chester asked.

"Well, if I'm being honest, my life isn't very interesting. If anything, I write to escape my pathetic life, not to illustrate it."

"Ah, but your pathetic life is all that matters. Without it, your story has no soul. You're trying to invent truth out of thin air when you have all the truth you need right in here." He reached across the table and pointed to Tobias' chest.

"And what truth is that?" Tobias asked with a bite of frustration in his tone.

"I can't tell you that. But it's going to be key to finding your ending."

Tobias could feel his eyes moisten and his cheeks warming as a lump formed in his throat. Anger welled up inside his chest and he fought to push it back down. He'd had just about enough of all these vague references to discovering his truth and listening to his inner voice. *What truth? What inner voice?* A part of him wanted to press for further clarification about this so-called "inner truth" but he was too embarrassed to admit that he needed it spelled out. He couldn't bear yet another reminder that not only was he an imposter to the world but apparently, also unto himself.

"OK, well, besides that," Tobias said, "Is it any good?"

Chester removed his glasses and exhaled sharply. "No."

Tobias deflated like an unplugged bounce castle. This was exactly what he was afraid of. "No? Just, no? Is there any specific part I could fine-tune? I know the whole Trandarian occupation kind of deviates from the main plot—"

"Main plot? What main plot? Your protagonist disappears for eight chapters and by the time he reappeared I thought he'd been killed off! You have at least six subplots, seven if you count the sentient ecology on Braxam, and none of them follow any semblance of story structure! Sorry, kid. You've got a great imagination. I'll give you that. But fiction is so much more than that. Fiction is . . . Well, fiction is *truth*."

"So what do I do now?" Tobias asked. "Toss the whole thing out?"

"Don't be so dramatic. There's good stuff in there. You've created some imaginative worlds and solutions to very unique predicaments, like when Bex discovers the Naak Trolls are prone to epileptic seizures and he's able to breach the time fortress with nothing but the strobe setting on his flashlight. That was genius! Like I said, you've got some imagination. You just need something to say, that's all."

"And that's my inner truth?" Tobias clarified.

"It's already in there."

Tobias didn't have the energy to protest or challenge him further. It's not so much that he disagreed with the brilliant satirist. He wasn't *that* arrogant. He simply hadn't the slightest idea what the man was talking about. He didn't want to risk exposing himself as a complete fraud, not only in the literary sense, but as a human being. "Thank you, Mr. Lang. I appreciate you taking the time."

"Time? I got that in spades."

"Mr. Lang, can I ask you a personal question?"

"Shoot."

"Why are you still here, in this in-between? Why haven't you walked through the door?"

Chester nodded in silence for a moment. He looked over at Beth who was wiping laminated menus with a damp wash rag. "I still got more yearning to do," he said.

"Well, I'll leave you to it then," Tobias said. "Thanks again." He tucked his manuscript under his arm and slogged back out into the street with a heaviness in his chest. *What am I trying to say?* he thought repeatedly as he walked along the tidy sidewalk toward the center of town.

The literary king did not beat around the bush when he stated his book was simply not good. It lacked soul. It lacked truth—whatever that was supposed to be? Regret overtook him as he pondered the years of futility this project represented. He had to admit finally that, in the end, none of it really mattered. His self-importance had been a performance for an audience of one—himself. He wasn't who he had convinced himself to be after all. He didn't feel much like writing anymore and considered for the millionth time in his adult life whether he should at long last give up writing altogether. *Who am I kidding?* he thought.

He came upon a trash bin near the intersection. It looked as though it had never been used. He took one last look at his colossal waste—a waste of time, and paper—and tossed it in. As soon as he released his grip, he felt a sudden jolt in his chest. He opened the lid of the trash bin and looked inside. The manuscript was gone. The trash bin was empty. A woman approached and tossed a coffee cup into the trash as she walked by. After she'd passed him, Tobias peeked into the bin. It was gone. *A magic trash can.*

With nowhere in particular to go, Tobias called a car and returned to his newly acquired writing cottage, which he no longer had any plans to use as such. He arrived and stood in front of the cottage for a while as the driverless car reversed itself and departed from the property. A wood thrush watched him intensely from the branch of a Wisteria tree in full bloom. It hopped and chirped aggressively as if Tobias, the death appropriating outsider, were intruding on its property. Tobias felt unsettled and he retreated inside.

Literary success, in Tobias' estimation, was a means for recognition, for validation—the merits upon which to justify his self-worth. He'd never considered another route. The idea that his worth, his value, could be appraised without having earned it, seemed outlandishly ideological and unrealistic— the stuff of fairy tales and delusion. These long-established assumptions were now being challenged and he kept finding himself on opposite sides of this mental wrestling match.

So what if he never published a book, so long as he had Mia's love. She didn't seem to have the same expectations he'd always placed on himself. He reflected on their conversations, none of them having anything in particular to do with writing or his aspirations to become successful. She liked him for no *reason* at all that Tobias could fathom. This confounded him. It was so unlikely from the very beginning that he had never bothered to impress her intentionally. There was no artifice or manipulation on his part and he had been perfectly willing to let it all go once she realized her error in judgment.

After their last night together, however, Tobias was beginning to believe that it was real—that she really did want to be with him. It didn't make any logical sense, but he was willing to accept that there might be something else at play—something bigger, spiritual even. Like love. That was the only reasonable explanation, because it would have to take something much greater than conventional logic for any of this to make any sense at all.

He spent a few days at the cottage awaiting Mia's arrival. The place was already tidy from when he first moved in and he tried to keep it that way, fluffing throw pillows on the couch, straightening framed art on the walls that were perfectly fine to begin with. He rummaged through old books that had been left on a built-in bookcase in the living room, maybe twenty or thirty all together. No Chester Lang. He only recognized a few titles including *Moby Dick* and *A Farewell to Arms*. He selected *A Scanner Darkly* by Phillip K. Dick and read on the back patio overlooking the ocean. A few chapters in, he was bored so he walked down the uneven railroad tie steps down to the rocky beach. He picked up a handful of sand and let it run through his fingers. *What is this stuff?*

On what he estimated to be the fourth or fifth day, he shuffled into the kitchen and opened the cabinets and refrigerator, mostly out of boredom rather than curiosity, and definitely not out of necessity. He might have been tempted to eat had the opportunity presented itself but the desire was not strong enough to motivate him to actually cook anything. He was surprised to find milk in there. There was no expiration date printed on the container and he gave it a sniff. It wasn't spoiled. He put it back.

He opened a drawer and saw a rolling pin, just like the one Mia found in his mother's kitchen. He stared at it for several minutes and wondered where Mia was. She said it would only be a couple days and it was getting closer to a week. He remembered what he'd promised her. He was supposed to be trying to let go. He took the rolling pin into his right hand and placed his left hand on the stone countertop. "This is all in my head," he said out loud to himself. "It's not real." Tobias raised the rolling pin above his head. "It's not real!" He slammed it down onto the back of his left hand.

The pain was so intense that he couldn't even scream. He buckled onto the tile floor cradling his wounded hand against his chest and pounded his right fist against the cabinets, enraged with his own ineptitude.

Although it hurt like hell, there was no damage to his hand. No broken bones. It didn't even swell up. But the pain was enough to deter any subsequent attempts. Instead, he read, took short hikes around the woods near the cottage, and walked down to the beach. Most of the time he laid about thinking of Mia and their future together. *Where is she?*

A knock came at the front door and Tobias started. *Mia?* He rushed into the living room, jumped over the couch, and knocked over a floor lamp on his way to the front door. When he opened the door, his smile quickly faded. His eyes widened and he pulled back. The intense, dark brown eyes peering back at him were unmistakable. "Khalil?"

"We need to talk," Khalil said in a deep and authoritative voice. "Can I come in?"

Tobias hesitated before acquiescing. "Yeah. Yeah, sorry. Come in." He could only imagine what Khalil might have wanted to discuss with him. Of course, it must have had something to do with Mia. He'd always presumed Khalil hadn't approved of Mia's friendship with him for reasons he'd never been given. Tobias picked up the lamp he'd knocked over and set it upright as Khalil entered the idyllic yet modest dwelling.

"It's about your parents," Khalil said.

"Oh, yeah, I wouldn't worry about it. My mom—she's all bark and no bite. I don't think she would ever sue anybody."

"What? No, it's not that. They're planning on taking you off life support."

Tobias heard what he said but had difficulty making

sense of it. "That's ridiculous. It's only been . . . how long has it been? A week?"

Khalil didn't blink for several seconds and then pushed his long dark hair back with both hands and exhaled dramatically. "You might want to sit down for this." Tobias sat placing his hands on his knees. "You've been gone for close to three months."

"What? No, Mia was just here and it had only been five days. She said she was coming back."

"Mia's not coming back."

"Wait. No, that can't be right." Tobias shook his head. "She was just here."

"Look, I don't have a lot of time. Can we please focus on the fact that your parents are about to pull the plug? We can't let that happen. We need to get you back before you're gone for good."

"Are you guys together?" Tobias asked, completely ignoring Khalil's warning. "I knew there was something between you two. I asked her and she said there wasn't anything going on—"

"There isn't. Tobias, please listen to me."

"I see what's going on here. Look, we're just friends. We haven't done anything, you know . . . sexual."

"I don't care! I didn't come here to talk about Mia. That's not important right now."

"Well, it's important to me! Why can't I see her?"

"Oh my God." Khalil dropped his head in his hands in exasperation.

"Why did you come here?" Tobias asked.

"I'm trying to save you!" Khalil shouted.

"Why? Why do you care? We're not exactly friends, are we?"

"That doesn't mean I want you to *die!*"

"I'm sorry. I'm just not buying it. I mean, what do you care if I live or die?"

"Look, I brought you here under my watch. I knew you weren't ready, and I made a judgement call that ended up going south real fast. I've been researching how to get you back and I've finally figured it out—just in time, too. I'm just trying to do the responsible thing. That's all."

"Where is Mia? Why didn't she come back?"

"This has nothing to do with her! Now listen, your health insurance has already refused to extend your coverage—"

"But she told me she was coming right back."

Khalil grabbed Tobias by the shirt and growled, "Tobias! Would you please listen to me?" He let go immediately and gave a surrendering gesture showing the palms of his hands and then straightened out the wrinkles on his shirt. He exhaled sharply before continuing. "Your parents are paying out of pocket to keep you on life support but as you know, they just can't afford to fund your vegetative state indefinitely. They may be able to keep it going for a few more weeks but once they run out of their retirement savings, that's it. You don't have a lot of time."

"OK, I get it but what am I supposed to do?" He was still rattled from being manhandled by the oaf.

Khalil locked eyes with Tobias. "You're going to have to go through the door."

"Wait. I thought once you go through the door you lose all your memory."

"That's true if you are running on residual consciousness. This is what I've been researching for the last three months. When you die your consciousness is disconnected and goes into a kind of backup mode until you're ready for the next stage where you get reconnected. *Your* consciousness is fully active though, which means you'll revert right back to where you're supposed to be, on Earth. As soon as you walk through the door, you'll wake up in your hospital bed and you can put all of this behind you."

"How do you know all of this? Why hasn't anyone else told me this?"

"Because they don't know how it works."

"And you do?"

"You have to trust me—it's the only way. Come on, we don't have a lot of time."

"Listen, I don't want to be disrespectful or anything but I'm going to need a second opinion on this whole door situation. What if I disappear forever?"

"Nothing disappears forever. Come on, I have a car." Khalil took hold of Tobias' arm. Tobias recoiled but lacked the physical strength to extricate himself from Khalil's formidable grip.

"Let me go!" Tobias pleaded as Khalil escorted him toward the front door.

Khalil reached for the doorknob with his free hand. Just as he was about to grasp it, his fingers passed through the doorknob. He was starting to glitch and flicker. Tobias pulled his arm back and Khalil attempted to reclaim it, but his ghostly hands became impotent to grip anything. Anger flashed upon his face, and he pointed at Tobias with a pixelated index finger. "You're making a big mistake."

And then, he was gone.

17

Tobias could still feel the residual force of Khalil's powerful grip around his upper arm, which he stroked tenderly with his opposite hand. Khalil's absence brought even more trepidation than when he was physically present. The anticipation of Khalil's return was spinning him into a panic. He looked out the front window to discover the vehicle Khalil had arrived in—a lime green Dodge Challenger with black custom rims. He didn't know where he was going but he was going to get there fast.

Tobias climbed into the car and gripped both hands around the steering wheel, taking in the smell of leather. He pressed the start button, and the engine awoke with a deep rumble. Still unsure where he was headed, Tobias slammed the shifter into drive and hit the gas. The car's rear spun sideways, kicking up gravel, before lurching powerfully down the unpaved driveway and out onto the winding mountain road. He located the call button on the steering wheel and shouted over the roar of the engine, "Call Remy!"

The phone rang twice before Remy picked up. "Yo, T, what up?"

"I'm in trouble, Remy. This guy's after me. He's trying to get me to go through the door. He says I've been here for three months, and Mia isn't coming back but I think he's lying. I need your help!" Tobias exclaimed in a single breath.

"Woah, woah, woah. Slow down, man. How do you know this guy?"

"He lives with Mia. He's a tourist, like me. I think he's mad about me and Mia and just wants me gone. He says if I go through the door, I'll magically return to my body on Earth but he's lying, right?"

"That's crazy. I mean, nobody really knows how the door works but you definitely don't return to your body on Earth. This dude is definitely tryna take you out, brah. Where you at?"

"I'm driving. Can I come to you?"

"Why don't you meet me at the library? That way we can get some eyes on this dude. See what he's up to."

"Yeah, OK. Good idea. I'll meet you there." Tobias hung up and shifted into overdrive as he careened down the mountain road hugging the turns around breathtaking rock formations. Had it really been three months? He was afraid to find out. Why was Khalil being so dismissive about Mia? Doubt began to worm its way into his anxious mind. When he arrived at the library, Remy was standing out front.

"Yo, man, if you tryna hide you sho picked a very conspicuous ride," Remy said, ogling the green sports car.

Tobias followed him into the library where they found an empty computer station. Remy logged in and pulled up the search screen. "What's his name?"

Tobias realized he didn't know Khalil's last name. The

thought occurred to him that perhaps he was with Mia. "Actually, can we check in on Mia?"

"Mia Navarro," Remy said out loud as he typed her name into the search field. He hit enter and a red message appeared: NOT FOUND.

"What does that mean? Not found?" Tobias asked. "Did you spell it right?"

Remy typed it in again and got the same result. "That's strange. I never seen that before. Lemme check something." He typed in his own name and hit enter. His name appeared along with the dates for his birth and death and the word: DECEASED. "That's what I thought. At least she ain't dead."

Tobias typed in Mia's name and double checked the spelling before hitting enter. NOT FOUND. "Must be some kind of glitch or something."

"So what else did he say?" Remy asked.

"Well, he did say my parents were taking me off life support."

"What? And you didn't lead with that?" Remy asked with a high-pitched inflection. "We need to talk about your priorities, man."

Tobias knew he was right. As much as he wanted to check in on Mia, he navigated back to the search screen and typed in his mother's name. He hit the live feed button and his mother appeared. She sat on a grey herringbone couch dabbing her eyes with a tissue. This couch was familiar. He recognized the elephant embroidered throw pillow to her right and the turquoise glass-blown figurine on the end table. He zoomed out and froze.

"Take your time, Barbara. Every feeling, no matter how uncomfortable, is valid and deserves to be felt," Dr. Macintosh said. His mother must have reached out to her to cancel his recurring appointments. He imagined Dr. Macintosh suggesting she come in herself, given the circumstances. The therapist wore a bulky cream-colored scarf that contrasted with the sharp edges of a navy blue pant suit. Tobias always felt she exuded an elegant and classy confidence. His mother, by contrast, appeared frumpy in comparison, wearing black track pants with a faded pink souvenir sweatshirt and athletic sneakers.

"I just feel so guilty. It's an impossible decision for a mother. How can I do this to him? He was making progress with you. He was getting better. It's so unfair!"

"You're angry. It's an impossible situation. I hear you. It feels like life is forcing your hand."

"Yes! It's not fair. Why do I have to be the one to make this terrible decision? Why do I have to be the one to end his life? I don't know if I can go through with it."

"What choice do you have?"

"I suppose you're right. We have nothing left in savings. We could sell the house but how long would that buy us? No, I know. It has to be done." Barbara took a deep breath and straightened herself as if to sluff off the weight of her guilt.

"You did everything you could." Dr. Macintosh looked at the clock on the wall behind the couch. "I'm afraid we're out of time." She exhaled sharply and smiled apologetically. "Same time next week?"

"Yes. Thank you so much. You've been such a great help—to all of us." Barbara stood and put on her jacket. She turned to face Dr. Macintosh. "Tobias never really clicked with any of his previous therapists, but I think he really liked you."

Dr. Macintosh smiled. "I liked him, too. He was a very special person. I'll see you next week," she said holding the door as Barbara passed through.

It broke his heart to see his mother so distraught. There had to be another way. Somebody had to know something about how this place works—something other than going through the permanent memory-erasing door. Then again, Khalil was telling the truth about his parents pulling the plug. If Khalil wanted him dead—if he wanted Mia all to himself, why would he bother coming to warn him? Why not just let him die naturally?

"Do you think he's telling the truth about the door?" Tobias asked Remy. "I mean, he was right about that other stuff."

"Man, I've told you everything I know about the door. But I don't know what I don't know. I hate to see you be the guinea pig for something so . . . final."

"Somebody has to know more about this, right?"

Remy stared blankly and slid both hands into his pockets. Tobias wondered how he could know so much and so little at the same time. His eyes popped open, and he sat up. He tried to remember the name of the counselor he met at the entrance. *Maggie.* "Come on," Tobias said. "We're going to the archway."

<hr>

They arrived at the archway a few minutes later. They walked past the fountain and up the stairs to where several counselors in white were greeting newcomers as they exited the orientation building.

"I'm looking for Maggie," Tobias said to the first available counselor. "Is she . . . working today?" It occurred to him that some people have jobs here even though money doesn't exist. He decided to put a pin in that question, among a growing list of others, since it wasn't pertinent to the task at hand. The counselor called to Maggie who had just finished helping another newcomer. He waved her over and Tobias thanked him.

"Maggie! It's Tobias," he said as she approached. "Tobias Munch. Do you remember me?"

"Of course! How are you, Tobias?" Maggie's voice was upbeat and pleasant. It reminded him of his first grade teacher, infinitely patient and kind.

"Well, I'm still here. Still not dead. Oh, this is Remy."

"How do you do, Remy?" She smiled warmly and shook Remy's hand.

"I can't complain," Remy said. "My friend Tobias here, on the other hand, he's in a bit of a pickle."

"You have to help me get back to Earth," Tobias said.

"I told you. I don't know anything about going back," Maggie said apologetically. "I'm sorry."

"You must know someone who does though, right? Isn't there someone who deals with . . . special circumstances? I'm not supposed to be here!" He said that last part more forcefully than he'd intended.

"I believe you are," she said.

"Excuse me? Why? What do you know?"

"I just mean, you know, everything happens for a reason. Don't you believe that?"

"No, I don't believe that!" He was almost shouting now. "That's just what people tell themselves to feel better when bad things happen. This was a mistake! A terrible mistake! I don't belong here!" His volume turned heads nearby and Tobias felt as if he'd crossed a line. "Look. I'm sorry," he said more calmly. "I just need some answers. There has to be someone else I can talk to."

"Maybe you should talk to the bishop," she said.

"The bishop?" *There's a bishop? Now we're getting somewhere.*

"Yes. He always has something helpful to say. You can usually find him at the bowling alley."

Why didn't you mention a bishop earlier? Tobias thought to himself. "Thank you! I'm sorry I got a little heated," Tobias said, rubbing the back of his neck as if massaging away the chagrin.

"It's fine, really." Maggie chuckled. "Good luck! I hope you find what you're looking for."

"Thanks for your time," Remy said and ushered Tobias back down the steps.

"You know where the bowling alley is?" Tobias asked as they walked back to the car.

"Do I? They make the best Philly cheesesteak in town. You wouldn't think it but trust me, it's bomb. I'll drive."

18

TOBIAS WAS NOT A RELIGIOUS PERSON. His mother was raised Presbyterian, but she rarely attended services herself and she never pressured him to come along. But even though he was not the least bit influenced by religious teachings, the thought that there was a bishop available to answer some of his most urgent questions about this mysterious dimension comforted him. The fact that he'd been instructed to find him at the local bowling alley, and not a church, hardly phased him, given the oddities he'd experienced so far.

The bowling alley was nothing special. In fact, many of the buildings and establishments he'd seen in the in-between were not exceptional. The diner, for example, was exactly like the kind of diner one might have patronized during the 1950's. The library was not especially modern or high tech, just a regular library. This bowling alley, too, was a regular bowling alley, the kind you might find in any American town. The stucco exterior was painted light gray with horizontal pink and blue stripes around the top. Neon bowling pins danced back and forth near the roofline.

When they walked through the automatic sliding doors, a wave of musty carpet and shoe deodorizer overtook them. The distinctive sounds of pins being bowled over complimented the 80's rock music blaring over the sound system. There were only a handful of bowlers scattered across twelve available lanes. Even though Tobias had never been to this particular bowling alley before, everything about it seemed familiar.

"Hey man, you go find the bishop," Remy said. "Ima score us some cheesesteaks!"

"Oh, no, nothing for me—" Tobias said after Remy had already walked away. He took a look around to find whoever was in charge. A stalky man stood behind the shoe rental counter spraying deodorizer into blue and red leather bowling shoes before replacing them onto numbered shelves. He wore a faded black heavy metal concert T-shirt tucked into ill-fitting jeans. A red beanie sat high upon his unwashed head so that it stood upright. His mustache dipped into a pair of mutton chops on the sides of his face. He appeared to be mouthing the words to the 80's power ballad blaring over the speakers and thrusting his head at certain inflections, which made the top of his beanie wobble comically above his head like a frantic muppet.

"What size?" asked the man without looking up from his task as Tobias approached the counter. His voice was annoyingly high pitched and he spoke with a Southern drawl.

"Oh. No, I'm not bowling," Tobias said. "I'm looking for the bishop. I was told I could find him here?"

"You found him." He put the aerosol can away under the counter and wiped his hands with a grease-stained cloth. He looked directly at Tobias who just now noticed the man had a glass eye, and not a very convincing one at that.

"You're the bishop?" Tobias asked dubiously. The man turned his back to Tobias and pointed to his leather belt, which was embossed with the name B I S H O P in white lettering. "Wow. That's crazy. Your name's Bishop? What a coincidence," Tobias said. "No, I'm looking for an actual bishop. You know, like a priest."

"Like I said, you're lookin' at him," he said briskly, placing both hands on the counter. "What do you want? A blessing? A baptism? You want to confess somethin'? What?"

"Sorry. Never mind. I'll get out of your hair." Tobias turned to leave. This was clearly not the guy.

"Now just wait a minute, tourist," Bishop said with a smack of hostility. "What makes you think I'm not a real bishop?"

Tobias froze. If he told him the truth, that the mustachioed rental shoe distributor looked more like a low volume meth dealer than a man of the cloth, he would surely invite verbal aggression at the very least, if not that of a physical nature. And Tobias had never been keen on physical confrontation. *Where is Remy?* he thought. Remy had a way of talking to people. He'd know how to respond in a way that would put Bishop at ease and they could get out of there. But he was nowhere in sight. Under the circumstances, he decided, he might as well go along with it.

"Oh no, I believe you," Tobias said. "I guess I'm just having second thoughts, that's all."

"Second thoughts about what?"

Tobias looked around the bowling alley once again. No Remy. "Ahh, I had some questions."

"Don't we all?" Bishop replied. "Go on."

"I want to know who's in charge up here. Who runs this

whole place? I need to talk to someone in charge. I'm not supposed to be here."

"No shit."

"I'm in a coma so I shouldn't even be here. I'm not dead."

Bishop brushed his mustache with his hand. "Let me ask you a question. Can you tell if I'm alive or dead?"

Tobias surveyed Bishop for a moment, trying to avoid looking into his glass eye, before answering. "No."

"No, you cannot. And do you know why you cain't tell the difference between the livin' and the dead? It's because you can only imagine life through the lens of cor-POR-e-al exis-tence. Life, as you know it, is limited by that physical body you keep wearing around like a dadgum Halloween costume. You look ridiculous."

Tobias looked down at his hands and then thrust them back into his sweatshirt pockets. "I don't care! I like having a body and I want to wear it on Earth, where I belong!"

"And you're sure that's where you belong?"

"Of course it's where I belong. I sure don't belong here!"

"Well, I cain't argue with that. Not with that ridiculous meat suit you insist on wearin'."

"I'm not *insisting* on it. I . . . I don't know how to take it off," Tobias said sheepishly.

"I can help you," Bishop said as he reached for Tobias. "Here, let me show you—"

"No! No, thank you. I'm good. I'm good," Tobias said, backing away.

"Suit yourself," Bishop said. As he heard his own words his eyes widened and he laughed. "Get it? Suit! Suit yourself! Aha ha ha!!"

"Yeah. Good one," Tobias replied unenthusiastically. He waited for Bishop to stop laughing. "Look, I'm really just interested in getting back to Earth. Is that something you can help me with? What do you know about the door?"

"Oh, yes. The door," Bishop repeated after gaining his composure.

"I was told that since I haven't died yet, that my consciousness is fully active, so if I were to go through the door, I'd end up right back on Earth. Is that true?"

"Who told you that?" Bishop asked furrowing his brow.

"This guy, Khalil. He's another tourist."

"Well, he sounds like an idiot."

"Yeah, well, I'm pretty sure he's coming after me. I think he wants me dead."

Bishop shook his head. "No, no, no. Look, there's only one way to go through that door and that's of your own free will. That's *litrally* the only rule. You have to choose to walk through it, voluntarily. Nobody can force you."

"Ok, but let's say I make that choice. Is there any chance Khalil is right? Is there a chance I could end up back on Earth and wake up from this coma?"

"Nobody knows what happens once you walk through the door. So theoretically speaking, I suppose there's always a chance. Then again, there's a chance you might disintegrate into nothingness. I wouldn't risk it. Why don't you just go back the way you came in?"

"I can do that? I don't remember much about it. I woke up in my childhood bed. I don't even know if it's still there."

"Never was. That was probably just a simulation to ease you in, so you didn't freak out. The portal's still out there though."

"Of course!" *Why didn't I think of that?* "I'll just go back the way I came!"

"Now hold on there, chief. You cain't go through like that." Bishop looked him up and down. "You won't fit."

"What do you mean? I came in like this."

"No, you didn't. The portal is this big!" Bishop made the OK symbol with his thumb and forefinger, looking through it with his one good eye. "You put that on after you got here 'cause it's the only way you know how to see yourself. And if you don't know how to let go of it, you ain't getting back through that portal."

"OK. So, what do I need to do? How do I learn to let go?"

Bishop crossed his arms. "How long did you say you been here?"

"About three months."

Bishop shook his head. "Brother, if you ain't been able to let go yet, I ain't sure you ever will."

Tobias slumped his shoulders and his face fell. He still hadn't a clue how to let go of his body. He couldn't even blink-nod to change his clothes on this imaginary meat suit. "This is hopeless," he mumbled.

"Not if you had a magic eye."

"A magic eye? Are you for real?" Tobias had no confidence this man was an actual bishop for any established Earthly religion. However, he'd been witness to enough strange phenomenon in the in-between that he was willing to concede the possibility that he might know something of the supernatural.

"What? You don't believe in magic?" Bishop said jutting his good eye menacingly toward Tobias.

"No! I mean, I don't *not* believe. What does it do exactly?" Tobias worried he'd offended the poorly dressed bowling attendant and self-proclaimed man of the cloth.

"Never mind," Bishop grumbled. "You're not worthy."

"What? Hey come on! I'm totally worthy." Tobias wasn't sure he was.

"Are you pure of heart?" Bishop was completely serious.

"Yep. Totally pure," Tobias said confidently, even though he had no idea what he might have meant by that. This line of questioning reminded him of a Knights of the Roundtable comedy sketch. At that moment Remy walked up with a Philly cheesesteak in each hand. *Thank God!* "Remy, tell the bishop I'm pure of heart."

The corners of Remy's mouth pulled downward as he nodded repetitively. "Yeah man, this dude here? Solid dude. Heart of gold."

"Alright then," Bishop said sufficiently satisfied. "What are you willing to sacrifice?"

"Sacrifice?" Tobias asked. "What do you mean?"

"Well, talismans aren't *free*! You gotta give something up. Something important."

"Like what? Like, no chocolate for forty days or something like that?"

Bishop dropped his head and then pushed his misshaped beanie up past his receding hair line. "You're wasting my time," he said. "You don't know the meaning of sacrifice."

It was true. Tobias really didn't know what it meant to sacrifice. His losses were abundant but none of them had ever been voluntary. He operated under the assumption that life had been taking advantage of him all along. It had been taking from him—swindling him at every turn. Getting his hopes up and then pulling that football out from under him and then laughing hysterically at his misery. The idea of his sacrifice being a payment for something he desperately needed felt like another con.

"You're right," Tobias conceded. "Maybe I'm *not* worthy."

"Hold up," Remy interjected. "Can I make a sacrifice on his behalf?" Remy asked Bishop.

"I'm listening," Bishop said raising one eyebrow.

"No," Tobias said. "You don't have to do that."

"No shit," Remy said. "That's what makes it a sacrifice—the fact that I don't *have* to." He turned to Bishop. "What if, in exchange for getting Tobias here back to Earth, I take over your shifts here at the bowling alley for one whole month. I'll spray shoes, vacuum the floors, whatever needs doing. Deal?"

"Well, I have been meaning to take some time off," Bishop said scratching his mutton chops. "OK, you got yourself a deal." He extended his pudgy hand and Remy shook it.

"Thank you, Remy," Tobias said.

"Don't sweat it." Remy turned to Bishop. "Alright, let's do this."

Tobias and Remy were horrified by what they saw next. Bishop proceeded to gouge his finger into his eye socket. The moist, squishy sound it made as his finger penetrated his skull caused both Remy and Tobias to writhe and gag. Finally, his eye dislodged and popped out of his skull like a miniature gooey cannonball. He caught it before it fell to the floor. Bishop held the glass eye, coated in a pinkish-clear slime, in the palm of his hand and offered it to Tobias. "Here. Take it."

Tobias was still half turned away from Bishop and his slimy eyeball. It was looking right at him. Tobias could have sworn the disembodied eyeball was following his movements. He shook his head.

"Come on! Don't be a pussy. Take it!" Bishop said. A pinkish-clear liquid oozed from his open socket.

"Why?" Tobias managed.

"Because it'll help you see the world as it actually is and if you're ever going to let go of your body you have to see things the way they really are. Now here." He extended the eyeball toward him.

Tobias could not remove the look of disgust on his face to save his life. He swallowed and carefully took the eye between his thumb and forefinger. "How does it work?"

"It's an eye! How do you think it works? You gotta look through it," Bishop said.

Tobias shook excess goo from the slippery orb and then wiped it on his sleeve. He reluctantly brought the glass ball up to his line of sight and closed his right eye. It was still a good twelve inches from his face and he couldn't make out anything from that distance. He slowly and deliberately inched the glass ball closer to his left eye until at last he could see it. With the glass ball directly against his own eye, Tobias could finally see the light.

It was just like the day Masha's ensemble played in the park. Bishop and Remy both appeared as indistinguishable gleaming beams of white light. Everything in his immediate surrounding appeared translucent and reversed like a film negative. He looked down at himself and his body had been replaced by radiant white light with no distinguishable features or parts—just a single beam of pure light. He pulled the glass orb away from his eye and everything appeared as it had before—everyone in their respective meat suits.

"See?" Bishop said. "Now all you have to do is get down to that portal and, as long as you can see yourself the way you really are, you should be able to slip right on in there." Bishop was sifting through a shoe box full of glass eyeballs. He selected one with a light blue iris, which did not match the brownish-hazel hue of his good eye and pressed it crudely into his gaping eye socket. He contorted his facial muscles and blinked repeatedly until he felt satisfied with its fit. He didn't bother to adjust the direction of its gaze, which was directed unrepentantly to the right.

Tobias wondered why the bishop didn't just give him one of the eyes from the shoe box. Why did he have to give him the one in his head? He thought maybe it was better if he didn't know.

"Are you sure this is going to work?" Tobias asked.

"No, but what other option you got?" Bishop asked.

"I guess you're right," Tobias admitted. He looked down at the glass eye in his palm. "Thank you."

"Thank your friend here. It was his sacrifice."

19

———————

TOBIAS AND REMY headed toward the barrens. Remy knew exactly where to find the portal since he'd been visiting it almost every day in hopes of meeting another tourist. He used his familiarity with the barrens to convince Tobias that he should drive the supped-up green Challenger, although Tobias didn't need convincing. He only chose that car because Khalil had left it sitting there in his driveway.

"If he had extra eyeballs in that box, why did he have to give me the one he was using?" Tobias asked. "That's just disgusting."

Remy laughed.

"I mean, I don't want to be ungrateful but that's just weird," Tobias said. "That guy was really *weird*."

"It takes all kinds," Remy said, smiling. "Besides he did provide you with a pretty good solution. I didn't know you could go back through that portal, did you?"

"No. I guess nobody's ever tried to go back early, before the tea wore off."

"So," Remy said, changing the subject. "Now that you're going back, you think you can do me that favor?"

It hadn't even occurred to him. Tobias was focused on getting back to Mia—to starting a new life. Remy's plan to obtain months old evidence from a teenager and have him go to the cops was a long shot and Tobias assumed his efforts would be wasted. Then again, Tobias *did* tell Remy he would help him before he found out he was in a coma. Remy *did* just volunteer to work at the bowling alley for a month so that he could return home, thereby saving his life. He couldn't think of a valid reason to refuse. "Yeah. Of course."

"You still have that piece of paper I gave you?" Remy asked, referring to the paper with the boy's address written on it.

Tobias checked his pockets, not because he thought he still had it but to demonstrate that he was just as concerned about it as Remy was, which he wasn't. Remy had blink-nodded him into these clothes *after* giving him that piece of paper. He didn't remember what he did with it because he really had no intention of following through with this favor in the first place. To his surprise, Tobias pulled out the folded piece of paper from his right front pocket. "Oh my God. Here it is."

"Cool," Remy said. "We're here."

He pulled to the side of the road. They stepped out of the car and walked into the open desert. Sand blew softly over the crests of far away dunes. The mystic portal that transported human consciousness from Earth to the in-between was nothing like Tobias had imagined. The portal was a rusty water pipe jutting two feet out of the ground with a simple faucet attached at the top.

"*This* is the portal?" Tobias asked incredulously.

"Yep," Remy said. "This is it." He didn't seem bothered by the unassuming nature of this portal to another dimension. "You got that eye ready?"

Tobias reached into his pocket and removed the magic eye. He frowned as it stared back up at him. He placed it up to his own eye and peered into it. Remy was now a single beam of pure white light and so was he. Tobias looked at the portal and it was no longer a rusty pipe but a pinkish shroud billowing around a vertical slit roughly four feet high. It was impossible to see inside the folds of fabric as the layers unfolded over multiple layers of itself.

Here goes nothing, Tobias thought to himself. He had no legs or arms to command movement, so he willed himself toward the portal and focused his attention at the center of the opening. There was a darkness behind the shroud that he couldn't quite reach, no matter how hard he pressed forward. The layers of undulating folds seemed to push him back toward the outer surface. He backed away and gathered his strength for one more powerful attempt but alas, he was unable to penetrate its barrier.

Tobias removed the magic eye and found himself crouched down around the mouth of the faucet. Remy stood cross-armed with a perplexed look on his face. A little embarrassed from being in this position, Tobias stood and brushed sand from his pants. "I couldn't get in."

"I can see that," Remy said.

"It felt like it was resisting me. Like it was pushing me out."

"I don't know what to tell you, man."

Suddenly, the portal began to quake, and they could hear the creaking sounds that old pipes make when they haven't been used in a while. "What's happening?"

"Get back, get back. Someone's coming through," Remy said, taking a few steps back.

Thick brown liquid began to ooze from the faucet, which shuddered and spat. Brown liquid gushed out full blast onto the sandy ground. It pooled in a thick sludge, inching its way toward their feet. They took a few more steps back as the remaining liquid spat forth from the rusty faucet. The kiddie pool-sized puddle bubbled and fizzed. It began to swirl clockwise in the middle and rose up, collecting itself like a garment as it grew upward into the figure of a person. The last of the ooze trickled upwards over its body and filled in the remaining details.

Tobias slowly stepped back as the new arrival solidified and revealed its identity. "It's him," he stammered. "It's Khalil!"

"I'm going to have to insist you come with me," Khalil said authoritatively.

Reflexively, Tobias threw the glass eye at Khalil. It hit him in the chest and then fell pitifully to the sand with a soft thud.

Khalil grabbed Tobias by the nape of his neck and escorted him towards the car. Tobias struggled but was no match for Khalil's strength.

"Hey!" Remy shouted. "Why don't you pick on someone your own size?" Remy was taller than Tobias but a good six inches shorter than Khalil. When Khalil turned around Remy clocked him squarely in his jaw.

Khalil released his grip on Tobias and rubbed his chin. The blow seemed to have barely had any impact at all. He pointed at Remy and said, "Stay out of this. You don't know what's going on!" He turned back to detain Tobias again but got a fistful of sand in his eyes.

"Let's go!" Tobias shouted and jumped into the car. Remy followed his lead while Khalil wiped sand from his eyes. Tobias started the car and slammed it into drive. The back tires kicked sand all over Khalil as they sped away. "This guy just won't stop," he said, as Khalil miniaturized in the rearview mirror. "I don't know what I ever did to him but he's been gunning for me since the very start. I'm pretty sure he has a thing for Mia."

"Where you gonna go?" Remy asked. "Sounds like he ain't giving up."

"What about your place?" Tobias suggested. "You have a house, don't you?"

"What do I need a house for?" Remy said. He didn't sleep. There were no harsh elements to seek shelter from because it was always 72° in the in-between. He had an endless wardrobe that existed in his mind and appeared on command. He had no need for storage nor any need to protect any belongings since everything in the in-between was free.

"Right," Tobias said. "Well, we need to go somewhere he'll never find us."

By now they had entered the city and Tobias decelerated, not that he had ever seen police in the in-between to apprehend him for speeding. They reached a detour sign before hitting Main Street where a Mardi Gras-style parade was in full swing. Colored smoke, streamers, and glitter erupted from dazzling floats with sequenced dancers. Brass instruments and drums cut through cheers from merry-making parade goers. Tobias pulled into a smaller side street and parked the car. Out of habit, Tobias locked the car using the key fob.

"Hey, let me see that," Remy said. Tobias tossed him the

key fob and Remy pointed it at the car. When he clicked the button, the green car turned yellow, then red, then gray. Khalil was less likely to spot a gray car than a bright green one. "That's better."

"Good thinking!" Tobias said.

"Come on!" Remy said and they ran toward the crowd. They pushed their way through smiling spectators, some of which were wearing feathered and sequenced masquerade masks. Remy took two masks from a vendor and handed a black one to Tobias. He kept a pink and purple one for himself. They donned their masks and attempted to blend in as they made their way further up the avenue.

They nestled themselves in with a rowdy group of parade goers. Tobias tried to blend in but couldn't bring himself to holler along with the drunken rabble. He kept looking around to see if Khalil had followed them there. This, of course, made him stand out even more. Remy, on the other hand, moved in sync with the cadence of the marching band as it passed by. He managed to pull off casual interactions with his neighboring partiers and even let out a convincing "Whoop, whoop!" It was almost as if he'd completely forgotten they were being chased.

The approaching rainbow-themed pride float elicited an eruption of cheers as it blared the first three notes of the all-too-familiar anthem "YMCA." It was rumored that the cast of dancers upon the pride float featured Glenn Hughes, the original Village People "Leather Daddy," who died of lung cancer in 2001. This particular cast included all the original characters from the 1970's disco group with the addition of a shirtless firefighter and a martial arts master, also shirtless. Everyone seemed to be generously forgiving of the well-oiled dancers' loosely choreographed dance moves.

As the chorus invited throngs of parade goers to participate, Remy enthusiastically threw up his arms to form the letters Y, M, C, and A, in that order. Tobias gave an unassertive attempt to play along but was distracted by one of the dancers. It was the Native American dancer who seemed to be looking directly at Tobias. Tobias tried to assure himself that he was masked and there was no way anyone could identify him, yet the dancer would not break his gaze.

As the float passed in front of them, the Native American began walking toward the back of the float, pushing past oblivious costumed performers, and doing his best to keep his eyes on Tobias. The headdress he wore snagged on the Leather Daddy's chains, which maintained its hold on the costume headpiece as he continued toward the back. Seeing him with his long black hair pulled back in a ponytail left Tobias no doubt. It was Khalil, only he looked even more menacing in war paint.

He had to shout to get Remy's attention. "Remy! Hey, Remy! It's *him*! He's the Indian!"

"Hey man, don't say that. It's *Native American*."

"Fine. The Native American is Khalil! Look!"

Khalil was climbing down the ladder at the back of the float as it passed them. Once on the street, parade goers mistakenly thought he must be doing crowd work, so they gathered around him, dancing enthusiastically, thrusting their pelvises at him with great gusto. When one man got too close and made contact with him from behind, Khalil reflexively elbowed him in the forehead, and he went down. He had temporarily lost sight of Tobias and craned his neck to scan the area where he'd last spotted him.

Tobias and Remy fought their way back through the crowds and into a mostly empty movie theater. It was a small vintage theater with only three screens and an antique popcorn machine in the lobby's concessions area. Before escaping into one of the dark theaters they were stopped by an usher who asked them for their tickets. He was wearing a red vest and tie with one of those old fashion bellhop caps with the flat tops.

"I thought everything was free up here," Tobias said.

"Yes, of course. Tickets are free but you still need a ticket to get in," the usher said politely. "The box office is right out front. You can't miss it."

Tobias looked at Remy who shrugged and then back to the usher. "We're kind of in a hurry. Can you just do us a solid just this one time?"

The usher looked over his shoulder and then leaned toward Tobias with the back of his hand against his mouth as if secretly conspiring in a frightfully devious scheme. "Which film are you wanting to see?"

Tobias looked around the lobby at the lightbulb-framed movie posters. "That one." He pointed randomly to the 1987 classic *Harry and the Hendersons*, a comedy about a family who adopts an endearing Sasquatch and tries to keep his legend secret.

"Ahh, yes. Delightful film. Very amusing. You'll be in theater one, just to the left," the usher said, unlatching the red velvet rope to let them pass. "Enjoy the show!"

They entered the darkened theater mid-way through the film and sat near the front. They slumped down in their seats. Remy leaned toward Tobias and whispered, "You want some popcorn?"

"What? No. Let's just hide out here for a bit and then we'll sneak out that exit." Tobias kept turning around to see if anyone else had entered the theater. There were only four other people in the entire theater.

Remy seemed to be taking advantage of the situation and actually paid attention to the movie. He laughed out loud. "Aw man, that shit's funny!"

"Shhhh! We're trying to keep a low profile," Tobias whispered. He looked back again. "I don't think he followed us in here. Come on, let's sneak out through there." He pointed to the nearest exit.

"Can't we just stay 'til the movie's over?" Remy asked. "I forgot how much I liked this movie!"

"You're kidding. No!" Tobias tried to conceal his annoyance with Remy who didn't seem to share the same level of concern for his safety.

He glanced toward the back of the theater once again. This time, his eyes widened into coasters. Khalil was standing at the back of the theater in war paint and brown suede pants, scanning rows of mostly empty seats. "He's here!" Tobias announced and pushed Remy out of his seat and toward the exit near the right side of the screen, out into a parking lot.

When they arrived at the car, someone else had parked behind it, boxing them in. Tobias had to maneuver back and forth a number of times to extricate the vehicle from its tight spot, only hitting the bumper of the car behind him twice. He looked in his rearview mirror and Khalil was running up the sidewalk toward them. He spun the steering wheel in the opposite direction and hit the gas but in his panic, forgot to put the car into drive. The car lurched backward over the sidewalk and pinned Khalil into a brick wall.

"Oh shit!" Tobias cried and flew out of the car. Khalil was slumped over the trunk, moaning. His bottom half disappeared into the red bricks, caved in by the car's back bumper. "I'm sorry! Please don't die."

Remy inspected Khalil. "He ain't dead. He's just a little . . . squished."

Khalil let out a groan and pushed his torso up from the trunk and rested on his elbows. He flung his long hair to one side facing Tobias. "What did you do that for?" Khalil eked out.

"I'm sorry! I didn't know you were behind me, I swear!" Tobias pleaded.

"I need to tell you something," Khalil said laboriously. "They're pulling the plug. You're out of time."

Tobias knew he was telling the truth. He'd witnessed his own mother admitting to having to make this very decision. He looked pitifully on Khalil, costume paint smeared with sweat running down his cheeks. "And the only way back is through the door?"

"Yes," Khalil said.

"Why can't I go back through the portal the way I came?" Tobias asked.

"Because it's a one-way portal."

"How do you know all of this?"

"Because I helped create the portal. We never had any reason to engineer a return portal because as long as you're alive on Earth, your consciousness does the work of bringing you back on its own. We never thought we'd need to return on command. But the door is different. The door reconnects your consciousness to whatever is beyond the door. But since you're still alive, your consciousness is a closed circuit, the door will just kick you back to your original state."

Tobias stood there blinking. Nobody else in this place seemed to have any answers at all. Even though he didn't understand any of it, Khalil's explanation was the only one he'd been given, and he seemed to know what he was talking about. Plus, he tried to go back through the portal, and it didn't work. Tobias was about to die. His parents were going to pull the plug and he was going to die. He realized the door was his only hope. If it didn't work out the way Khalil said it would, well, he'd be dead anyway. If it did work, he'd get to see Mia again.

"Alright," Tobias said.

"For real?" Remy asked, surprised.

"What other choice do I have?"

"You need to move fast," Khalil said. He appeared pixilated. "It's happening tod-d-d-day." He glitched like a bad video conference call. "I'll see y-y-you on the other side."

"Will you tell Mia I'm on my way? Tell her I'll be right there!"

Khalil appeared frozen in place for a moment, and then he was gone.

20

———————

REMY DROVE as Tobias stared blankly out the front passenger window. He had a strange feeling that he was going to miss the freedoms he'd experienced in the in-between. He wasn't looking forward to going back to work at a job he hated. He wasn't looking forward to his pathetic apartment. His mind returned again and again to Mia. Maybe now he finally had the chance to be with her in real life. On the other hand, would reality be sufficient to sustain a love created in a limitless mystical dimension? Self-doubt surfaced right on cue.

"We're here," Remy said. They arrived at the end of the road, which stopped near the foothills of a picturesque mountain range. They hiked toward a massive gorge sliced into near vertical canyon walls. As they made their way along the dried riverbed, a mysterious light spilled into the gorge from a cleft in the rocky canyon wall. An ambient tone resonated throughout the gorge and grew more pronounced as they approached the source of the light. It wasn't exactly a melody, but it carried a musical quality, nonetheless.

At last, they turned a corner and stopped. A commercial steel door embedded itself flush against the canyon wall. It was the kind of door one might see in a school building leading into the gymnasium or cafeteria—solid, gray, and unadorned with a horizontal push bar instead of a doorknob or handle and a reinforced stainless steel kick plate across the bottom. There were no signs or markings on or surrounding the door.

"This must be it," Tobias said.

"Must be," Remy said.

Tobias looked around along the canyon walls for any kind of instruction. "So I guess . . . just walk right in?"

"I guess so. There ain't no magic words."

"OK, well, I guess this is it." Tobias was surprised to feel a lump forming in his throat. He was genuinely going to miss Remy. He wished he could have met him on Earth when he was alive. "It's been really nice knowing you. I'd be lost here if it wasn't for you. You've been a real friend." Tobias realized Remy might be his only friend. He held out his hand.

Remy stood looking downward with his hands on his waist. "You know what? Fuck it," Remy said. "I'm going with you."

"What?"

"That way, if for whatever reason this don't work, I'll be there with you for whatever comes next."

Tobias was deeply touched by the offer. He felt ashamed to admit to himself that he was far too selfish to have done the same for Remy, had the shoe been on the other foot. No one had ever put themselves on the line like that for him. "Thank you. That really means a lot, but I have to do this on my own."

"You sure?"

"Yeah. Plus, if this *does* work, I can still help you. I'm going to find that kid and we're going to put those cops in jail."

Remy smiled and his eyes appeared glassy. He nodded. "Alright then. You ready?"

Tobias glanced back at the door and nodded. "I'm ready."

Remy wrapped his arms around Tobias. "Remember what you learned up here. You got a second chance now, so make it count. Now go live your life. Make it great." He gave his back two hard pats and released him.

Tobias nodded at Remy and turned toward the door. He took a deep breath and let it out. Tobias placed both hands on the push bar and pressed. The door opened into a dark space. He closed his eyes and took a step into the darkness, and then another. He heard a metallic latch click as the door closed behind him. He was too afraid to open his eyes, but he could feel a shift in temperature as he advanced into the void. He could hear muffled voices in the distance but couldn't make out what they were saying.

Tobias could no longer feel the ground beneath him, and he had the strange feeling that he was suspended in air. He tried to take another step but couldn't. He tried to wave his arms out in front of him, but his limbs remained at his sides. He felt cold and shivered. The voices grew louder, and he sensed there were people around him but when he tried to open his eyes, they would not comply. Tobias flew into a panic.

Fear pulsated wildly in his chest. His body shook violently to maintain warmth. A ravenous hunger made its introduction after months of contentment. The voices were becoming more distinct and sounded distressed. A rapid beeping followed the rhythm of his heartbeat.

"Nurse!" a familiar voice called. "Nurse!"

"Is everything OK?"

"His heart rate just shot up!" His mother's voice was unmistakable. It worked. He was back on Earth—back in his body. Khalil was telling the truth and he couldn't understand how he knew or why he cared. Tobias felt cold hands on his face and arms. More voices and shuffling. A bright light bore into his left eye and then his right.

"Tobias, can you hear me? Tobias! Tobias, squeeze my finger if you can hear me! Can you squeeze my finger?"

Tobias attempted to squeeze. He wasn't sure if it was working. He made an effort to speak but as soon as he engaged his vocal chords, a wretched pain strangled his throat and tears streamed down both cheeks.

"He's trying to say something," his mother said.

"Tobias, I'm going to get this tube out of your throat now and you're going to feel some pain, but it will be over very quickly, OK? On three. One. Two. Three."

It felt as though his entire trachea and lungs were being yanked from his throat. He let out a pathetic whimper. Tears streamed from his eyes. His mother practically laid on top of him as she embraced him. "Toby, oh, Toby! You're back! You're back! My baby is back!" Her words devolved into sobs.

For the next couple of hours, Tobias was inundated with medical attention. He was encouraged not to speak, which went without saying because his throat was on fire from being intubated. Of all the painful experiences he'd endured, the extubation procedure was by far the most hellish. The second was his ferocious hunger but in order to allay that problem he'd have to swallow, and he would rather die of starvation. He could wiggle his fingers and toes but larger muscle movements were quite difficult. He wanted to stretch and move his body, but this took an immense amount of effort.

His mother Barbara sat at his bedside through the entire ordeal and kept reminding Tobias to relax and just rest. His father was there, too. He read in a chair by the window most of the time, occasionally looking over the top rim of his glasses at Tobias. His mother was proving to be as attentive and nurturing as he had always known her to be and for the time being, he needed this reliability of comfort and normalcy more than ever, especially after what he'd experienced in the in-between.

A nurse entered the room with a small plastic container of apple juice and a straw. She encouraged Tobias to try to drink something, acknowledging that it might be a little painful at first. *A little?* Tobias turned his head toward the window, away from the nurse. His stomach groaned in protest.

During the course of the next hour or so, he learned that he would be staying with his parents once he left the hospital. Due to his situation, they managed to terminate his lease agreement without incurring extra fees. He also learned that his position at the company had been filled and he was no longer employed. They had generously agreed to donate the next six months of his salary to his parents for hospital expenses, long after his insurance denied coverage. He learned that it may be months before he could walk normally again. He would require intense physical therapy to reverse muscular atrophy and re-establish motor neural connections.

His thoughts returned to Mia. They always did. He wondered if she knew today was the day—the day he was scheduled to pass on from this life and walk through the archway, not as a tourist, but as a legitimate resident of the in-between. He wondered if Khalil had informed her and was half hoping she'd walk through his hospital room door. He had no way of contacting her since he never had a chance to retrieve his phone from the hospital after his initial stay and never got her phone number. He no longer had access to a viewing room to check in on her. He only vaguely remembered where she lived. He knew the area but not the exact address. He licked his lips and attempted to say "Mom," but quickly winced in pain before any vocalization could be made.

"What is it, dear? Hold on . . ." Barbara dug around in her purse and procured a small stationary pad and a pen. She placed the notepad on the adjustable over-bed table and oriented his bed into a sitting position. She placed the pen in his hand. "Write it," she said.

Tobias gripped the pen with merely twenty percent of his normal dexterity and placed the pen's tip against the floral bordered notepad. He scribbled: FIND MIA NAVARRO.

"Mia Navarro?" Barbara read aloud. "Isn't that the girl who hit you with her car?"

Tobias nodded slightly. The pen fell onto the table and Barbara secured it back into his hand. He wrote: I LOVE HER.

She stiffened her face to conceal the worry behind her eyes. "Oh, honey. I think that's the medication talking."

Tobias shook his head and furrowed his brow. He underlined the words I, LOVE, and HER. He did his best to say, "Please," without using his vocal cords.

"Alright, dear. I'll see what I can do." She slung her purse over her shoulder and left the room. Tobias turned toward the mounted television in the corner of the room. He hadn't been paying attention to the 24-hour news network and only caught the tail end of a segment on cryptocurrency before falling asleep.

He dreamt of Mia. It started off peaceful enough and at some point, he was with her again in that small plane where she tried to teach him to let go of his body. He was in the pilot's seat, and they were approaching the side of that mountain. He realized he didn't know how to pilot an airplane and started hitting buttons and pulling levers at random. He yanked at the center stick, and it broke off in his hands. Mia smiled at him and blew him a kiss. She jumped backward from the aircraft and into the clouds. When he turned back around, the mountain had turned into a giant stone carving of his mother's face. "Wake up," she said.

"Wake up! Tobias, wake up, dear," his mother said. "You were having a bad dream."

Tobias sat up and caught his breath. *It was just a dream*, he thought. For a second he thought maybe all of it had been a dream—Mia, Remy, the whole thing.

His mother wiped his head with a damp cloth. "Honey, I'm afraid I have some bad news." She wore a sorrowful expression. "It's about that girl. Honey, that girl died three months ago. She was in a plane crash. I have the obituary right here." She pulled up the obituary on her tablet and handed it to him. "I'm so sorry."

In that moment, all the physical pain in his body disappeared to make room for shock and disbelief. He stared at her picture on the screen and the few words that summed up her existence on this planet, yet he couldn't bring himself to acknowledge the devastating truth—Mia Navarro was dead.

Sadness does not describe what Tobias felt upon discovering his only chance for happiness had vanished. He thought he was returning to a life that finally made sense but as soon as he arrived, the opportunity disintegrated like a mirage. He wondered why Mia hadn't arrived in the in-between when she died. At least he assumed she hadn't. If she had been there, why wouldn't she have come to see him? She knew he was waiting for her. He was right back where he was before meeting Mia. Only now, he had no job, no apartment, and he couldn't walk. He turned distant and unresponsive.

Tobias spent the next two weeks in his repurposed childhood bedroom. It was a guest room now. All his old furniture remained but the walls had been repainted a neutral beige, covering up the black accent wall his mother reluctantly allowed him to paint his sophomore year of high school. The bedding and curtains had been replaced with matching patterns in hunter green. A throw pillow with the word HOME embroidered on one side attempted to reassure him that this was still, in fact, his home.

The Pulp Fiction movie poster, electronic dart board, and framed Beastie Boys concert tour print had been replaced with matching oil on canvas pieces his mother purchased from a big box discount home goods retailer. His desk, which had always been cluttered with various miscellaneous items, had been cleared, revealing random scratches and ink stains, most of which were covered by a large vinyl desk mat. A cheap decorative globe sat in one corner concealing the Nine Inch Nails logo he had carved into the wood surface as an angsty teen. It was his room. But also, it wasn't.

He attended physical therapy three days a week, and while compliant with instructions during the sessions, his efforts lacked any internal motivation to recover. His minimal progress was noted in his medical records, and he was referred for a psychiatric evaluation. By the sixth session he should have been able to walk short distances around the house without the aid of a walker but after falling down in the hallway on his way to the bathroom one day, he lost the will to complete the journey and soiled himself.

He refused to join his parents for meals in the dining room. His mother delivered his meals bedside and later cleared the dishes, which remained mostly untouched. He bristled whenever she would try to communicate to assess his wellbeing and unfairly levied undue scorn in her direction. Her generosity of spirit and genuine care somehow felt particularly unbearable—the burden of undeserving love, which he could not summon the strength to reciprocate. He had lost twenty-seven pounds during his hospital stay and he failed to gain much of it back as his doctors had predicted.

The psychiatric evaluation confirmed his previous diagnosis of Major Depressive Disorder, Recurrent, Severe Without Psychotic Features. Had he chosen to disclose any information about his three-month interdimensional travel during his evaluation, he certainly would have been diagnosed with psychosis. The treatment suggestions included an increase in his current anti-depressant with the addition of another for good measure, and weekly psychotherapy.

His mother contacted Dr. Macintosh, who cleared an hour the following week to make room for Tobias on her schedule. Tobias felt a trace of optimism at the mention of his therapist's name. At least Dr. Macintosh was familiar with his feelings for Mia and would empathize with his loss, so he allowed himself a measured amount of anticipation for the upcoming session. Of course, he wouldn't tell her about the in-between or how he spied on her session with his mother from the viewing room. She was one of the only people he could trust to tell him the truth. She carried no agenda or bias the way everyone else in his life did, especially his mother. Dr. Macintosh might be the only person on Earth who truly understood him. And more than anything, Tobias wanted to be understood.

21

———————

HE WOKE up early the following Thursday with a newfound energy. His appointment with Dr. Macintosh was scheduled immediately following his physical therapy session that morning. He surprised his parents when he shuffled into the kitchen fully dressed. Instead of his usual t-shirt and sweatpants, he had put on a button-up shirt, which took him a good five minutes to button given his limited motor coordination. He even attempted to tie his own sneakers but was unable to pull the strings tight enough for them to last a trip down the hallway. His parents stole glances at one another as he ate all of his scrambled eggs, bacon and toast with jelly, and drank a full glass of orange juice. He'd eaten more in one sitting than he had in the last two days.

His mother drove him to his appointment. She rode with him up the elevator and offered to wait with him in Dr. Macintosh's waiting room. She confessed she had seen Dr. Macintosh for a few sessions while he was in a coma and wanted to make sure he didn't feel weird about that. He did but he told her he didn't care. He stared at the abstract charcoal painting in the waiting room. It reminded him of the archway.

The door to Dr. Macintosh's office opened. "Tobias?" She smiled warmly.

"Yes," Barbara said after Tobias failed to respond. "Hello, Joelle."

"Hello, Barbara. It's good to see you."

Barbara helped Tobias to his feet and made sure he was stabilized with the support of his walker. She gently guided him toward the office door. "I need to run some errands, but I'll be back here when you get out. OK, honey?" She patted his hand.

Tobias nodded and entered the office. He sat in his usual spot and glanced around the office. Everything was exactly as he remembered it. Dr. Macintosh sat across from him in her chair, clasping her hands and resting them on her lap.

"It's good to see you, Tobias. Your mother filled me in. How is your recovery coming along?"

Tobias shrugged. He wasn't interested in discussing his sluggish progress in physical therapy. He was there to talk about Mia. "Did she tell you about Mia?"

"No. What happened with Mia?"

"She died in a plane crash." His voice was steady and monotone when he said this.

"Oh, Tobias. I'm so sorry to hear. Would you like to talk about that?"

He thought he did but couldn't find the words to describe what he was feeling. How could he explain without going into insane territory? "No," he said finally.

"No?"

"I don't really know what to say about it."

"Maybe you could start by telling me about the accident."

Tobias made eye contact with her for the first time since entering her office that day. He wasn't entirely sure which accident she was referring to. His mother must have told her about Mia hitting him with her car. "Oh, you mean the car accident?"

"Yes."

"OK. Well, yeah. She hit me with her car. It was the same night after our last session. I tried to talk to her, by the way, after I left your office. I went in to her work but she didn't see me. Anyway, it was so random. That night I was just walking around downtown and—"

"What were you doing downtown?"

"Oh, I got into an argument with my parents and—"

"What about?"

"Huh? Oh. My mom had my ex-wife's book! Yeah, I guess Everly ran into my dad and asked him if he wanted a signed copy before it came out and he said yes. I guess it's not that crazy, but it just freaked me out and I needed to get away." He looked at her for validation that he was making sense. "Anyway, so I was crossing the street down there and she hit me with her car. The paramedics came and took me to the hospital. The next morning she was there!" His eyes lit up.

"Mia visited you in the hospital?"

"Yes! She apologized for hitting me and then offered to take me home."

"And what did you think of that?"

"I couldn't believe it! I figured she was just feeling really guilty and felt obligated to offer some kind of help. I don't know."

"So did she take you home?"

"Yes, but when we got to my apartment, I realized I forgot my keys and we were going to go back to the hospital to get them but, I don't remember why but we ended up at her house and she made me a sandwich. And *then* . . ." His eyes nearly popped out. "And then she took a nap with me!"

Dr. Macintosh matched his energy as he recounted these events. "In her bed?"

"Yes! I was freaking out. But I fell asleep for a while and then we went out to get some food. Oh, something I forgot to mention. She smokes a *lot* of weed. Like multiple times a day. And so she offered me some and I finally accepted, and I got *really* high. I never smoke. I just never really liked the way it made me feel. But anyway, I got real high and then—" Tobias chuckled to himself. "This is a little embarrassing but . . . no, I can't."

"You can't leave me hanging now," she said with a smile. "Tell me."

"Oh my god. I . . . so suddenly I had to go to the bathroom. Like number two. And all they had were these porta potties and . . . long story short, I shit my pants."

Dr. Macintosh yelped and covered her mouth. "Oh no!"

"Yeah. I was so embarrassed. I mean, I didn't tell her about it or anything but still."

"Then what happened?" Laughter lingered in her accepting eyes.

"So then we went back to her house and there was a party going on. She lives with these roommates by the university, and I guess they have parties all the time. I wasn't really feeling it though because I was still high but not in a good way and I was super tired, so I went upstairs and fell asleep again. But *then* . . . oh my God." He continued with a subdued tone. "One of her roommates came in there and tried to seduce me while I was still asleep."

"What?!" Dr. Macintosh said in his defense.

"Yeah, it was weird. I think she must have been super drunk. Anyway, I shut that down right away and I was worried she was going to tell Mia that I did something to her, so I went looking for her and I found her out back with some other people and they were . . ."

"They were what?"

Tobias realized he was about to get into incriminating territory, so he quickly recalibrated his story. "Uh, they were . . . They were just drinking around the campfire, yeah. So that's about the time I fell into the coma."

"What's the last thing you remember?"

"Um . . . I sat down by her, and I guess I just closed my eyes and passed out. Weird, right?"

"Indeed. And that's the last thing you remember before waking from your coma three weeks ago?"

He hesitated a beat too long. "Yes."

"I've read about people who dream while they're in a coma. Do you have any recollection of dreaming while you were out?"

If Tobias had been dreaming this whole time, it was the most vivid dream he'd ever experienced, and while he might have certainly described certain aspects of his time in the in-between as dreamlike, the experience was continuous and followed a linear timeline. He decided perhaps the most plausible answer he could provide, given Dr. Macintosh's apparent knowledge of coma dreaming, was to admit he had dreamt but he would keep it vague and restrict any details.

"Sure," he said. "Just the usual stuff, you know."

"What usual stuff?"

"Oh, you know. Random things."

"Did you dream of Mia?" She wasn't going to make this easy.

"Um ... yeah, I'm sure I did."

"It would seem unusual if you hadn't, especially after spending a whole day with her and having pined for her for so long."

"Right. Yeah, I think I did, actually. I dreamt we were riding a Ferris wheel." He attempted a chuckle but even he could tell it sounded forced. Dr. Macintosh refused to mirror his deception.

"What else did you dream about, Tobias?" She slowly leaned in placing her chin atop her closed fist. Her eyes burrowed into his.

"Oh, I don't know. I met the late Chester Lang, the author. He read my book."

"And? Did he like it?"

"No. He didn't, actually."

"What a shame," she said. "Can you remember anything else you might have dreamt about?"

Tobias hadn't expected such persistence on her part and was feeling uneasy with her probing. "It's all kind of fuzzy. Nothing really stands out at the moment."

Dr. Macintosh stood and walked over to her desk and picked up a red folder. She walked back to her chair and began flipping through some of the pages. "This is your medical report from the hospital. It shows that the coma was caused by damage to the reticular activating system in your brain. Is that right?"

"I think so." He wasn't paying that close attention when the doctors were explaining because he'd just found out about Mia's death, and he tuned most everything else out.

"This part of the nervous system is responsible for sleep-wake cycles and if there had been significant damage to it, you would not have been physically able to enter dream states."

"I don't understand."

"Well, Tobias, either you are not being honest with me about dreaming, or . . ."

"Or what?"

"You tell me." She removed her glasses and fixed her gaze on him.

Tobias could feel heat rising into his face. He shifted in his seat. He shouldn't have said he was dreaming. Was it possible that she knew about the in-between? "Or . . . I was really there?"

"Where is *there*?" she pressed, tilting her head in the other direction.

He swallowed hard. *Here it comes.* "The in-between," he said, more as a question.

"Tell me about this in-between."

What am I doing? Tobias thought to himself. "It's . . . It's a place people go when they die—before they pass into the great beyond. It's a place where you learn how to let go of your physical body because you can't take your physical body with you into the Great Beyond."

"And did you learn how to let go of your body?"

He scoffed. "No. I tried. Everyone else could do it but for some reason, I just couldn't figure it out."

"Interesting." She jotted something down on her notepad.

A full ten seconds passed. "Do you think I'm crazy?" Tobias asked.

"We don't use that word," she said admonishingly.

"You don't believe me though, do you?"

"The question is whether *you* believe you."

"I mean, it felt pretty real to me, at the time."

She placed her glasses back over her eyes and flipped through a few more pages of the medical report. "It says here your blood tested positive for cannabis, which you told me about. And psilocybin? Did you take mushrooms, too?"

"Yeah," Tobias said sheepishly. "It was a tea. Mia did it, too. That's how we got to the in-between. She and some of her friends go there sometimes."

"And you wanted to experience this for yourself."

"I'm not sure I really believed it was a real place at first. I thought she was being, you know, like metaphorical. I just wanted to be a part of her world. I was tired of feeling like an outsider looking in. I thought maybe if we could share an experience together, maybe I'd have some kind of chance with her."

"I understand," she said with melancholy in her voice.

"You do?"

"Of course, Tobias. We all want to be a part of something special. We all want to belong." Her eyes were warm and motherly—the closest thing to a hug without making physical contact. "Can you remember what that felt like—when you were with her?"

Tobias reflected on the brief moments they shared. A few seconds here, a few seconds there. A lifetime of happiness in a glance, a smile, a touch—brief and light, yet intentional. "Yes. I remember."

"Do you feel it now?"

Tobias nodded.

"Show me where you feel it."

Tobias placed a hand over his chest. "Here," he said. A single tear trickled to the corner of his lip.

"Isn't that proof that it was real—that you belong?" she said.

Tobias craned his neck to the right to conceal his vulnerability and wiped the tear from his face.

"You belong," she said again.

Tobias shook his head. His face reddened and his lips contorted to suppress an avalanche of emotion.

"You. Belong."

The avalanche gave way to heaving sobs. It *was* real. He couldn't deny what he felt in that moment. He clutched the front of his shirt and acknowledged what he'd never before allowed himself to fully own—his own experience, his own truth, and nothing could ever take that away. *I loved her*, he thought. *I* love *her. I love you, Mia.* He could almost feel Mia's arms around him. He rocked softly in her ethereal embrace. Between breaths he heard the faintest of whispers, like the secret call of the ocean inside a seashell: *I love you, too.*

22

———

THEY PASSED the bookstore on the way home and Everly's display window had been replaced with the newest bestseller of the month. Old Tobias would have been glad not to have been reminded of her success but instead, he missed seeing it there. He'd always seen that book, and the relative ease in which her work had risen to prominence, as a personal affront. He realized for the first time, Everly hadn't rejected him. *He* rejected *her*—for years.

He was too focused on his own struggles, his own short-comings, his own failure, that it never occurred to him to think of what *she* needed. She carried him through it all and got nothing in return. She gave and gave until there was nothing left to give. He could see it now and for the first time, Tobias felt proud of her. And although the divorce had been final for over a year, he finally decided in that moment, in the passenger's seat of his mother's car, to let her go.

Familiar streets and buildings seemed slightly smaller, somehow less threatening, as they swept past the passenger side window. His thoughts turned to Remy and how quickly he was willing to let go of finally getting to see his murderer put in jail, just so Tobias wouldn't have to walk alone into the Great Beyond. It didn't make any sense until now. He was loved and he did *nothing* to deserve it. Nothing. He realized that he had been the ungrateful recipient of so much unconditional, unearned love his entire life. He remembered something Remy said: *You see what you need to see when you need to see it.* Tobias wished he had seen it sooner, but he could finally see it clearly now. His heart felt like it would burst through his chest.

Tobias decided he wasn't going to waste any more time and he recommitted himself to Remy's mission. He hoped it wasn't too late. He remembered Remy giving him a piece of paper with the witness' information. *What did I do with that piece of paper?*

When he got home, he went straight to his closet and sifted through his clothes to find the jeans he was wearing the day he was discharged from the hospital, which his mother had since washed. He reached his fingers into one pocket and felt around—nothing. He reached into the other pocket and his fingers met the straight edge of a folded piece of paper.

He retrieved the folded paper with two fingers. The washing and drying had pressed it into a single matted square about an inch wide. Using his thumb nail, he found the crease where two halves had been pressed together and gently pried them open. He did it again a second time to reveal the nearly completely faded words: NICO ALVAREZ 834 FORMOSA, APT 6

Tobias reached for his phone and pulled up the Uber app. He typed in the address and summoned a ride. *What if he's not there? What am I even going to say?* Tobias put his jacket on as the driver pulled up.

"Where are you going?" Barbara asked with fear in her voice as he made his way down the driveway with his walker toward the car. "Toby! Be careful! *Toby!*" Barbara cried.

"I'll be back, mom! I love you!" he shouted as he closed the back passenger door. The driver placed the walker in the trunk and gave Barbara a quick wave.

On the way there, he did a search for Remy Williams and pulled up some old local news articles from six months ago. There were very limited details in these stories, but he did find the names of the two officers on the scene: Darren Beatty and Will Turner. He bookmarked the page and scrolled further down. He clicked on an article from a local music reviewer. The article featured Ophelia Day, the jazz singer Remy played guitar for. The main photo centered on Ophelia singing live at Reeds Lounge in a sequence gown, and in the background, Remy. The stage lights put most of his body in the shadows but illuminated the body of his guitar and his upturned face, mouth opened in a state of elation. He bookmarked the page.

"We're here," the driver said.

Tobias looked out the window and confirmed the number on the building. The driver got out to get the walker and placed it on the sidewalk. He helped Tobias out of the car until he had a firm grip on his walker.

"Thank you." He walked slowly to the rundown apartment building, passing an overturned shopping cart and a sun-faded plastic playhouse for toddlers along the way. *Number two. Number four. Number six!* He walked up to the front door that looked like someone had thrown up on it. He could hear the muffled sound of Spanish television coming from inside. He tapped gently on the sullied front door. The volume on the television turned down and he heard steps coming toward him. The door opened to the extent that the chain lock would allow and a stern looking elderly woman peered at him through the opening. She must have been the kid's grandmother.

"Qué quieres?" the woman asked with a challenging stare.

"Oh, uh, do you speak . . . Habla inglés?"

"Sí. Qué quieres? What do you want?"

"Uh, I'm looking for Nico Alvarez. Does he live here?"

"Sí. Por qué? Are you with the school?"

"No, I just wanted to speak with him for a minute. Is he home?"

"He's at school. Cómo se llama? What's your name?"

"Tobias. Tobias Munch."

"OK, Tobias Munch. I tell him you came by." She shut the door and locked the dead bolt.

Tobias stood there for a moment considering knocking again to ask when Nico would be home and then decided against it. He sat on the stoop to call another ride when he heard the *ppsshhh* of air brakes just around the corner. He used the walker to stand as the school bus door opened and four or five teens filed out and started walking in different directions. A skinny boy, maybe fifteen, with curly dark brown hair protruding around over-ear headphones and a low-slung backpack, walked toward him.

Tobias waved stupidly to get his attention. "Nico? Are you *Nico*?"

"Yeah," Nico said warily as he slowed his steps and pulled his headphones down around his neck. "Who are you?" He stopped a good ten feet away. Smart.

"I'm Tobias," he said, placing an open hand on his chest. "Can I talk to you for a minute?"

Nico looked around, probably to assess his safety. Tobias realized he was putting this poor kid in an awkward situation. "Whachu want?"

"Listen, I know this is going to sound weird, but do you remember what happened here about six months ago, when that guy got shot right over there?" Tobias pointed toward the crime scene.

"Are you a cop or somethin'?"

"No! *Psshh*. No, definitely not." He assumed the teenager might have been suspicious of law enforcement. "In fact, I think cops, *some* cops, are really bad dudes. You know what I mean?"

Nico put his thumbs under the straps of his backpack and cinched them tighter toward the middle of his chest. He looked away and then back at Tobias from the corner of his eyes.

"Hey, you're not in any kind of trouble or anything. I'm just wondering if you can help me out."

"I don't know nuthin'," Nico said.

"Can I tell you what I know?" He waited for Nico to give him the slightest up-nod. "I think those cops killed that man for no reason. And to justify what they did, they planted a knife on him after he was already dead so they could claim self-defense." He waited for a response, but Nico just shook his head and shrugged as if to say, *so, not my problem.* "You sure you don't know anything about that? You sure you didn't see anything?"

"Nope," Nico said with a snap of defiance.

Tobias hung his head. "Look. Those cops are going to get away with it, which means they'll probably do it again. Who knows, maybe to someone you know. We need to stop them. We can't let them get away with this!"

"Who's this *we*?" Nico said. "I said I don't know nuthin'. I gotta go." He turned sideways to slink past Tobias and jogged the rest of the way to his apartment.

"Wait! Nico, wait! Can I at least give you my number just in case you think of anything? You can call or text me anytime. Please, can I just give you my number and then I won't ever bother you again? Please."

Nico took his hand off the doorknob. He slowly walked back toward Tobias and took out his phone. He unlocked it and handed it to Tobias. For a split second, Tobias had the notion to take the phone and run but, since he could barely walk, decided that was a terrible idea. He took the phone, entered his name and number, and handed it back. "Thank you. If you think of anything or remember anything, please don't hesitate to call or text me, anytime, day or night." Nico took back his phone and ran inside. This was going to be harder than he thought.

He was physically exhausted when the Uber arrived to take him home. He had exerted more energy in a single day than he had since leaving the hospital two weeks ago. He wondered if Remy had seen him from the library viewing room trying to convince Nico to turn over the evidence. Had he tried hard enough?

They passed through the warehouse district, which was lined with one and two-story brick buildings that had been gentrified and turned into yoga studios, smoke shops, hair salons, and a boutique grocery market. At a stop light Tobias noticed a neon sign in a window between a comic bookstore and an old-world barbershop. In the middle of the window was a hand with an eye in its center and the words Psychic Medium at the top and Palm Readings at the bottom. "Stop the car!" Tobias demanded from the back seat.

There was no open or closed sign in the window, but he took the lit neon sign to be a good indicator that the establishment was indeed open for business. The door was tight in its jam but with a little push it sprung open and he stepped inside. The tiny waiting room, which felt more like a hallway than a room, consisted of three dining room chairs and a small end table. On top of the end table stood a table lamp with a stone carved statue of the elephant god, Ganesh, as its base. A wooden business card holder held a stack of lilac cards adorned with a sun and moon. The name on the card said, Moira St. Claire, Psychic Medium, Tarot, Palm Reader.

A curtain separated the waiting room from the back of the shop. "Hello?" Tobias called back. When no answer came, he sat in one of the chairs. He'd had his palm read once before. It was in New Orleans and he was with Everly about a year into their marriage. Neither of them believed in any of this "woo-woo crap," as he put it, but the reading promised them a lifetime of happiness and good fortune. Or maybe that was just hers.

A middle-aged woman with razor thin eyebrows pulled back the curtain and waved him toward the back. *This must be Moira.* He thought maybe he should have called ahead or made an appointment. He wasn't sure how any of this stuff worked. "I'm Tobias," he said as he sat down at a round table that had been draped in a gold-colored tablecloth. A crystal ball sat at the center of the table. The room was dimly lit by lamplight and a few candles. Incense burned from somewhere that he hadn't identified. The room was small and cluttered with books, crystals, and other mystical objects Tobias was unfamiliar with.

"Hello, Tobias," she said as she sat across from him. Her voice was alarmingly deep. "I can see that you are mourning. You've lost someone recently?"

"Yes." *How can you tell?* "I did lose someone. Are you able to talk to people on the other side?"

"I can do more than that. I can let you talk to them," Moira said. "Who would you like to speak to?"

Tobias reminded himself that he was there to speak to Remy, not Mia. As much as he wanted to know her whereabouts and why she never arrived in the in-between after she died, he resolved to following through with the task at hand. "His name is Remy Williams."

"Do you have anything of Remy's, a piece of clothing or some other item he might have been in contact with?"

"Will this work?" Tobias reached into his pocket and pulled out the folded piece of paper with Nico's information on it. Remy had been in contact with it after all. He handed the paper to her.

Moira held the paper with both hands and closed her eyes. After a few moments she began to moan. Tobias watched her face closely as she made contact. Her eyelids parted enough for Tobias to see the whites of her eyes, which were rolled up in her head. "Take my hand," she said and thrust her bangled arm across the table.

This is really weird, Tobias thought. As soon as he made contact with her the air was filled with the sound of static. Muffled voices, some in other languages, broke through in choppy segments like a radio tuner seeking a stronger signal. "Hello?" came a faraway voice. Tobias concentrated and the voice repeated, "Hello?"

"Remy?" Tobias said. *This is incredible!*

"Yo T! I didn't think you was ever gonna call."

"I'm sorry. I should have called sooner. Listen, I talked to the kid."

"And?"

"I couldn't even get him to admit he had the evidence. He was pretty guarded."

"Damn. Well, you tried. I knew it was a long shot."

"There's got to be another way though, right?"

"You got me. Not a whole lot I can do from up here."

Tobias had an idea. "Maybe there is."

"Whachu mean?"

"That piece of paper you gave me, remember? It was still in my pants pocket when I got back to Earth. So, I think if you could somehow copy that video of your murder from the viewing room computer and save it to a thumb drive or something, I or someone, could bring it back to Earth. What do you think?"

"I think we'd need to act pretty fast. The trial is next week."

"Wow. OK. I'll have to find Khalil. I don't know if he'd be willing to let me return after all that."

"It's worth a shot."

"You're right. I'll see what I can do. Go ahead and get that video."

"I'm on it," Remy said. "Hey man."

"Yeah?"

"Thanks for doing all this. I appreciate it."

Remy's voice was starting to break up, fading in and out like a cell phone out of range, and Tobias couldn't make out what he was saying. Moira cut in.

"I lost him," she said. "I'm sorry, Tobias but I can only

hold the connection open for so long. It takes a lot out of me." She wiped her forehead with a handkerchief.

"It's OK. I got what I needed. Thank you," Tobias said. "Can I ask you a question?"

"Yes."

"Does everyone go to the in-between when they die?"

"The in-between?" Moira asked a bit confused. Was it possible she didn't know?

"Can I ask you to contact someone else?"

"I'm tired but I can try. I may not be able to establish a connection but I might be able to sense something. Do you have an item?"

He didn't have anything of hers. He pulled out his phone and logged into Instagram and found her account. The last post was on November 23rd—a selfie from inside an airport with Gate 23 in the background. The caption read: *Headed to L.A. to see my mama!* She must have been visiting her for Thanksgiving. "I don't have a physical item, but I have this photo."

Moira took the phone. "She is so beautiful!" She concentrated on the image for a few seconds and then focused her attention into the crystal ball with her hands hovering around its edges. She began to moan again. This part made Tobias uncomfortable. It went on far longer than it had with Remy. The ball filled with a cloudiness, and he wondered what she might be able to see from her side of the table. Finally, she stopped moaning. "I'm sorry. I didn't find her."

23

___

THE NEXT MORNING, Tobias showered and dressed himself. When he tied his shoes, he observed that he had noticeably more dexterity in his fingers than the day before. He did some light stretching as he'd been instructed to do at home by his physical therapist and entered the dining room where his parents were eating breakfast. Tobias announced that he was visiting a friend today. Although his mother expressed her concerns about overexerting himself, she was happy to see him starting to take initiative. The mention of even having a friend was encouraging since he hadn't mentioned having any friends before.

Of course, the term *friend* was a bit of a stretch. Although he credits Khalil for saving his life, they'd never had any semblance of rapport. Frankly, he was scared of Khalil and despite his good deed still saw him as an adversary.

"Where did you say this friend lives?" Barbara asked with concern in her voice.

"By the university," he replied. His car was parked in the

driveway, but he wasn't confident in his ability to drive just yet. "I'll take an Uber."

His father spoke without looking up from his crossword. "I can take you." Tobias and Barbara both looked at Arthur as if he was a talking chair. "I have to go down there today anyway." Arthur had a friend in the History department at the university and they always had some kind of collaboration or academic related event that he never went into much detail about. Or maybe Tobias had never really cared that much to ask.

They didn't say much on the drive over to Khalil's house. Tobias welcomed the silence. It gave him a chance to rehearse in his mind his proposal to return to the in-between. If Khalil wasn't amenable to allowing Tobias to go, he would ask if Khalil might go himself and retrieve the thumb drive from Remy. Of course, he thought, he should probably open with an apology for backing a car into him. It's important to get off on the right foot.

"I've been meaning to apologize," Arthur said out of nowhere. "For the whole book thing. I didn't think about how you might feel about that." He was referring to Everly's book, *The Courage to Start Again*.

Tobias was taken aback. He couldn't remember his dad ever apologizing to him for anything before. "Oh, you don't have to apologize. I overreacted. In fact, I was thinking I actually might read it. Maybe it's time I buried the hatchet."

Arthur nodded. "I think so, too. Are we getting close?"

"It's just past that vegan place."

Arthur pulled into the driveway since there were less steps getting to the front porch. "If you need a ride home just give me a call," he said as he placed the walker in front of Tobias and helped him out.

"Thanks, dad."

He made his way up the concrete steps onto the front porch and rang the doorbell. His dad waited until someone answered the door before driving away. It was Frankie. *This is awkward*, he thought. She was barefoot, wearing a pair of boxer shorts and an oversized anime t-shirt. She was also wearing a gaming headset—the kind with a microphone reaching around to the front of her mouth from the earpiece. Tobias could clearly see the outlines of her nipples through her white shirt and must have been staring a bit too long when Frankie jutted her chin forward and shook her head.

"What do you want?" Frankie asked, annoyed. "No, not you," she said to whoever she was gaming with online.

Tobias blushed. "Um . . . Is Khalil home?"

Frankie rolled her eyes and opened the door wide for Tobias to enter. She turned and walked back into the den while pointing toward the back porch. She plopped down on the couch and demanded he shut the door behind him. Tobias walked through the old house—floorboards creaking underneath him. Khalil was sitting on a patio table on the back deck reading a book. He looked up from his book when Tobias appeared at the glass-inlaid backdoor.

Tobias managed to get his walker through the door and pulled it shut behind him. Khalil tucked his long, dark hair behind his ear and propped one knee up on the chair as he pulled rolling papers and a small tin from his shirt pocket and started rolling a joint. "So . . . you finally listened," he said.

"I want to apologize for that," Tobias said. "You were right."

Khalil scoffed lightly through his nostrils. "I know."

"How did you know though?"

"I tested it for myself. I had already proposed a theory about the door, but it hadn't been tested. I went through the door three times to make sure it worked before I came to you," he said and licked the rolling paper along its edge.

"Well, I'm sorry I crushed you with the car. I honestly didn't mean to."

Khalil lit the joint and took a drag. He held his breath and his eyes squinted. He held the joint out in front of Tobias, who waved his hand to decline. Khalil exhaled a stream of smoke over his right shoulder. "Don't worry about it," he said. "It's not like you did any permanent damage. Didn't even hurt really."

"Right. Of course. I should have listened to you though. You saved my life. I appreciate it."

"Why are you using that walker?"

Tobias figured it was obvious. "They said it'll be months before I can walk normal again. I'm in physical therapy."

Khalil snickered.

"What's funny about that?" Tobias asked.

"Didn't you learn anything up there? Why do you think we go there? Do you think it's just for fun?"

Tobias was under the impression it *was* just for fun, but he could tell this was a rhetorical question and that the answer must have been no. "Why *do* you go there?"

"What you learn in the in-between applies here. Same principles. If you let go of your body in the in-between, you can let go here, too."

"Well, that's the thing. I never could let go."

Khalil raised an eyebrow and took another drag, held it for a few seconds, and exhaled. "Really?"

"Yeah." Tobias felt embarrassed and decided to change

the subject. "So, Mia. How . . . how are you doing? I mean, I'm assuming you were close?"

"We were. We *are*."

Tobias wasn't sure how to phrase this next question. "Have . . . have you seen her?"

Khalil shook his head. "Not exactly."

"Why didn't you tell me she died? When I told you she was coming back you knew she was dead, and you didn't say anything."

"She isn't dead."

Tobias had the impression Khalil was pulling something. "What do you mean? I read her obituary."

Khalil took another hit from his joint. He exhaled and paused dramatically. "Have you ever ridden a skateboard down a really steep hill?"

Tobias couldn't help but assume this was the weed talking. "Yeah?"

"Well, what would you do if at the bottom of that hill was a landmine and you would surely die if you hit it?"

"Jump off the skateboard?" Tobias said slowly in the form of a question.

"Right. Because you're not glued to the skateboard. It's not a permanent part of you. It's a separate thing and you can either use it or not use it. And if it came down to sacrificing yourself or the skateboard, you'd probably let that skateboard go, right?"

"So, you're saying, since Mia knows how to let go of her body, and she can do that on Earth just like in the in-between, that she like, jumped out of her body before the plane crashed?"

"Wouldn't you do the same if you knew how?"

"I guess so. But her body—"

"Toast."

"That actually kinda makes sense. When I tried to find her from the viewing room the search result said *not found*. Then I went to see a medium and she couldn't find her either."

"There you go."

"So where is she?"

Khalil nodded and looked toward the sky using his hands to demonstrate. "Everywhere."

"That's not as comforting as you might think it is," Tobias said. "Will I ever be able to speak to her again?"

"Of course. She's not dead. She is very much alive. Only her body is dead. Very dead. They didn't find any identifiable remains."

"That's really gross, Khalil. So you're saying she's alive, just without a physical body."

"Correct."

"So how can we contact her?"

"You can't. But she can contact you. My guess is she's been trying to. You have to be open to it."

"Are you saying she's like, a *ghost*?"

Khalil paused to consider the question. "She is technically a disembodied spirit, so I suppose you could call it that. Traditionally, ghosts come back from the in-between and get stuck here. Mia never went to the in-between. She never died. That's an important distinction because ghosts are not evolved. They didn't choose to leave their bodies like Mia did. But, like other ghosts, she is probably trying her hardest to materialize. That's what makes it possible for her to communicate or to appear to us lowly humans. Some ghosts look as real as you and me. They walk among us every day."

"That's a bit unsettling."

"Indeed. So what did you need anyway? Did you really just come here to apologize?"

"Actually, there is something. When I was up there, I met this guy—really great guy. Anyway, I said I'd help him out with his situation. He was murdered by the police, actually and they planted a knife on him so they could claim self-defense. I told Remy—that's the guy's name—that if he made a copy of what he saw in the viewing room, I'd take it back with me to Earth and prove his innocence."

"Is that the guy who punched me?"

"Yes, but that was only because he thought you were trying to kill me."

"That is quite the promise," Khalil said.

"I know but if I can do it, I think I should. He'd do the same for me."

"So you want me to help you get back to the in-between, is that it?"

"Or . . . or you . . . I mean, if you were planning to go back anytime soon, maybe you could bring it back with you?"

"I knew there was something," Khalil said, shaking his head.

"Wouldn't you want to help out an innocent man and put some racist cops in jail?"

"You make a strong case. However, I used up all the tea trying to track you down. This stuff is in very limited supply. It might be another month before I can get any more."

"This has to happen before next week! That's when the trial takes place for those cops. Are you sure you don't know anyone else who has any? Who do you get it from?"

"Oh no. I can't ask for more. She is very strict about rations."

"Who?"

"The Doctor. Like I said before, La Seta is a sacrament in our community. It's not a party drug. If she knew we were using it for anything other than spiritual enlightenment, she would cut me off."

"How would she know?" Tobias asked.

"Trust me. She knows," Khalil said. "In fact, she's the one who sent me to bring you back. Once I proved my theory about the door and she heard about them taking you off life support, she sent me to bring you back."

"How does she know *me*?"

"I don't ask questions. All I know is if I didn't bring you back before your parents pulled the plug, there was going to be serious consequences." Fear surfaced from behind Khalil's eyes. Whoever this Doctor is, Khalil seemed to be afraid of her.

"Who is this doctor? Doctor what?"

"We just know her as the Doctor. She created the training program we have been working through. New recruits are often initiated through the partaking of La Seta and then, if it's something they want to go forward with, she helps guide them through the program. Mia was a trainer. You were supposedly her newest trainee."

"What? So she was just trying to get me to join some psychedelic cult?" Tobias felt betrayed—betrayed by Mia but also by his own judgement. It made sense though. She was quite intent on showing him how to let go. She would always bring the conversation back to letting go of his body. He didn't think much of it at the time but now it made sense.

"You would not have been my pick. But she was convinced you were the right guy. Said the Doctor selected you for a reason."

Tobias figured that must have been what Mia was arguing with Khalil about that day at the house. Khalil didn't agree he was cut out for the training program. In retrospect, he guessed Khalil was right.

"But why did the Doctor select *me*? How does she know me?" Tobias asked.

Khalil shrugged. "I honestly don't know how she makes her selections. Like I said, I don't ask questions. If the Doctor says you're the guy, then you're the guy."

Tobias had an idea. "What if I went to the Doctor myself? If she already knows about my situation, I don't know. Maybe she'd be willing to give me another shot."

Khalil shook his head. "I don't think that's a good idea."

"Why not?"

"Because this isn't for you, Tobias. You should have never gotten roped into all this."

"If it's all the same to you, would you mind calling this Doctor and ask if she'll meet me?"

Khalil shook his head. "It isn't all the same to me. I already stuck my neck out for you once and we all know how that turned out."

"Please," Tobias pleaded. "Can you just ask her if she'll meet me?"

Khalil lightly tapped the end of the smoldering joint into the grain of the wooden tabletop to put out the remaining ember and then slipped it back into his shirt pocket. "Wait here," he said and walked into the house.

Tobias wasn't sure he was making the right decision. Maybe he should quit while he's still *alive*. But Remy was counting on him. Plus, his curiosity about the Doctor and how he became a target for her spiritual training program was eating at him.

A few minutes later Khalil returned. He stood in the doorway with a bewildered look on his face. "She said 'yes.' She said she has some other important plans for you."

"What kind of plan?" *Oh God, this was a bad idea!*

"I haven't the slightest. She'll meet you now. We have to go, now."

24

Tobias rode shotgun in Khalil's open-air Jeep to the outskirts of town. He still felt a bit wary and unsure of himself around the dark-haired statuesque action-figure of a man. Khalil was younger in age yet still older somehow—wiser. He certainly knew more about the in-between and about the subtleties that differentiate the living and the dead—a subject that never much interested Tobias before. He wanted to know more about this Doctor and her spiritual program from an academic sense but didn't want to be prose-lytized to.

"So how does it work?" Tobias asked.

"How does what work?" Khalil asked.

"The tea. Like literally, how does it work? How does it transport you to the in-between?"

"La Seta acts on certain neurotransmitters in the brain, like any other form of psilocybin, but it's infused with compounds that act on other areas of the brain that have to do with our vestibular and somatosensory processing, the parts that essentially tether us to our bodies in three-dimensional space. With me so far?"

"I think so." He wasn't.

"Well, without getting balls deep into the neuroscience of it all, without that connection we simply float up to the next level—like cutting the string from a helium balloon. And when I say *we*, I mean our consciousness. Our bodies stay here, on Earth."

"Why did I get stuck?"

"That part I'm still trying to work out. Normally, what happens is your brain will eventually re-establish that connection on its own. Imagine a sentient cord that gets severed underwater and the two severed ends just float there until by chance the current brings them together again and when that happens the two pieces recognize each other as the same cord and a connection is re-established from memory. But with you, because the coma de-activated the memory from either of these severed pieces, even if they randomly bumped into each other, they couldn't recognize each other as the same cord so they just kept floating unattached. That's my theory anyways. Does that make sense?"

"Sort of. I mean, I don't know if I'll ever fully understand it. How do you know all of this?"

"I have a Ph.D. in Applied Neuroscience from Stanford. But all my work with La Seta has been with the Doctor and her program. It's the kind of thing you have to experience first-hand."

"I imagine so."

"Let me ask you something," Khalil said.

"What?"

"Why you? Did Mia say anything about why you were

chosen? I mean, the Doctor wouldn't make a special appointment with just anyone."

"I don't know." He sensed Khalil wasn't buying it. "I swear. I have no idea. I thought, you know . . ." Tobias turned his gaze outside the passenger window, ". . . she liked me."

"Why would you think that?" Khalil seemed genuinely perplexed.

Good question, Tobias thought. "I don't know. I guess we got along OK."

"You actually thought Mia *liked* you? Like you thought she wanted to *date* you?" A condescending smirk sprouted from his lips—the first approximation of a smile Tobias had ever witnessed on Khalil's face.

"No," Tobias blurted defensively. "Not at first. I was just as surprised as you seem to be right now. No, that first day I was like 'Why is she still hanging out with me?' But then the day just kept going and I was just feeling lucky to be there, you know? But then we ended up in the in-between and it felt like, I don't know, like maybe she might actually be into me."

"Did she say that?" Khalil's smirk hadn't completely dissipated.

"No. Not exactly."

"Well, what *did* she say?"

"She just wanted me to learn how to let go of my body and she tried to show me some things, but she never explained why it was important or anything. I just thought this is what you guys did for fun up there."

"But you couldn't do it for some reason. That's what I don't get. What would the Doctor need you for if you can't let go of your body? What are these important plans?" He was asking himself these questions out loud.

"Is it bad?" Tobias asked. "Am I in danger?"

"That's what I'm trying to figure out. What makes you so fucking special?"

Tobias didn't respond. Was he special or was he in danger? He was having second thoughts about seeing the Doctor. He just wanted to help Remy if he could, but he wasn't so sure about the Doctor's new plans for him, whatever it might be. "What kind of danger are we talking about here?"

Khalil remained silent.

"Khalil?"

"Sorry. I was just thinking. I honestly don't know. I'm sure you'll be fine." He turned and looked directly at Tobias. "You don't ever have to do anything you don't want to do."

Tobias debated with himself whether this was a good idea or not. *What am I getting myself into?* He reasoned that whatever danger he might be confronted with would have to be his decision. He was just going to see what she had to say. More information couldn't hurt. He was curious how the Doctor knows him.

They had taken a dirt path off the main farm road several miles outside of town in the piney woods. Had they not been in an off-road equipped vehicle they wouldn't have made it this far into the woods. All that was left of the path were two tire tracks littered with pine needles cutting through dense tree coverage. A fallen pine tree laid across the path and Khalil slowed to a stop. "Wanna give me a hand?" Khalil said, hopping out of the Jeep.

"With what?" Tobias was basically an invalid.

"Never mind. Just stay put." Khalil muttered something that trailed off as he walked toward the fallen tree. Tobias looked on as Khalil reached his arms around the massive trunk and hurled it to the left side of the path like it was nothing. Khalil climbed back into the Jeep, ignoring the astonished stare Tobias couldn't seem to relinquish and continued down the bumpy forest trail. Khalil literally had superpowers.

At last, the reflection of the sun off a metal roof caught his eye. Tobias spotted a cabin in the distance. It was much larger than he expected—more like a retreat center than a tiny cabin in the woods. "Is that it?"

"That's it," Khalil said.

"Are you coming with me?"

Khalil shook his head. "No. I wasn't invited to this meeting. This is between you and the Doctor. Don't worry. I'll be right outside."

Gravel crunched under the brawny off-road tires as they turned into the driveway from the dirt path. Tobias slowly disembarked from the Jeep and lost his balance when the ground turned out to be much further down than he'd anticipated. He steadied himself and reached for his walker, which he'd stowed in the back seat of the open-air vehicle. Khalil made another comment about how he didn't need that walker, but Tobias pretended not to hear him.

He began walking unsteadily toward the house when the foot of his walker caught on a rock, and he fell directly on top of it as it tipped forward in slow motion. Tobias stood slowly, wiping pine needles from his shirt and hair. He straightened his glasses and looked back at Khalil sitting in the Jeep shaking his head reproachfully. *God, he must think I am such a loser.*

The cabin looked old yet well-maintained. He imagined this is where the Doctor might conduct her spiritual trainings. He stepped onto the front porch where wind chimes hung and clanged together in the soft breeze. A stone Buddha reclined among potted succulents and Adirondack chairs. Tobias approached the front door, dark walnut with a multi-colored textured glass inlay. He knocked.

A young, bald, albino man answered the door. He wore a white flowy tunic and matching trousers that reminded Tobias of a monk or some kind of religious disciple. He was barefoot. A soft smile rested upon his serene face, and he bowed respectfully. "You must be Tobias," he said with an English accent.

"Yes."

"The Doctor is expecting you. Come in." He opened the door wide and bowed his head as Tobias entered the wood accented foyer. "Please. Take a seat," the albino said with an outstretched hand directing him to an open seating area beneath a wood-beamed vaulted ceiling.

The space seemed so much larger on the inside than he expected. A stone fireplace hosted a crackling fire in the corner of the room. Windows from floor to ceiling occupied the entire far wall, allowing the beauty of the surrounding forest to blend into the minimalist natural decor. Scandina-vian furniture clustered around a live edge wood coffee table in the center of the room. He made his way to a pristine white couch and sat on the edge of the cushion observing the resort-like surroundings.

"Would you like a glass of water?"

Tobias started. He didn't hear the albino man standing right next to him holding a tray with two recycled green glass tumblers and a matching bottle of water. "Yes, please," he replied. He was incredibly thirsty from the trip.

The man opened the swing top stopper on the quart-sized bottle and poured crystal clear spring water into a matching drinking glass. "The Doctor will be here shortly," the albino said and walked stealthily out of the room.

Tobias drank the entire contents of the ten-ounce glass in four swallows. He felt the cool water coating his insides like rain on the cracked desert floor. He poured himself another glass and drank half of it. Tobias allowed himself to scoot back in his seat and lean against the back of the couch, holding his glass with both hands between his legs. He took a deep breath and slowly exhaled through his mouth to steady his nerves. *What's taking her so long?* he thought. He wondered what this new age, psychedelic-promoting, cult leader might be like. He found himself equally curious as he was skeptical.

He tried to organize his thoughts according to what questions he wanted answers to the most—questions about the in-between, how to help Remy, and most importantly, how did she know him and what does she want? There were so many that it seemed impossible to prioritize them but the one question that kept resurfacing was *Where is Mia? And, When can I see her?* He had already accepted that Mia had never been in love with him and was simply trying to recruit him to their spiritual community. He felt foolish for ever thinking otherwise. Still, he wanted to hear it from her perfect lips. It might hurt but it would appease his logical mind and free him from the disappointing temptation of needless and unfounded optimism.

The sound of heels clopping against the hard wood floors approached the main room from the hall. The Doctor appeared in a flowing two-piece white linen outfit, similar in style to what the albino wore. A turquoise beaded mala hung from her neck, the golden tassel reaching the middle of her torso. Turquoise accented her ears, fingers, and the tops of her open-toe shoes. A light breeze of Jasmine and Lavender wafted through the room as she entered.

"Hello, Tobias."

Tobias froze. His voice caught in his throat. His mind scrambled to re-establish a sense of order in a wild and chaotic universe. "Dr. Macintosh?"

25

Dr. Macintosh sat opposite Tobias in an armchair that was more art than chair. Her warm gaze held his like a wounded bird in the hands of a benevolent healer. "You must have some questions for me," she said with a familiar and reassuring smile.

Tobias nodded. The questions he had been prioritizing in his mind had collapsed into a disorganized pile when he recognized his therapist, who was also apparently, a cult leader. He opened his mouth to say something but then closed it again when he reconsidered its relevance to the moment. His next attempt allowed him to utter the word, "How . . ." and then he stopped again.

"I'll start," Dr. Macintosh said, rescuing him from his ineptitude. "You know me as Dr. Joelle Macintosh, psychologist. That is my real name and profession. I am also the founder of La Seta, a community of spiritual explorers that emerged from the discovery of a new chemical compound in 2012. You have experienced this for yourself. Here, I am known simply as 'The Doctor.' I help travelers obtain a unique skillset for accelerated spiritual enlightenment. We believe that if you can let go in the in-between, you can let go in human form as well."

"But I was never able to let go up there," Tobias interjected.

"Yes, I know. Did you know that you have spent the longest uninterrupted amount of time in the in-between than anyone since the very first travelers? That, of course, might be interpreted as accidental, and many do explain it as such. But I do not believe in accidents. Mia tried to help you, but her mission was cut short, as you know."

"What happened to her? Is she a ghost?"

"Ghosts . . ." She shook her head. "Ghosts are sad creatures. They have very little power to do much of anything in this dimension in the limited capacity they embody. Most of them don't even know they're dead. It's very sad. No, Mia is . . . something else. She's the second human to voluntarily shed their material body and remain fully in this dimension. She's been here all along and she is more powerful than any physical being alive today. Technically, she is a demigoddess."

She was already a goddess to him—a goddess in a barista apron. "You said she was the second human to let go of their body. Who was the first?"

The Doctor extended her palms face up and gave a slight bow.

"You?" Tobias asked. "But you have a physical body." He examined her closely wondering if she might be some kind of hologram. "Don't you?"

"Right now I do. It takes time to learn how to materialize. Believe it or not, it's actually quite limiting to manifest physically. The only useful reason to materialize would be to interact and communicate with other humans—like when I see my patients. Mia is learning how. You'll see her again soon."

"How soon? When can I see her?"

"You must be patient, Tobias." At that moment dark clouds amassed above the tree line and the room darkened. Rain began tapping on the metal roof above. Suddenly, a downpour. The Doctor laughed. "Right on cue! Say hello to Mia."

"Did Mia just make it rain?" Tobias asked astounded.

"She's showing off," the Doctor said with a wink.

"How do you know that's her?"

"Did you see rain in the forecast? No, it's Mia. She wants you to know she's here and that you have nothing to worry about."

"Can she hear us?"

"Of course. What would you like to say to her?"

Tobias looked up toward the wooden beams in the ceiling and shouted, "If it's really you, stop the rain!" Immediately, the rain stopped, and the room was eerily silent.

"She's not a street magician," the Doctor chided. "What do you *really* want to say?"

Tobias looked at the Doctor and then up toward the ceiling. He swallowed hard and looked at the Doctor again for some kind of guidance. He trusted her and had always longed for her direction even though, in the service of helping him learn to trust himself, she often refused to provide it.

"Go on, *say it*," she said. She was giving him that knowing smile. She knew how he felt about Mia, and it seemed like there was only one thing to say.

He looked up toward the ceiling again. He swallowed hard as he tried to formulate the words he'd been waiting the last three months to say out loud. "I love you, Mia," he shouted. "I know you don't feel the same about me and I understand. I don't know why I thought we could be together. That was stupid, I guess. Well, now you're . . . whatever you are, and I wish we could just talk face to face like humans. That's . . . I guess that's all." At that moment, the sun broke through the clouds and filled the room with light.

"She must have heard you," Dr. Macintosh said. "How do you feel?"

"Kind of silly to be honest." His face was flush, and he could feel his heart beating in his neck. "I know she was only trying to recruit me to La Seta. She never actually had feelings for me. I'm such an idiot."

"Don't be so hard on yourself, Tobias. You don't know her heart. Did I plant her in that coffee shop next to your place of business in hopes of engineering a serendipitous encounter? Yes. Did I send her to the hospital with flowers after she hit you? Yes. But that doesn't mean she couldn't have developed real feelings for you after you were acting on your own. Right?"

"Huh. Yeah. I guess that's possible." Tobias scratched his head. "So the car accident—"

"That was *not* a part of the plan. Trust me, she felt terrible about that."

"Why didn't you recruit me yourself? You and I had a pretty good rapport. I probably would have tried anything you suggested."

"I may be a demigoddess, but I still have professional boundaries."

"Why me?"

"Psychotherapy works well for most patients. Some need a more aggressive approach. It's not that you weren't making any progress—you were. But I thought you could use a little push. Plus, I liked you. I wanted to see you succeed. And I knew you'd be taken with Mia."

Tobias chuckled to himself. "Khalil made it sound like I was special or something."

"You are!" she exclaimed.

"Yeah, I know. I'm special like everyone is special in their own way."

"No. You weren't special at first."

Ouch, he thought to himself.

"But after you fell into a coma—that turned out to be a very unique revelation. You showed us a way to extend our time in the in-between, which means we can train for longer periods at a time. So, you could call it an accident, but it led to a ground-breaking discovery."

"So you're going to put new trainees in comas? That doesn't seem very safe."

"No, no, no. See, the portal, the one we currently travel through, is unreliable and slow. It's like a single synapse that we have to jump across one at a time. We need one that can facilitate multiple travelers at a time. Essentially, we need broadband."

"I don't follow."

"If we had a full consciousness dedicated to facilitating travel, that would essentially take care of all our training needs. What we discovered with you being there so long and being unable to let go of your body is that we finally have a way to supercharge our spiritual mission."

"What do you mean?"

"Tobias, *you* could be our portal!" The doctor's eyes lit up.

Tobias was utterly confused. He thought about that rusty faucet in the barrens. "What does that mean? I could be the portal. How can a person be a portal?"

"It would be just like before. You liked it there, didn't you? Of course, you wouldn't be in a hospital. We'd have to keep this whole thing top secret, at least until we can figure out the legalities. We have people, doctors, that can monitor your body here on Earth. You, in fact the only you that really matters, your consciousness, can live out the rest of your life in the in-between. You can have or be anything you want up there."

"Wait. Let me get this straight. You're saying that you want to put me back into a coma so my consciousness can be a broadband portal for your training program, and I get to live the rest of my life in the in-between, *as a tourist*?"

"Oh, I *hate* that word. They don't know the true purpose of our presence there."

"But why *me*? Anyone can be rendered comatose."

"Yes, but most people are capable of letting go of their bodies and you seem to be particularly resistant to doing so. It's uncanny. It is that resistance that allows the portal to remain open and tethered to the material world."

His face became flushed. He was special alright—special for having *less* abilities than everyone else, not more. He was valuable only because of his handicap. He avoided eye contact and rubbed his thighs. "So, if I do this, I can't return?"

"Of course you can! But Tobias, why would you want to? Imagine never getting sick, never growing old, eating whatever you want and never gaining any weight? Imagine finding love, or many loves. Imagine being limitless! And by the way, as the new portal, you would be the most respected and revered figure in our community. You would be *worshipped*. I believe everyone has a path. This is a chance for you to fulfil your potential. Isn't that what you've always wanted? To be the best version of yourself possible?"

"Can I think about it?"

"Of course. Take your time."

Tobias felt reassured that this was entirely his choice. "There is something else I was hoping you could help me with."

"Anything."

"Before I agree to do this coma thing again, I'm helping a friend and I need to bring something back from up there. It's a video of his murder. If I can get it into the right hands, his murder will be avenged, and he can finally go through the door and be at peace."

"That sounds like a very noble reason to travel. I'll allow it." She called for the albino, "Bastian!"

Bastian entered the room and bowed. "Yes, Doctor?"

"Prepare La Seta."

"Right away, Doctor." He exited as quietly as he arrived. When he returned, he held a tray with a single cup of steaming tea. He bent at the waist as Tobias took the cup from the tray.

"Thank you," Tobias said.

"You're welcome, sir," Bastian said. He turned and left the room with the tray tucked under his arm.

He wasn't expecting to travel right then and there but he figured it better to take advantage of the opportunity and get that evidence as soon as possible. He lifted the cup to his lips when the Doctor interrupted. "Ah-ta-ta-ta," she said. "Close your eyes," she said in a soothing, hypnotic voice. "Slow your breath and bring it to an even in and out . . . in two, three, four . . . out, two, three, four . . . in, two, three, four . . . out, two, three, four . . . Rest your awareness on the breath as it moves in and out at a steady, unhurried pace. Feel your body sitting there . . . breathing. Allow your observing self to see your body as a physical form. Notice yourself . . . noticing. *You* are not your body. Your body is safe right where it sits and it will be right there, breathing calmly, when you return to it. Take a moment to give thanks to La Seta as it frees you from the limitations of the flesh and lifts you to sacred realms of true freedom."

Tobias lifted his cup to his forehead in thanks, as he had seen Mia and the other travelers do the first time. He carefully brought the cup to his lips and took a sip. The taste was repulsive. The Doctor softly reminded him to drink the rest of the contents quickly. He tipped the cup back and swallowed the rest of the tea. He placed the cup back on the table and laid his head on the arm of the couch. The Doctor kept her eyes closed as Tobias melted like warmed butter into the couch.

26

THIS TIME, when Tobias arrived in the barrens, he awoke without the comfort of his childhood bed. He picked himself up off the sandy ground and straightened his glasses before realizing he didn't need them up there. He removed his glasses and tucked them away in his shirt pocket. The soreness in his legs, arms, and back had vanished. The dunes rolled for miles in every direction, but he knew that within seconds a car would arrive, and he'd be in the middle of the city before he knew it.

He reached into his back pocket and secured his phone. He called Remy.

"Yo, T! Where you callin' from?" Remy said when he answered.

"I'm in the barrens. Did you get that video?"

"Sho did. I got it right here."

"Meet me at that diner—the one with the waffles."

"I'll see you there."

Tobias realized that not long after he completed this task, Remy would be ready to walk through the door. It was hard to imagine living up here without him. Sure, he'd make new friends in time but eventually they too, would walk through the door.

When he arrived at the diner, Remy was seated at the counter where they sat before. The waitress had already placed a cup in his spot next to Remy and was pouring the coffee. It was a different waitress than the one who'd served him before. This one was a bit older with orange hair and unusually large front teeth.

"Thank you," Tobias said as he hopped up on the bar stool. It had been weeks before he had even considered hopping. It felt good to hop. He patted Remy on the back. "It's good to see you!"

"You, too, man. I didn't think you'd ever come back after all that."

"I might be coming back for good." He looked into Remy's eyes to study his reaction.

Remy furrowed his brows. "Whachu mean?"

Tobias looked around the diner with his palms up. "I like it here."

"Is it that girl? She here now and you want to stay here now, too?"

"No. She's not here. She was never really into me after all."

Remy's face fell into a sickened frown. "So what is it? You not considering, you know . . . suicide?"

"No! No, nothing like that. I can go back into a coma indefinitely."

"You wanna be a permanent tourist?" Remy was still frowning.

Tobias shrugged. "Yeah, why not? There's nothing for me

down there anyway. I don't have a job. I live with my parents. Mia's gone. I can barely even walk."

"How you gonna put yourself back into a coma? And who gonna pay for that?" Remy asked with a sideways grimace.

"It's a long story. I don't know if I'm actually going to do it. I haven't made up my mind yet." Remy didn't respond and turned back to his plate to cut another bite of waffle. Tobias noticed a slight shake of his head and searched for a change of subject. "So do you have that thumb drive?"

"Oh yeah." Remy reached into his front jacket pocket and removed the silver drive. "Here you go. I got the whole thing —all of it. I got that shit zoomed in and everything. If that don't lock 'em up, nothin' will."

"Perfect," Tobias said taking the drive and stuffing it deep into his right front jeans pocket. "Now when I go back this baby is coming with me." He raised his coffee cup and clinked it against Remy's.

Tobias looked over to where Chester Lang sat day after day, but he wasn't there. Tobias asked the toothy waitress if she'd seen him.

"He walked through the door last week," she said.

"Really? Huh."

"Did you know him?" she asked.

"Briefly. Does Beth still work here?"

The waitress smiled. "Didn't you hear? One day, he asked her if he could take her to the movies across the street. She said 'yes.' I couldn't believe it. Next day she came in out of uniform and tossed her apron over the counter and announced they were getting married. You should have seen the smile on that cranky ol' bastard's face. They got married the next day and just last week, they walked arm in arm, right through the door."

"Now that's a great story," Remy said nodding his head.

Tobias thought maybe his little intervention, the one Chester had begrudged him, had done some good after all. Maybe he had played some pivotal role in getting the old man to take some action. *Good for him*, he thought.

"You wanna refill, hun?"

"No thanks," Tobias said flatly. *Who else was going to leave?* he thought. If he becomes the portal he could see many people come and go.

"So," Remy said. "How long do you think you got 'til you fade away?"

"I don't know. A couple hours maybe?" This was only a guess, of course.

"Alright, so the dude you're looking for, the prosecutor— his name is Cecil Bryant. I'm not sure if there's a cut-off point before they no longer accept new evidence so you want to make sure he gets it as soon as possible."

"Got it. Cecil Bryant." He typed the name into the Notes app on his phone. "So, Remy, what are you going to do once this is all over? Once these guys get sentenced, that is."

Remy leaned back on his stool and drummed the counter with his fingers. "I guess I'll go through the door. Nothing left for me here. Some people want to stick around until their loved ones pass. You know, so they have a familiar face to greet them when they get here."

"Don't you want to wait for your parents?"

"I ain't never met my dad. My mama got a lot of years left. Women on my mama's side live a long time. My great granny lived to a hundred and four! I'm not sure I want to stick around another thirty years."

"Yeah, that is a long time. So what do you think is on the other side of the door?"

"Something. I mean, I don't think it's nothing. Some people think that's it. Like you go through the door and you just cease to exist anymore. I don't think that. I think there's something else out there. I don't know what but something."

"Right. Like what's the point of this place if there's nothing else to transition to?"

"Exactly. Besides, I've done everything there is to do up here anyway. Ain't nothing to really look forward to anymore."

Tobias felt despondent. Here they were—in Heaven, if you want to call it that—and even limitlessness had its limits. Apparently, the one thing death cannot free you from is boredom. Once you've lived your purpose, what else is there? Did he even have a purpose? Helping Remy was a kind of purpose but then what? Mia was never an option. She didn't think of him the way he thought of her. This realization still ached deep in his chest like a bruise. His writing was terrible, and it was terrible because it lacked purpose. Because *he* lacked purpose.

Perhaps the Doctor's proposal could be his new purpose. Maybe this is what he was meant to do. He still lacked a comprehensive understanding of her mission but as far as he could tell it wasn't nefarious or evil. He could see the value in helping others become more spiritually enlightened. He was unclear as to what end and he hadn't given it much thought but surely the Doctor would explain everything in more detail before enlisting him as the new portal. He liked the idea of being needed—useful. Maybe this *was* his path.

They spent the next few hours strolling around town with nowhere in particular to go. Tobias explained to Remy about the Doctor and how she had a plan for Tobias to become the new portal. "But like I said, I haven't decided what I'm going to do yet."

"Man, that's crazy. Your *therapist*? Seems a little . . . I don't know, unethical."

"Yeah, but she's not exactly like, a regular human. She's . . . I don't know. Evolved? She's mostly spirit, or something."

"And you said Mia's like her now, too?"

"Yeah. She made it rain."

Remy shook his head. "Man, I thought I heard everything. So you just get to live here permanently and all you have to do is be a portal for other tourists?"

"Travelers. That's what the Doctor calls us. I don't have all the details yet but that's my understanding so far."

"So how does that work? I mean, with the old portal you literally go through it. How they gonna come through you?" Remy had a disgusted look on his face.

Tobias shrugged.

Remy was distracted by a selection of guitars hanging in a music shop window. Tobias followed Remy into the shop where Remy picked up a vintage Les Paul, plugged it into an amp and started riffing. Tobias nodded along to the blues riff he was playing when the long-haired stoner-looking shop keeper walked over with an electric bass and placed it over Tobias' shoulder.

"Oh, no. I don't play," he said. Remy nodded at him, and he felt put on the spot. He placed his fingers along the neck of the bass and rested his other hand over the strings as he continued to nod along. Remy stopped and arranged his fingers in a roots-and-fifth pattern on the guitar's neck and plucked the correct strings in order. Tobias nodded even though he wasn't sure he quite had it down. Remy started over and would occasionally widen his eyes or nod his head at certain intervals. Tobias reflexively plucked at the bass strings, mostly hitting the wrong notes but occasionally he'd get it right and Remy would smile.

Afterwards, they strolled down to the boardwalk and raced go-karts and ate snow cones. The longer time stretched on, the more Tobias grew concerned about his inevitable return. He knew it would be pointless to ask how long it had been, given the in-between's rebellious and unpredictable version of time.

"What's wrong?" Remy asked.

"Nothing. I'm just wondering when this is going to wear off."

A disquieted look appeared on Remy's face.

"You don't think . . ." Tobias furrowed his brow and shook his head. "There's no way she—"

"No way your therapist would put you in a coma without your consent?" Remy asked, finishing his thought.

Tobias was stricken silent as color faded from his face.

"OK," Remy said. "We need to get down to the viewing room and check on you. Come on!"

When they arrived at the library, Remy found an open station and logged in. He typed in *Tobias Munch* and hit the Live Feed button. Their eyes nearly doubled in size. Remy covered his gaping mouth. Tobias was in a bed with an IV in his arm, oxygen tube in his nostrils, and electrodes sprouting from his head and bare chest like a cybernetic spider. He wasn't in a hospital. The wooden accents and minimalist furnishings confirmed he was still at the Doctor's cabin.

"I can't believe she did this!" Tobias said. He couldn't believe he fell for it!

"Alright, let's calm down and think this through." Remy interlaced his fingers behind his neck.

"What if I just go through the door again?" Tobias suggested.

"I don't know. It might get you back in your body but do you think it'll be safe there once you wake up? I mean, if she's capable of doing *this*, what would stop her from . . . I don't know. You said it yourself—she's not a regular human."

Tobias zoomed out to see if the Doctor was anywhere nearby. A spiky-haired woman in a white lab coat checked the monitors and scribbled onto a clipboard before leaving Tobias alone in the room. Tobias zoomed back in and noticed the slight rise and fall of his chest. He was breathing on his own and he wondered if they would eventually intubate him. The thought caused him to shiver.

Tobias noticed the subtle movement of his hair and the thin wires of protruding electrodes as if a breeze had swept through the room. A warm glow gradually accumulated around his body and gathered around his head and chest. He heard a faint whisper, lightly punctuated by near consonants. He turned up the volume and drew closer to the monitor's speakers trying to make out any perceptible words, but they were much too faint and drawn out to discern. The light grew brighter and concentrated more densely above his head.

"What is happening?" Tobias said.

The ball of light grew to an intense brilliance and Tobias had to avert his gaze momentarily from the monitor. The ball of light, roughly the size of a fist now, spun itself above his resting face and suddenly, unpredictably, escaped *into it*. His body rose slightly like a pool float receiving a burst of air. His entire body emitted a flash of light before deflating and falling back into its previous resting state. The machines at his bedside continued to beep at a steady cadence just as before.

"What the hell?" Remy said in a high register.

"I think I'm going to be sick," Tobias grumbled. He placed both hands on his belly and leaned forward in his seat.

"You alright, you alright, just breathe," Remy said reassuringly, patting Tobias on the back. "Come on, breathe."

Tobias stood sliding the wooden desk chair back, which made a loud and disruptive scrape against the tile floor, inviting irritated glares from other viewers in the room. He turned and ran behind the nearest bookcase and doubled over. Remy followed him around the bookcase and watched in terror as Tobias opened his mouth wider and wider until the top half of his skull hinged back at a ninety-degree angle. The rest of his body froze in a horrific catatonic position as he heaved silently. A clear-brownish liquid dripped from the corners of his ever-expanding tooth-lined skull cavity. Tobias shivered and convulsed as a column of brown sludge gushed forth from his gaping mouth.

Tobias fell to his knees and immediately placed his hands over his mouth and face, which had reverted back to its normal shape. He wiped tears from the corners of his eyes with the back of his hand and coughed.

"Are you OK?" Mia asked.

27

───────

MIA REACHED for Tobias and lifted him to his feet by his arm. "Are you OK?" Mia asked again as calmly as if he had simply choked on his own saliva. She didn't appear as he imagined a highly evolved spiritual being to look. She was dressed casually in an olive-green romper and white sneakers. She wore a yellow-billed trucker hat that was too big for her head yet endearingly cute.

"It's you!" Tobias said. "You're *here*." He turned to Remy. "Look, it's Mia."

"I see that," Remy said with a look of utter disgust on his face. "That was some exorcist shit, right there. Damn!"

Mia giggled. "I just *had* to be the first. This is so exciting!"

"The first what?" Tobias asked.

"The first to travel through the new portal, silly! I can't wait to tell the others," she said. "This is going to be a game changer. What was it like?" Her bright eyes danced with anticipation.

"Not good!" Tobias screeched. "I did *not* like that one bit."

Mia's face fell into a frown. She tucked a ribbon of blonde hair behind her ear. "Oh no! Did it hurt or something?"

"Yeah! It hurt. I didn't know that's what it would be like. I don't want to do that ever again!"

"I'm sorry," Mia said with a pained look on her face. "I didn't think it was going to hurt. Maybe you'll get used to it? Like build up a tolerance?"

"No! No, I don't want to get used to it." If this is what being a portal is like he didn't want any part of it. "I don't want to be a portal anymore."

Mia scoffed. "Tobias, don't you know what this means? This is a miracle! It's your destiny."

"Hacking up tourists like a cat with a hairball is his destiny?" Remy asked scornfully.

Mia exhaled sharply and crossed her arms. "OK, fine. Can we just put a pin in this for now? I was hoping we could catch up. It's been a minute. How have you been?"

"Was that really you at the cabin, with the rain?" Tobias asked.

Mia shrugged and a coy smile returned to her face. "That was me. I can do weather and tides and stuff like that. Still working on materializing. The Doctor does it so effortlessly. She's amazing."

"So you knew she was my therapist this whole time?" Tobias asked.

Mia nodded bashfully, biting her lip. "I'm sorry. Do you hate me?"

"No." He really didn't. He couldn't hate Mia if he tried.

"Listen, what you said back at the cabin," Mia said. "I want you to know . . ." She took a deep breath and let it out. "I feel the same."

Tobias blinked. What did he say that she could have possibly felt the same about? "What do you mean?"

"At first, yes, I was just trying to recruit you. I wasn't expecting to develop feelings for you but . . . I did."

It was exactly what he had been waiting to hear for months but somehow this long-awaited revelation could not quite reach his deadened heart. He looked at Remy who had been patiently waiting in the wings. Remy raised his eyebrows and gestured with his head as if to say *Go on! Say something.*

"I, uh . . . I wasn't expecting that." He wondered if this was another con. He wasn't going to fall for that again.

Mia drew closer. "I know a way that we can finally be together."

"How . . . how would that work?" Tobias asked, genuinely curious.

"Now that you're the portal, I can exist in both dimensions. I can live with you here and travel back and forth for . . . business. A demi-goddess and a portal. How perfect is that?" She leaned in closer. "I mean, if you'll have me." She placed her hand on his chest and tilted her head up so that her parted mouth came within inches of his own.

Tobias took a step back. "Wait."

Remy dropped his head in disappointment.

"What's wrong?" Mia asked, reaching for him.

"I didn't give the Doctor permission to induce me," Tobias said sternly. "I told her I would *consider* it. She had no right to do this and you know it. Why would you let her do this to me?"

Mia crossed her arms again and huffed. "Tobias, don't freak out. It's not a big deal. I can just ask her to wake you up, alright?"

"Not a big deal?" Tobias shouted.

The librarian turned the corner and stood with her fists dug into her hips. She locked eyes with Tobias. "You!" The librarian marched toward them until Mia waved her hand in a quick circular motion, lifting her into the air. Mia pulled the librarian toward her open hand as she shrank down to the size of a jawbreaker. Mia held the miniature librarian between her thumb and forefinger and crushed her into powder.

"Damn!" Remy blurted.

"Holy shit!" Tobias squeaked. "Did you kill her?"

"Of course not!" Mia said. "She's already dead, remember? She'll be fine." She brushed librarian dust from her hands. "It's rude to interrupt. Now, where were we?"

Tobias thought twice about challenging Mia too strongly after witnessing the ease in which she might pulverize him. It also occurred to him that while her smite may not prove fatal in the in-between, had they been on Earth, it most certainly would've been.

"Listen," Tobias said cautiously. "I need to get back to my body." He pulled the thumb drive from his pocket and showed it to her. "I need to get this to somebody down there. If I don't, Remy's murderers are going to get away with it and he'll have died for nothing. This is a time-sensitive issue. Can we circle back to this whole portal business after I do this thing?"

"Yeah. Fine. Whatever," Mia said holding her elbows and looking snubbed. She looked up to see both Tobias and Remy looking at her. "What? Now?"

"Yes, please," Tobias said.

"Fine. Pull your pants down and bend over."

"Excuse me?"

"Well, I can't go back the way I came, sooo…"

"Oh, hell no," Remy said, covering his eyes.

Tobias darted his eyes back and forth between Mia and Remy. *Is she serious?*

"Let's do this. Come on," Mia said clapping her hands.

Tobias opened his mouth and stammered. Mia broke out into boisterous laughter. "Oh my God! You should see your faces right now!"

Tobias remained stunned. Remy's face looked as if he had just gotten a whiff from inside a dumpster.

"Tobias, come on," she played. "It was a joke!"

"Not funny," he muttered.

"I'm sorry." Mia put both hands on his shoulders. "I was just playing around," she said much softer.

Tobias loosened up a bit and attempted a smile. "Alright, so you'll just go back and ask the Doctor to wake me up?"

"Yes," she said. "But will you promise to think about it? Think about us? We could be *so* happy here."

"Yeah. Yes, of course."

"I'll be waiting," she said seductively. Mia pulled him to her and kissed him. It was everything he ever dreamed it might be—soft, passionate. He tightened his grip on her waist and pulled her body against his. As their mouths sealed together, a soft glow illuminated throughout her body and increased in radiance as their kiss deepened. The light gradually consumed her, and she vanished through their kiss and into Tobias.

Remy waited until the glow radiating from Tobias had subsided. "Hey man, you good?"

"Yeah," Tobias replied, patting his torso and chest.

"That was some crazy shit, bruh."

"Yeah."

"So? Whachu gonna do now?"

"I'm going to get back to Earth. And I'm going to avenge your murder, that's what."

"And then?"

"And then . . . and then I'm going to tell the Doctor I'm not interested in being the portal."

"What about you and Mia?"

Tobias scratched the side of his neck and shook his head. "There is no me and Mia."

"Whachu mean? She just told you she wanna be wichu, man. Ain't that what you been waiting for this whole time?"

"Yeah. I don't know. Something doesn't feel right. How could she just stand by and let the Doctor put me in a coma without my consent and not think anything of it? She's obviously aligned with the Doctor on this. She lied to me from the very start. How do I know I can trust her?"

"Plus, she straight wasted that librarian like she was nuthin'," Remy noted. "That was some pretty cold-blooded shit. I believe they call that a *red flag*."

They shared a laugh at such an understatement. Tobias continued laughing far longer than Remy, who's smile turned sour as Tobias began to heave violently. His face reddened and large blue veins bulged from his neck and forehead.

"Hey man, you alright?" Remy asked, reaching his hand out to steady his struggling friend.

Tobias opened his mouth and the top half of his head rotated backwards again like before and a torrent of brown sludge gushed forth from his unhinged skull.

This time the Doctor appeared with seraphic wings that expanded ten feet from end to end and then folded in behind her back. Tobias felt unnerved and fearful in her regal presence. He scooted back against a bookcase and pulled himself to standing.

"You have nothing to fear, Tobias. I would never harm you." Her voice was calm and reassuring.

"Why did you put me back into a coma?" Tobias asked meekly. "I wasn't ready. I didn't agree."

"I had to see it for myself. And it's beautiful! *You* are beautiful. Can't you see? We can be a family. You, me, Mia. We can do so much more *together*. You see, the old portal is only one-way. Travelers can reach the in-between through it but once the effects of La Seta wears off, it is their physical bodies on Earth that bring them back. I no longer have a physical body and neither does Mia. We need *you* in order to travel back and forth. You are essential to our cause."

"I thought you could materialize," Tobias recalled.

"I can. But it takes a great deal of energy to maintain a physical body and if I were to travel, I would lose conscious-ness on Earth and my material body would disintegrate. I can do many things, but I cannot be in two dimensions at once."

"So you could get here but you'd be stuck without a phys-ical body to return to. Is that it?"

"That's exactly it. Now do you understand how important you are?"

"I guess."

"Uh, can I say something?" Remy said stepping forward after taking in the interaction from a distance. The Doctor appeared annoyed at his interjection but he continued anyway. "Listen, I know this is none of my business but uh, shouldn't Tobias be able to choose for himself? It doesn't seem like you're giving him much of a choice."

"Well, of course it's his choice," the Doctor declared. "But it's a very easy choice to make. I am simply providing the information he needs to make it. He can either choose a life without limits, with his true love I might add, fulfilling a destiny worthy of adoration and praise. Or, he can live a shortened existence in a feeble body with no prospects for love or financial gain. The choice seems quite clear to me. What am I missing?"

Tobias thought about Mia's declaration of love and measured it against reason once again. "Mia *says* she wants to be with me but that's only because I can do this thing for her, not because she actually loves *me*. I'm special only because I have some sort of handicap that benefits you."

"Unbelievable! I am offering you boundless freedom here!"

Remy interjected, "It's not really boundless freedom if he's beholden to your travel plans."

The Doctor made a fist with her hand and Remy crumpled like a wad of discarded paper. She flicked her finger and he flew backwards against the wall and fell to the floor with a single, pitiful bounce.

"Hey! That's my friend!" Tobias shouted.

"Let me make this absolutely clear. You are the portal now. You can either take your honorable place within our divine family with all the benefits and privileges that come with that, or you can live out the rest of your years as a truck stop toilet! Either way, you will serve your purpose. What's it going to be?"

Tobias looked over at Remy, a crumpled wad rocking subtly from side to side with two frightened eyes peering back. He hated seeing him like that. Tossed aside. Pathetic. Remy didn't deserve this. He was a good man—a true friend. Tobias wondered if he'd ever be as giving, as loyal, as his only real friend. Would he forever be so preoccupied with his own shortcomings? So self-absorbed? This was his moment. The time had come to finally do something right. "Fine! I'll be the portal. But you have to promise to do something for me."

"I'm listening."

Tobias reached into his pocket and removed the thumb drive. "Will you please give this to Cecil Bryant? He's a city prosecutor. This will prove Remy's innocence and he can finally rest. If you do this one thing for me, I will be your portal."

The Doctor took the drive from his hand. "It's the least I can do," she said.

"Thank you," Tobias said. He looked at poor Remy. "And could you—"

The Doctor waved her hand in an upward flourish and Remy began to uncrumple slowly back into a standing position. He straightened his denim jacket and repositioned the driver's cap on his head in an attempt to restore some dignity. "There," she said. "No harm, no foul."

"Easy for you to say," Remy mumbled under his breath.

Tobias blinked rapidly as the color of nearby objects began to pale. His vision blurred, and a tingling sensation radiated through his hands and ears. He lifted his hands in front of his face, and he could feel himself fading. He flickered off and on like a lamp in a storm.

"What is happening?" she asked with a fearful wavering in her voice.

Tobias felt faint. Sounds were distant and his vision was now completely blurred. He could no longer feel his limbs.

"What. Is. Happening?!" she cried. "No! No, no, no, no!" The Doctor dove toward him but before she could make contact, Tobias was gone.

28

────────

THE SORENESS in his joints and muscles had returned like a flashback from an old injury. The natural light flooding into the room caused him to squint. Tobias was back in his feeble body again. *How did I get back?*

"We gotta move!" Khalil said as he plucked electrodes aggressively from his head and chest. "Can you walk?"

"Khalil? What happened?"

"I'll tell you on the way home. I got to get you out of here —now!"

"Where's the Doctor?"

"Come on," Khalil said, ignoring the question and pulling him into a sitting position. He placed shoes on his feet and didn't bother to tie them. He pulled a t-shirt over his head and Tobias managed to get his arms through the sleeves on his own at a snail's pace.

Tobias noticed the spiky-haired woman in a white lab coat tied to a chair in the corner of the room. Duct tape covered her mouth. *Did Khalil do that?*

"Let's go!" Khalil shouted.

Tobias placed his feet on the wood floor, a bit too slowly for Khalil's liking. His knees buckled when he tried to stand. Khalil groaned impatiently and picked him up, slinging him over his shoulder like a crash test dummy. As soon as they made it into the hallway, two men spotted them and cried out, "Hey, stop!" The men pursued Khalil down the hall and before he reached the great room, Bastian turned the corner blocking them in. He was holding a pistol and took aim at Khalil's head.

"Bastian! You don't want to do this," Khalil said. "The Doctor is finished. She can't protect you anymore."

The two men in white coats caught up to Khalil and took Tobias into their custody. Bastian kept his aim steady. "Of course she'll be back. Once the portal is secured, she will return, and you will face the consequences of your actions." He ordered the men to return Tobias to his room.

"No!" Tobias cried. "No!" Tobias violently swung his body in a twisting motion like a madman in a straight jacket trying to free himself from the men's restraint. When he looked up again, he noticed that Bastian had now fixed his aim on him instead of Khalil.

"Oh, right," Khalil said, shaking his head. "You're going to kill the portal? What will the Doctor think about that?" Khalil moved slowly toward the gunman who aimed at Khalil again. The albino's hand was shaking now.

"Stay back! I'll shoot!" Bastian cried backing away from Khalil.

"I dare you." Khalil was now a few steps away from Bastian.

The shot echoed against the vaulted ceilings in the great

room and Tobias reflexively covered his ears and descended into a squat. As the echo faded, he opened his eyes and checked himself for any damage. One of the men had been shot and slumped against the wall. The other ran in the other direction. Bastian's eyes widened in terror. He dropped the gun and ran out the front door, tripping off the front porch, and scrambling into the woods. Tobias could see clean through the bullet hole in Khalil's chest. There was no blood.

"Oh my God," Tobias stammered. "Are you OK?"

Tobias observed the bullet hole closing in on itself like rising bread dough. His flesh was good as new—not even a scar remained. He was like some kind of superhero—powers he'd learned in the in-between, which were available to him here on Earth. *This is why they go there*, he thought.

"I'm good," Khalil said. "You?"

"Good, I think."

"Good. Let's get out of here."

Tobias followed Khalil out to the Jeep and climbed into the passenger side. He realized he'd forgotten his walker but decided not to mention it. Khalil started the engine and quickly made his way back through the forest. Tobias waited until the cabin had faded from view before speaking. "What now? I mean, is the Doctor coming back?"

"Not without a portal," Khalil said.

Tobias suddenly became fearful that he'd be forced back into a coma. He also felt curiously guilty that he was the reason for the Doctor's imprisonment in the in-between. She had been such a good therapist. Khalil saved him—again. What did he stand to gain from this? "Why did you wake me up?"

Khalil pretended not to hear him at first, but he couldn't

extricate himself from Tobias' gaze. "I didn't realize she wanted to use *you* as a portal. It was all theoretical—until it wasn't. I can't believe it worked! This is partly my fault. It was *my* science. Anyway, I didn't know what was happening until it was too late."

"How did you find out?"

"Mia. She was so excited about it. I couldn't get a word in edgewise. And then she was gone. I knew I couldn't stop the Doctor. She is much too powerful. I had to wait until she traveled before I could wake you up."

"But you must have known that she'd be stuck up there once I came back."

Khalil let out a deep sigh. "I couldn't let her get away with this. It's wrong. She is too powerful a being to be using humans this way. I've been loyal to her for many years. I created the first portal and when I postulated the possibility of a two-way portal, she wouldn't let it go. She became obsessed. As spiritual beings go, she's still pretty new at this. I could just see her going down a dark path. I had to put a stop to it."

"Aren't you worried she'll find a way back?"

"We'll cross that bridge when we get there. For now, Mia's in charge. Let's just hope she sees things my way."

"She told me she loves me," Tobias blurted.

"She did?" Khalil asked incredulously.

"Maybe she was just saying that to get me to go along with the Doctor's plan."

Khalil shook his head. "That doesn't sound like Mia. She's not conniving. As unlikely as it seems that she would fall in love with you, it makes even less sense for her to play you like that."

"But our whole meeting was a set up from the very beginning."

"That was different. She was trying to help you. Mia trusted the Doctor had your best interest in mind. If she knew this was going to hurt you, I don't think she'd continue to go along with it. Plus, with the Doctor out of the picture, it's her call. If she truly loves you, she'll do the right thing."

———

When he returned home, his mother called from the kitchen. "Oh good! You're home. I saved you some lunch—chicken salad. How was your visit?"

"What?" He wondered what time it was.

"With your friend. You were gone almost four hours. Did you have a nice visit?"

Tobias felt as if he'd been gone for days, not hours. "Uh, yeah. It was . . . nice." That's not how he would have described it, but his mother liked it when things were nice. He came into the kitchen and gave her a kiss on the cheek.

"Where is your walker?"

Shit! He failed to consider she would notice a thing like that. "I feel like it's been holding me back. I need to start walking on my own. Isn't that what the PT said?" The physical therapist *had* encouraged him to rely less on the walker.

"Well, yes but you could barely walk *with* it just a few days ago. Let me see you." She looked him over. "You seem different."

Tobias wasn't sure what she could see but he did feel a newfound energy. "I think I'm starting to feel better, actually."

"Well, I think that's just wonderful," she said. "Oh, your

sister called. She'll be in town this weekend. Maybe we can all stroll around the botanical gardens if you're up to it."

"Yeah, that sounds great, mom. I'm going to lay down for a bit. I'm a little tired." He wasn't though. He needed to figure out his next move.

"OK, well I'll just keep your lunch in the fridge for whenever you're ready."

"Thanks, mom." He paused before heading back to his room. He felt an inclination to say something else, something sincere but she beat him to it.

She palmed his cheek. "I love you, son."

He laid down in his bed with his hands interlaced over his chest. He had given the thumb drive with Remy's evidence to the Doctor who was currently trapped in the in-between. Without a two-way portal, she had no physical body to return to. Who knows how long it would be before they find another portal? He couldn't think about that now. He had to figure out how to get that evidence from the kid and he didn't have that much time.

He looked up Cecil Bryant online and dialed the number. He got a voicemail and left a message about video evidence in the Remy Williams case. An hour later, he got a phone call.

"Hello?" Tobias answered.

"I'm returning a call for Tobias . . . *Munch*?"

"That's me."

"This is Dana Cummings with the city prosecutor's office. You said you have information on the Remy Williams case?"

"Yes. Well, I don't exactly have the evidence, per se. But I know someone who does."

"What kind of evidence?"

"It's a cell phone video of the whole incident. It shows

officer Beatty killing Mr. Williams and then planting a knife in his hand."

"And you've seen this video?"

"Uh, well, no but—"

"Mr. Munch, whoever has this alleged evidence can provide it to our offices no later than this Wednesday at 5:00 PM. Will that be all?"

"I tried to get it from him but he denies even having it. I thought maybe you guys could try—" The line disconnected. *That was rude*, he thought.

Tobias racked his brain for possible solutions. He was going to have to attempt to convince the kid once again. Maybe this time he would be more amenable, having had a few days to think it over.

Tobias felt a light breeze against his face, which was strange since neither the ceiling fan in his room nor the air conditioner was running. The small scrap of paper on which Nico Alvarez's information had been written wobbled and slid across the surface of his desk as if being blown with puffs of air. He sat up to observe it more closely. The front cover of a Chester Lang paperback he had recently dug up from his boxed belongings fluttered along with the first few pages. The ceiling fan, previously motionless, now turned ever so slightly. The green leaves from a plastic fern bobbed in its ceramic pot and a pencil rolled off the surface of a dresser, onto the carpeted floor.

What's happening? Tobias thought. The paperback's pages fluttered open, and the ceiling fan turned in a steady rotation now. The blinds bumped unevenly against the window and a framed family photo fell flat on its face. The wind grew stronger as Tobias scooted himself into a corner and squeezed a pillow across his chest, his eyes darting here and there at the effects of a mysterious wind. And then he heard a faint and distant voice originating from nowhere in particular.

"Mia?" Tobias asked. "Is that you?" He was equally terrified as he was curious with her enigmatic presence. Was she there to punish him for trapping her spiritual mentor in another dimension? "I didn't mean to!" Tobias called into the whirling gusts. "Khalil brought me back. It wasn't me!"

The wind stopped. The ceiling fan blades slowed, and a single piece of paper floated like a leaf to the floor. His bedroom door opened just an inch.

"Toby, is everything OK?" his mother asked without showing herself behind a cracked door. "I thought I heard you talking to someone."

"It's fine, mom. I'm just going to get some rest now."

"OK, hon. Rest up."

She closed the door as gently as she opened it. The full-length mirror on the back of the door became clouded so that he could no longer see his own reflection in it. Letters appeared on the surface of the mirror like fingers tracing over a steamy shower door: *LET GO.*

He read the message written in steam and blinked as he tried to comprehend. Let go? He couldn't let go of his body in the in-between. Why would Mia think he could do it now? Steam filled in where her invisible fingers had traced those words and new words appeared: *COME HERE.*

"Where?" Tobias asked. "Come where?"

A handprint appeared under the words—her hand. Tobias stood and warily approached the mirror. He placed his hand over hers and when he made contact with the surface, it rippled outward and he felt a strange kind of magnetism that drew his hand toward hers. He reflexively pulled his hand back from the odd sensation like warm static electricity. He heard the voice again but this time it was clearer. "*Come here.*" He looked closer into the steamy surface. Through the letters he could make out an unmistakably female form. It was Mia and she was naked. She reached her hand toward him from her side of the mirror. "*Come here.*"

Tobias extended his hand again and felt the warmth of hers on the other side. *Here goes nothing.* He closed his eyes and walked resolutely toward the mirror. His face smashed up against the mirror's surface followed by the rest of his body, which staggered backwards. He checked his reflection to make sure his nose wasn't bleeding.

"Are you OK?" Mia exclaimed in a kind of hollow and echoey voice.

"I think so," Tobias said. He approached the surface of the mirror once more and cupped his hands on either side of his face to get a better view. "Where are you?"

She giggled with an eerie echo and appeared again, faintly. Thin traces of light raced over the curves of her naked body—except there was no body. "I'm sorry."

"It's OK. I'm sorry I ruined your plans. Maybe you can find another portal."

"I don't need another portal."

"But you were so adamant about it before."

"I just wanted to be with you. We can still be together, like this for now, and as soon as I can materialize, I'll be as real to you as I was before." The light tracing the outline of her body sustained a quasi-solid form, something in between a gas and a liquid, that shimmered and refracted light when she moved. Her hair flowed like iridescent strands of gold suspended in weightlessness.

"I don't understand."

"I love you, Tobias. I want to be with you."

Tobias scoffed. "I mean, I want to believe that. Forgive me if I'm a bit skeptical."

"I understand. You have every right to be. Let me prove it to you."

"How?"

"I want to show you something."

29

———

THE DENSE WHITE fog that surrounded her cleared and he found himself peering into a dimly lit dive bar. At a table near the dartboards sat officers Darren Beatty and Will Turner in blue collar civilian attire. Mia floated toward the pair, and it was clear by the lack of attention anyone there paid the naked sprite, that she must have been invisible to them. The officers seemed to be in good spirits, as if their careers or their freedom wasn't on the line in the least. They were laughing and sharing a pitcher of domestic lager.

"That prosecutor ain't got nuthin' on us," Darren said. It was Darren's idea to plant the knife on Remy after he shot him. He was a seasoned officer and he seemed unusually confident, acting as though he'd done this sort of thing before. "You just stick to the story, and we'll be fine—trust me."

Will Turner, the younger officer, adjusted his baseball cap and cleared his throat. "You said 'freeze' and he reached down and pulled a knife on you. You had to protect yourself," Will said, rehearsing the fabricated story once again. He trusted his senior officer who was well-respected on the force. Will was a rookie cop and learned most of the job under his partner's tutelage rather than from the scripted police academy training, which couldn't possibly cover every scenario, especially how to cover up a murder.

"Worst case scenario, I get suspension *with* pay." Darren said. "Lucky me!" They laughed and clinked their beer mugs together.

Tobias observed their pre-celebration with disgust. "How can he be so cavalier after killing an innocent man like that and then covering it up? How does he sleep at night?"

"Wanna make sure he doesn't?" Mia asked in an eerily mischievous tone.

Mia's stormy arrival earlier that day was terrifying enough and that was a friendly introduction. He shuddered to think of what she might be able to accomplish with vengeance as her goal. "Do you think you could get him to confess?" Tobias asked.

"I'm going to try," Mia said. "And you're going to help."

"How?"

Mia explained her plan and provided detailed instructions before dissolving into the dense white fog. Tobias changed his clothes and grabbed his car keys. He hadn't driven since the night Mia hit him with her car. He crawled out of his bedroom window and fell into a shrubbery. His car was parked in the driveway. He put it in neutral and released the emergency brake allowing it to roll down the driveway and into the street before starting the engine. He didn't want to alert his parents that he'd left.

The goal was to get a written confession from Officer Beatty that he had planted the knife on Remy to justify his killing and claim of self-defense. He may have gotten off with a slap on the wrist even without the planted weapon. He could have confessed to killing him solely based on fearing for his life and still remain on the force. Maybe he'd have to work behind a desk for six months, but he wouldn't have been convicted of murder or had to serve time. It was too late for any of that now.

Darren Beatty lived with his wife Shirley in a newly constructed planned community on the west side of town. Each lawn meticulously manicured with saplings planted in each front yard and hanging plants on every front porch. Shirley was the esteemed chair of the local rotary club and ignorant of her husband's corrupt activities. She had also had her share of ghostly experiences throughout her life and believed staunchly in paranormal phenomenon, much to her husband's chagrin.

It was well past sunset and the moon reflected off a man-made neighborhood pond directly across the street from the Beatty house. Tobias parked a few houses down along a well-tended hike and bike trail that meandered along the reedy banks of the pond. He could see lights flickering inside the house and the curtains swaying on their rods. Mia had assured him the security system would be disabled and the doors unlocked. In addition to manipulating the weather, Mia had learned how to infiltrate electrical circuitry. Shirley's screams could be heard from the front porch. The haunting was underway.

Tobias, dressed in all black, pulled a ski mask over his face before walking through the unlocked front door. He followed Shirley's screams to the master bedroom where Darren held his wife on the bed. Framed pictures were shaken loose from the walls and the wooden blinds slapped aggressively against the windows. Tobias stood silhouetted in the doorway of the bedroom. Mia stood in front of Tobias and projected Remy's image onto him.

"Remember me?" Tobias asked. He was surprised to hear his voice was distorted and amplified. The monstrous sound of it gave him chills. "You won't get away with this, Beatty."

"Who are you?" Shirley shrieked, her fingers still covering her eyes.

"Tell her, Officer," Tobias boomed. "Tell her who I am. Tell her what you did!"

"Who is that, Darren?" Shirley asked through her hands. But Darren was too frightened to speak.

"What is my name?" Tobias asked.

Darren stuttered and a loud clap of thunder shook the house. They huddled and whimpered under a useless comforter.

"Remy! Remy Williams! I shot you!" Darren cried.

"Tell her about the knife, Officer," Tobias implored.

Darren was sobbing and choking on his spit. "I . . . I p-p-put it in his hand after I killed him t-t-t-to make it look like he was armed."

A look of shock and dismay shown on Shirley's face.

"Now you're going to pick up that phone and tell the captain what you just told her."

Shirley was glaring at Darren through her tears, slowly shaking her head as if to ask: *How could you?* Darren's mouth opened and closed like a catfish gasping for air. He looked back and forth between his wife and Remy's ghostly projection.

"I'm sorry!" Darren cried. "I'm sorry! Please! I can't—" Another thunderclap reverberated in their ears. Darren's hand shook as he reached for the phone charging on the nightstand. He picked up the phone and glanced back at his wife who was sniveling and pressing her face against the headboard in terror. Darren suddenly dropped the phone, opened the nightstand drawer and pulled out a loaded 45. He aimed it at Tobias and pulled the trigger. When Tobias didn't fall, he fired two more rounds.

Tobias was astonished to find all three bullets hovering in mid-air, inches from his chest and head. Mia had managed to create enough force to stop them in their tracks, then let them fall to the wooden floor. Tobias slowly tilted his gaze upward and met Darren's gawking eyes. Darren pulled the trigger three more times in succession: *click, click, click*. He threw the gun at Tobias and jumped out of bed, leaving his wife clutching the bed sheets to her neck. Tobias released a menacing roar and pursued Darren down the hall. When he arrived in the kitchen, Darren knocked over bar stools and a baker's rack in an attempt to slow his pursuit.

Darren managed to escape into the garage wearing only boxers and a white undershirt. He didn't wait for the garage door to fully open before lurching his truck back into the driveway in reverse, taking the lower panel of the garage door with him. Thunder cracked as rain pelted the truck's windshield. Lightning illuminated the twilight sky and struck a nearby tree which caught fire and fell into the glistening street. Still in reverse, Darren swerved to miss the burning tree and then again in the opposite direction to avoid hitting a parked car. In his panic, he accidentally slammed his foot on the accelerator instead of the brake and launched his brand-new full-sized truck backwards into the pond across the street.

Tobias removed the ski mask and the rain subsided. Neighbors emerged from their homes in pajamas and bath robes. Darren slid out of the driver's side window as water began to fill the cab. He sloshed out onto the bank of the pond as his truck slowly rolled backward until only the hood and grill peeked above the surface like a watchful leviathan.

Police arrived a few minutes later followed by a tow truck. Darren, wrapped in a silver emergency blanket, ranted wildly about ghosts as the arresting officers traded pitying glances at one another. They placed him under arrest, read him his rights, and placed him in the back of the patrol car. Neighbors whispered to each other, shaking their heads. Tobias avoided speaking to anyone, especially the police.

Tobias received a text message from an unknown number with a link to a YouTube video. He hit play. It was Nico's raw footage from his apartment across the street from Remy's crime scene. When the clip ended, the knife planting sequence was enhanced and repeated in slow motion so that there was no question about the cover up. The entire video was seven minutes, twenty-seven seconds long. The caption gave details about the men involved with a call to action inviting people to protest at the courthouse on the day of the trial. So far, the video had been viewed 2,034 times and the numbers steadily increased with each passing second.

Tobias replied to the text.

Thank you!

Sorry I lied. I didn't know u.

You did the right thing.

U think it'll work?

It already did.

Tobias snapped a photo of the cop car as it drove away and sent the image. Nico replied with a raised fist emoji.

The next morning it was a national story. By the time of the trial, the video had been viewed over eight million times and shared across every social media platform with the hashtag #JusticeForRemy. Ophelia Day, the jazz singer Remy played for, spoke on his behalf on national television and sang at a concert to raise awareness for police injustice. Celebrities and politicians spoke out, calling for sweeping police reform.

On the day of the trial, hundreds showed up to the courthouse in an overwhelming show of support for Remy, holding signs and chanting, "Hey, hey! Ho, ho! These racist cops have got to go!" Media gathered on the courthouse steps to report on what had become a national event.

Remy's mother sat in the front row of the courtroom gallery wearing all black, the same outfit she wore to her son's funeral six months ago. Tobias sat in the back of the courtroom when the jury re-entered the court with their verdict. He looked up toward the ceiling and wondered if Remy was up there watching from the viewing room. Would he be alone, or would others have gathered with him for moral support? Tobias decided it was probably the latter. He wished he could be there with him to see his face when the judge read the verdict.

The bailiff took a slip of paper from a jury member and handed it to the judge. Judge Santos proceeded with the verdict. "On the count of perjury, the jury finds the defendant—guilty. On the count of obstruction of justice, the jury finds the defendant—guilty. On the count of second-degree murder . . ." He paused and the Tobias leaned forward in his seat. "The jury finds the defendant—guilty."

He removed his glasses and addressed Darren directly. "Darren Beatty, you took the life of an innocent man—a man who has made a significant contribution to the arts and to the music education of many of our community's youths. Remy Williams was forty-seven years of age when you took his life. I am hereby sentencing you to forty-seven years, for each year that Remy lived among us, in the state penitentiary. Your actions have cast a blemish on our city's esteemed police force. You will be ineligible for service in law enforcement in perpetuity." The gavel came down and chatter erupted from the gallery. Darren Beatty was escorted out of the courtroom with his head hung. Tobias exhaled a sigh of relief.

Remy's mother wiped tears from under a black veil. Shirley Beatty, who was sitting across the aisle from Ms. Williams approached her with tears in her eyes. "Ms. Williams, I can't imagine what you've been through. I know it might not mean much but please accept my sincerest apologies for my husband's actions. After hearing what he did, I can no longer stand by him. I know this doesn't bring your son back, but I want you to have this." She handed the elderly woman a check. "It's my husband's pension from the force. He doesn't deserve it and I don't want it. If there's anything you need, I want you to know I'm here for you."

Shirley turned and walked toward Tobias. He hoped she wouldn't notice him from the night he commiserated with Mia in their haunting but since he had been disguised as Remy, she didn't recognize him. He felt a twinge of guilt that he had put her through that. She was a good one.

Tobias approached Ms. Williams as she stood. "Hello, Ms. Williams. My name is Tobias. I was a good friend of Remy."

"Nice to meet you." She shook his hand.

"He meant a great deal to me. I learned a lot from him. In fact, I'd say he was the best friend I ever had. He stood up for me—a couple times, actually. I never got a chance to pay him back."

She smiled sweetly. "Well if you were his friend, you'd know that he would never expect you to pay him back."

Tobias nodded. "You're right about that, Ms. Williams. He wouldn't. I've never met anyone as generous and giving as Remy." Tobias scanned the mostly cleared room. A few people were gathered in small clumps but most everyone else had left. Ms. Williams was alone. "Do you have a ride home, Ms. Williams? I'd be more than happy to give you a ride.

"Oh, how nice of you," she said. "It's quite alright. I take the bus."

"Are you sure? It would be my pleasure."

"Well, alright then. Thank you."

Tobias escorted Ms. Williams down the steps of the courthouse through a sea of celebratory cheers, camera flashes, and pleads for comment from reporters. He walked her to his car and paused only briefly to scan the cheering crowd. *You did good*, he thought. This was by far, the best thing he'd ever done. After helping her into the passenger seat of his car, he pulled away leaving reporters, with their microphones and cameras, behind with the merry making masses.

"Oooh Lord, I can't believe all this!" Ms. Williams said, looking out the back window at the celebratory crowds.

"They're saying this ruling is going to change policing laws all around the country," Tobias said.

"That would be something, wouldn't it?"

"I just wish it didn't cost him his life."

"You know Remy. If he knew this much good was gonna come of it, he woulda laid down his life voluntarily. I just know he's up in Heaven right now celebratin'."

"I believe he is." Tobias looked up toward the clouds and smiled. "I believe he is."

30

────────

SIX MONTHS PASSED and while the headlines of Remy's case had disappeared, the effects were being carried out in municipal ordinances and state laws across the country. Will Turner, who was tried eight weeks later, was convicted of perjury and obstruction of justice. He was dishonorably discharged from the force and sentenced to three years in the state penitentiary.

Congress passed a robust police reform bill that was headed to the Senate for a vote in the next couple of months. Ms. Williams took the money Shirley had gifted her and donated it to several charities and civil rights organizations. The non-profit music school for underprivileged kids where Remy volunteered, accepted a large donation and renamed their school *The Remy Williams School of Music*.

Tobias tried to contact Remy after the trial, but Moira St. Claire informed him he was no longer there. Remy must have done what he had planned to do all along. Once justice had been served, Remy walked through the door. Although Tobias often wondered where Remy went, he always felt a sense that he was still here somehow. He couldn't explain it. That's just how it felt.

Tobias finished his book, *Odyssey Intergalactic*. He had all but given up on it until Chester Lang appeared to him in a dream one night. He didn't speak directly to him. His back was turned, and Tobias could hear the sound of keys being typed on a vintage typewriter. Tobias couldn't quite see over Chester's shoulder. A woman called from another room, "Dinner's ready!" Tobias assumed it must have been his new bride, Beth—who else? Chester put out his cigarette, removed his glasses, placing them gently on the desk, and stood to join her. Tobias sensed Chester was happy because he was humming some bygone ditty as he left the room. Tobias approached the typewriter to see what he'd written. There was only one sentence on the page. It read: *Who do you think you are?* Tobias woke from this dream and couldn't get those words out of his head.

He had an epiphany and sprung to his laptop. The protagonist in his novel was the heir to an ancient kingdom that had colonized a distant planet. His entitlement, his birth right, becomes the source of all his troubles and pain throughout his epic journey. In the end, he arrives at his promised kingdom only to find it has been destroyed. He climbs a heap of rubble to a dilapidated throne and declares himself King of Nothing. The casual reader might categorize the story a tragedy. But for Tobias, the protagonist finally finds freedom. He'd let go of the idea of being anyone at all.

He'd managed to pare it down from a sprawling 879 pages down to 524 pages, still quite robust but within the accepted range for a science fiction novel. After a final round of editing, Tobias considered an offer his ex-wife made before their divorce was final. She said that whenever he finished his book, that she would be more than happy to use her connections to help him get it published. He stared at her contact card in his phone for several minutes, giving his former resentment plenty of opportunity to resurface. He was surprised that it hadn't and instead, felt an overall sense of peace. He hit the call button.

"Tobias? Is everything OK?" Everly asked with genuine concern in her voice.

"Yeah. I'm good," Tobias said. "How are you?"

"I'm good," she said a bit suspiciously. "I'm in San Francisco doing this book tour. Two more weeks to go. I can't wait to be done."

"Congratulations! You did it again."

"Thank you. I—" She was interrupted by someone on her end to whom she replied, "OK, I'll be right there." She returned to the line. "I'm so sorry, I'm at this book signing and they want me to go out there." She produced an exasperated grunt. "I haven't heard from you in so long. Are you sure everything is alright?"

"Yeah. I just wanted to let you know that I finished my book."

"That's wonderful! Tobias! Oh my God! That's *really* wonderful. Do you have an agent?"

"No, not yet. I thought I'd reach out and see if, I don't know, if you had any advice or whatever but I don't want to keep you. I can call you later."

"Send me the manuscript. I'll pass it on to my publisher."

"Really?"

"Of course! I'm so sorry. I have to get out there. Can I call you later? I'd like to catch up."

"Yeah. That would be great."

"I'm so happy for you! Talk to you soon. Send me that manuscript!"

And he did. Unfortunately, as it turned out, her publisher rejected the manuscript—a hard pass. Instead, she passed it onto her agent, who passed it onto a new agent in his company, who wasn't in love with it necessarily, but as a favor to Everly Bronson, shopped it to a number of smaller publishing houses. It was eventually accepted and published by a small press specializing in science fiction and horror. Tobias received an advanced payment of $600. When he opened the envelope, he laughed at the paltry sum, which paled in comparison to the four-and-a-half million Everly made up front for her latest book. But it didn't matter. He'd finally done it. Tobias Munch was a published author.

Of course, being published didn't proffer the fame and notoriety that he had imagined it would all these years. He chuckled at himself that such an unlikely outcome had ever been conceived. What he realized, having accomplished an eight-and-a-half-year goal, was that he could no longer blame his depression and sense of otherness on his unpublished status. Now that he'd put his best out there for the world to judge, he could no longer use that as an excuse. He was who he was, published or not. He remembered what Dr. Macintosh said, before he knew she was the sociopathic leader of a psychedelic cult, when she was simply his therapist: *There is no wall.*

Tobias put his advance toward a deposit on a new apartment closer to his parent's house. His mother tried to convince him to stay longer but Tobias was more than ready to have his own place again. Tobias could have gotten his job back with the consumer goods company he worked for before. His position had been filled twice in the few months he'd been away and it was vacant once again. Tobias would have rather been in a coma than do that job again, especially since he no longer felt the need to use his title to justify introducing himself as a writer.

He got a job as a barista at the Higher Grounds Café, the same coffee shop he frequented on his way to work for the past year, where he first met Mia. The pay was not great but he enjoyed the work and the hours moved much quicker than they had at the consumer goods company. He took the early morning shift so that his afternoons were free to write. He started a new project—a portal fantasy bromance adventure across multiple dimensions of time and space with Remy as the main character.

Mia continued to develop her supernatural abilities, including her ability to materialize. She could appear and manipulate physical objects, but she wasn't quite solid enough to interact convincingly among human society the way Dr. Macintosh had done. She appeared to Tobias regularly and they would speak for hours on end, about life, death, and everything in between.

With the Doctor out of the picture, Mia became the new head of La Seta and she chose Khalil to run operations until she was fully able to manifest physically. His first order of business was to abandon the quest for a new portal. At first, nobody returned to the in-between for fear of what the Doctor might do. Specifically, they feared she might try to coerce a vulnerable traveler into being the new portal, which everyone agreed was inhumane no matter what promises the Doctor made. But after several preliminary explorations, Khalil determined that with no real power in a non-physical world and nothing to teach, Dr. Macintosh must have surrendered to the Great Beyond.

Tobias slumped in a plastic stacking chair at a folding table with twenty hardback copies of *Odyssey Intergalactic*. He looked up occasionally as a customer entered the locally owned independent bookshop, each time ringing a quaint brass shopkeeper's bell suspended above the door. This was his first book signing since the release of his debut novel and, after an hour and a half, hadn't sold a single copy. His name written in chalk on the sandwich board out on the sidewalk didn't do much to entice foot traffic from the stretch of bohemian boutique shops and cafes. The only person who even approached his table was a bookshop employee who read the back cover and commented on the novel's length, pumping the hardback up and down in his hand to demonstrate its heft.

The book had been reviewed a handful of times with a three-and-a-half-star rating on Amazon. Besides the glowing five star review his mother had posted, reviews ranged from embarrassing to moderately charitable. One simply stated: *This is space garbage. And way too much of it.* It was the kind of exposure therapy Tobias needed as he discovered a growing ambivalence toward the trifling opinions of complete strangers.

With a half hour left in his author event time slot, Tobias started packing his books back into a cardboard box. The shopkeeper's bell rang but Tobias had resigned sizing up potential readers.

"Hey buddy!"

Tobias looked up. It took a second for him to recognize the man who was speaking to him with a silly open-mouthed grin. "Carl?"

Carl, his old boss, approached the table with a copy of *Odessy Intergalactic* in his hairy hand. "You still signing books? I ordered this the day it went on sale. Good stuff!"

"Thanks. I'm glad you liked it."

"Your hand getting tired yet?" Carl said. He chuckled at his own unfunny joke.

Tobias looked around the nearly empty bookshop. "No. It's been pretty dead in here."

Carl looked around bobbing his head. "Yeah, I guess you're right." He handed Tobias his copy. "I don't know if you heard but your old job is still available if you're interested."

Tobias signed the title page of the book and pushed it back across the table. "Thanks, Carl. No, I got a job at Higher Grounds, that coffee shop right next door to your building."

"I've been meaning to check that place out," Carl said.

"You should stop by."

"You really bounced back after that coma. How you feeling?" Carl asked.

"I feel good. I couldn't be better," Tobias said with confidence. This was a true statement. At any given moment one can only be exactly what they are, no better . . . or no worse, for that matter. "So, you really liked the book, huh?"

"Yeah! I love that part when Bex realizes he's the illegitimate grandson of Aldous Nan and has to come to terms with his shameful lineage. He says something I thought was really profound. I underlined it. Hold on, let me find it." Carl flipped through some pages. "Here it is: *A man's destiny is not in the arc of his lineage or in the tale of the stars but only in the heart of a man can he find his own way. His story is etched by choice. What he chooses is what is written, and it is written as he goes.* Man, oh man! That really spoke to me. It's like, it's never too late to create your own story. I love that!"

Tobias smiled graciously. *He gets it.* "I'm glad."

"Welp, I better get home. Promised Cindy I'd put the baby crib together today."

"That's right! You were having a baby." Tobias had completely forgotten.

"Yeah! Little Nora. She'll be six months next week. Look here." Carl pulled up a photo on his phone and held it out for him to see.

"She's beautiful." *She must have taken after her mother,* Tobias thought.

"Yeah, that's our little nugget. She still sleeps in our bed, and I just never got around to putting her crib together. It's still in the box."

"Do you need a hand?" Tobias asked without hesitation.

"Really?" Carl was genuinely surprised at the offer, as if he'd waited years for it.

"Sure." Tobias shrugged. "I mean, I'm not all that handy but I can turn a screwdriver. Plus, I'd love to meet Cindy and Nora."

"Well, I . . . I'd love that. Let me just give her a call and let her know you're coming."

Tobias continued packing up his books while Carl stepped away to call his wife. Tobias curiously looked forward to spending time with his weird, ex-boss and this made him sneer to himself. Sure, Carl was kind of an odd fellow but then again, Tobias supposed, what's wrong with that?

He wasn't paying attention when Mia entered the bookshop. She walked confidently up to the table wearing a sunflower printed mini shift dress. She put her hands on her hips and gave Tobias a flirtatious spin.

"What do you think?" she asked looking down at her newly materialized body.

"Mia! Oh my God. You did it!" Tobias said and then lowered his voice. "You *materialized*."

"Feel me," she said holding out her arm. She bounced with delight when Tobias gently squeezed her upper arm.

"You feel *really* warm."

"I do? It takes a lot of thermal energy to materialize. I'm still learning how to regulate my body temperature. It's weird, I don't get hungry or sleepy but oh my God . . ." Mia leaned across the table and whispered, "I get so *horny*. Maybe because it's been so long but I don't remember ever feeling this aroused before." She glanced over her shoulder to see if anyone was around and then whispered, "I can't stop touching myself!"

"Dear God!" Tobias blurted, suddenly flush and noticeably aroused himself. Luckily, he was standing behind a stack of books.

"So anyway," she said, bouncing back and tossing her hair. "I thought we could hang out once you finish up here. Did you sell any books?"

"Ha! No. Not one."

"I'm sorry." She bit her bottom lip and made an apologetic face.

"It's fine."

"So . . ." She clapped her hands together in a prayer and brought them to her chin. Her stunning eyes danced with anticipation. "What do you want to do?"

"Well, actually, I made plans to hang out with an old friend after this. It's my old boss, Carl. I think I told you about him."

"The guy that says, 'later dater'?" Mia said in a goofy voice.

"Yeah, that guy. Anyway, I said I'd help him with something."

Mia's shoulders dropped. "Oh. OK, I just thought . . . You know what, that's fine. We can hang out another time, I guess." She pasted a smile onto her mouth, but disappointment lingered in her eyes.

"Are you sure? I'm really excited for you. I know you've been working hard on this. I just made these plans right before you got here."

"No, it's fine, it's fine. You guys have fun. Seriously! I'm immortal, remember? I'll be around."

Carl was purchasing a couple of children's books and a stuffed armadillo at the register. He spotted Tobias talking with Mia and gave him the most conspicuous and hopelessly juvenile thumbs up. Tobias grinned and shook his head, both at Carl and at himself for choosing to spend the afternoon with him instead of the most beautiful woman he'd ever met —a woman with the power to wield the elements but whose desire, inexplicably, burned for this very average, very unimpressive mortal.

"Are you free later tonight?" Tobias asked.

"Take me to dinner!" Mia beamed. "Nothing fancy—just a normal human meal with like, people and music and normal things."

"Normal would be nice for a change," Tobias agreed.

"It's funny," she said thoughtfully, twisting the ends of her hair around her fingers.

"What?"

"Just this idea that being human is a problem to be solved in the first place. I always thought the answer was to transcend it—to rise above it. But in the end, I just want to be human again."

"You never stopped being human."

"You know what I mean."

"Yeah." He glanced at the book he was holding—the one that he'd expected would hoist him over that imaginary wall. "I do."

AUTHOR'S NOTE

Thank you, dear reader, for coming along on this crazy ride with me. I hope you had as much fun reading it as I did writing it. Please take a few minutes to rate and review *Tourist Trapped* on Amazon, or anywhere else it may be listed.

Subscribe to my Substack for all the latest: jbvelasquez.sub stack.com.

ACKNOWLEDGMENTS

I'd like to thank my best friend Jason Jenkins, who read along as I drafted this story from the very start. His early impressions and ongoing support encouraged me to stay the course. As often as I questioned my creative capacity, he never did (or at least, I don't think he did). During our bi-weekly FaceTime calls, he never failed to ask me how my book was coming along. For a writer, that means more than you know. Thanks, bud.

I'd like to thank my beta readers, Meghomala Bhowmik, Abigail Ted, and Hannah Shipley Williams. Lucy Dupliak was my developmental editor who helped shape the story structure, humanize my characters, and lend plausibility to so many elements of this story. This book would be seriously lacking without her experienced eye. And thanks to my copy editor, Omer Hassan, this book would have had a lot more typos and hundreds less commas.

Thanks to Eve Hard, who designed my cover. The concept came to her immediately with only a brief synopsis and I think it's absolutely perfect!

And to my amazing kids, Sofia and Greyson, who are still too young to read this filth, I love your sweet little faces. Thank you for laughing at all my stupid jokes.

ABOUT THE AUTHOR

J. B. Velasquez has always been an avid reader and lover of witty, satirical, and thoughtful fiction. His writing reflects upon his own inquiries and observations about life through the lens of interesting and deeply flawed characters.

J. B., a psychotherapist by trade, lives in Tucson, Arizona where he is raising a menagerie of lovable critters, two of which share his DNA. He co-founded the Tucson Author Alliance in 2024.

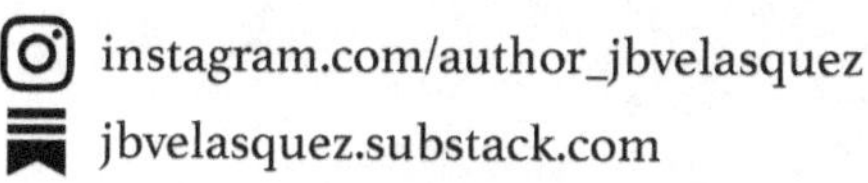

instagram.com/author_jbvelasquez

jbvelasquez.substack.com